Ulla Montan

Peter Høeg, born in 1957 in Denmark, followed
various callings—dancer, actor, sailor, fencer,
and mountaineer—before turning seriously to
writing. He is the bestselling author of five novels
and one short story collection. His work has been
published in thirty-three countries.

Also by Peter Høeg

Smilla's Sense of Snow

Borderliners

The History of Danish Dreams

Tales of the Night

The Quiet Girl

Praise for

The Woman and the Ape

"[A] cunning new suspense fantasy . . . The denouement is both biting and sweetly romantic."

—*San Francisco Chronicle*

"Erasmus is a remarkable fictional achievement . . . Madelene is easily as engaging a heroine as Smilla and readers should look forward to following her. . . . An expertly executed entertainment."

—*The Boston Book Review*

"Peter Høeg's humor and scathing social commentary successfully dovetail."

—*Chicago Tribune*

"This is a fable where we can't wait to see what happens next. . . . Høeg's book is sweet and thoughtful and passionate all at once."

—*Men's Journal*

"[A] swift-paced, lacerating new work . . . Thought-provoking . . . Too fresh in its writing and its perceptions to fall into the sentimentality one might expect . . . Don't think *King Kong*, this is much subtler. Highly recommended."

—*Library Journal* (starred review)

"An energetic fable about relations between the animal kingdom and its human exploiters . . . Høeg is an adventurous and intelligent writer whose future course seems, happily, impossible to predict. He has made himself, in a few short years, one of the essential contemporary novelists."

—*Kirkus Reviews* (starred review)

"The reader will want to stop to prolong the pleasures of Høeg's instructive, witty parable, which only flags for a few idyllic pages before leaping into its dramatic, shocking, humorous, and utterly unpredictable ending. . . . Høeg writes tautly and poetically."

—*The Hartford Courant*

The Woman and the Ape

Peter Høeg

Translated by Barbara Haveland

Picador

Farrar, Straus and Giroux

New York

THE WOMAN AND THE APE. Copyright © 1996 by the Lolwe Foundation and Munksgaard/Rosinante, Copenhagen. Translation copyright © 1996 by Barbara Haveland. All rights reserved. Printed in the United States of America. No part of this book may be used or reproduced in any manner whatsoever without written permission except in the case of brief quotations embodied in critical articles or reviews. For information, address Picador, 175 Fifth Avenue, New York, N.Y. 10010.

www.picadorusa.com

Picador® is a U.S. registered trademark and is used by Farrar, Straus and Giroux under license from Pan Books Limited.

For information on Picador Reading Group Guides, please contact Picador.
Phone: 646-307-5259
Fax: 212-253-9627
E-mail: readinggroupguides@picadorusa.com

Designed by Abby Kagan

All author royalties from the sale of this book go to the "Lolwe" Foundation, which provides aid to women and children in the Third World. "Lolwe" is the East African Luo tribe's word for the infinite space seen in the west, across Lake Victoria, where the sky meets the water and beyond which lies the world of the gods. In Dho-luo, the language of the tribe, this word means an initiative which it is hoped will spread to the limits of the known world.

The "Lolwe" Foundation has been set up by the author himself.

Library of Congress Cataloging-in-Publication Data

Høeg, Peter.
    [Kvinden og aben. English]
    The woman and the ape / Peter Høeg ; translated by Barbara Haveland.
        p. cm.
    ISBN-13: 978-0-312-42712-2
    ISBN-10: 0-312-42712-3
    I. Haveland, Barbara. II. Title.

PT8179.18.O335K8513 1997
839.8'1374—dc20
                                                                96-27289
                                                                    CIP

Originally published in Denmark by Munksgaard/Rosinante, Copenhagen,
as *Kvinden og aben*

First published in the United States by Farrar, Straus and Giroux

First Picador Edition: November 2007

10 9 8 7 6 5 4 3 2 1

part one

one

An ape was approaching London. It sat on a bench in the open cockpit of a sailboat, on the lee side, all hunched up with its eyes closed and a blanket around its shoulders. Even in that position it made the man sitting across from it seem smaller than he actually was.

The man was currently going by the name of Bally, and there were just two things in this life he still had any time for: the moment when he arrived in a big city and the moment he left it. That was why he now got to his feet, crossed to the rail and stood there, looking out toward the city, and in so doing made the first and last mistake of the voyage.

His absentmindedness transmitted itself to his crew. The helmsman switched over to autopilot, the deckhand worked his way aft from the foredeck, both gravitating toward the rail. For the first time in five days the three men stood idle, lost in the sight of the electric lights of suburbia, like fireflies dancing past the boat and fading away astern.

The wind had risen during the night. The Thames was now overlaid with fluted bands of white foam, and the boat, besides having the wind dead aft and a billowing mainsail, also had a large foresail hoisted. Carrying this much sail was verging on recklessness, but Bally had been hoping to make it in while it was still dark.

He was not going to manage it, he could see that now. There was a change in the air, with the first light of this spring morning spreading like a gray pelt across the buildings. Reminded of the ape, Bally turned around.

It had opened its eyes and leaned forward. One hand rested on the little switch on the dashboard for adjusting the autopilot.

Bally had always brought the animals with whom he sailed up on deck because it lessened the risk of their dying of seasickness, and this approach had never brought him anything but good results. They had been attached to lifelines, wrapped in blankets and given half a milligram of an effective neuroleptic per pound of body weight twice daily. Well secured and with no clear idea of their surroundings, they had dozed the voyage away.

This procedure would now, he thought to himself with the speed at which thought is occasionally possible within a space of time too short to allow for any physical reaction, apparently have to be altered.

Lagging—though only slightly so—behind the ape's hand, the autopilot turned the bow of the boat a few fatal degrees out of the wind. It pitched awkwardly on the choppy waters. Then it jibed.

At that instant the ape was looking straight at the three men.

Many years before this, Bally had discovered that life consisted of a series of repetitions, each less savory than its predecessor—an overall distastefulness in which man himself was but one more repetition. He was also well aware that the reason he had, throughout his life, sought such close contact with animals had something to do with the fact that amid this general and automatic loathing there was a kick to be gotten out of having power over machines of a lower order than one-self. This notion of the lifelessness of all things was now being challenged. The ape's movements were purposeful and well thought out, but that was not the worst of it. The worst thing, the thing that, even though it lasted for only a fraction of a second, was to make itself felt throughout the rest of Bally's life, was what he saw in its eyes.

For this he had no words—for this, at that point, no one had any words. But it was in a way the opposite of automatic.

The vessel's mast was fifty-five feet tall, its mainsail had an area of more than fifty square yards, so the swing when it came was quicker than the eye could follow. All the three men had time to register was a slight list and a crack like a gunshot as the boom snapped two steel shrouds on the port side. Then they were swept into the Thames.

With a groan of overtaxed bearings the autopilot adjusted to the new tack and corrected course accordingly. At its own speed of twelve knots plus two knots from the incoming tide, the boat carried on toward London, now with the ape as its sole passenger.

Fifteen minutes later the first call to *The Ark* went out over the shortwave radio. This and the two subsequent calls went unanswered, and after that they ceased.

But behind the smoked glass of an observation window in a low tower near Deptford Ferry Road a member of the River Police put down a microphone and lifted a pair of binoculars. Slowly but intently the city's immune system was being activated to detect a breach of rules.

Downriver from Tower Bridge, at the yacht haven by the Pool of London, St. Katharine's Yacht Club has a café. Here, during the summer months, breakfast is served on an open-air terrace between the Thames and St. Katharine's Dock, and on this morning, even at such an early hour, some dozen guests were already seated there.

The Pool is said to be the only spot at which the Thames is blue. It is here that the royal yachts anchor. From here legations to London sail out to have lunch on their national training ships. Here, one September day in 1866, 100,000 people watched the famous race between the two tea clippers the *Taeping* and the *Ariel*.

Something of the expectancy of that earlier time was now aroused on the Yacht Club terrace at the sight of *The Ark*. Everyone there recognized the boat as an Ocean 71, built at Poole, a speedy but nevertheless classic English ketch. And by its casual approach and rash spread of canvas they could tell that this was a skipper of the old school, a traditionalist, heading into port under sail alone. A few minutes later, over the gilded dolphins on the bow, they caught a glimpse of the man himself, wearing neither oilskins nor sunglasses, not even a cap. Just a sober gray overcoat. A hush fell over the terrace; everyone knew what was going to happen next because they had heard how the real pros did it, dropping anchor at the last minute, every inch of canvas brought down with a clatter and the boat gliding smoothly and neatly around the chain and into the quayside. As *The Ark* came through the open sluice gates, they prepared to applaud, a few already had their hands in the air, but by then it was too late. With an apocalyptic screech of splintering wood the ketch plowed into the outermost of the moored yachts, sliced it in half and sparked off a domino-style chain reaction along the serried ranks of mahogany and rosewood hulls.

None of the breakfasters came to their senses quickly enough to see how the gray overcoat leapt from the cockpit and across a foundering hull and then disappeared—swiftly, if haltingly—around the side of a building. But two others did. In the sluice-gate control room a lockkeeper employed by Taylor Woodrow, the company that owns and runs St. Katharine's Dock, laid down his binoculars and reached for his telephone. And on the east side of the dock Johnny broke into a run.

two

What Johnny was running toward was a truck parked on the side of the dock facing the Wapping industrial park. In this he had followed *The Ark* from the prearranged docking point at Klein's Wharf on the Isle of Dogs and then into central London.

This truck was Johnny's only home and sole possession and yet it was never locked, not even now. Instead, on the door hung a sign showing the silhouette of a dog and some words in very small lettering. This sign was not there for decoration. In the bunk behind the driver's seat lay a hundred-pound Doberman by the name of Samson who had spent five years as one of the champion dogs in the illegal running dog-fights held in Britain's immigrant communities. Johnny had bought him when he was starting to lose and was, therefore, about to be put down, and it had taken a year to wean him off the life of a sports star on a strict diet and with a drastically increased lung capacity and stroke volume and make him both his watchdog and his best and only friend.

Johnny had two names, the second of which was every bit as important as if not more so than his given name. This was Golf Zulu India Thirteen Foxtrot Whiskey, his ham radio international call signal. On the dashboard in front of him was his radio transmitter, and now, while starting the car with one hand, with the other he tuned in the receiver to 148 MHz—the Metropolitan Police wave band—in time to catch the tail end of the first vague description of the man in the gray overcoat and the order to seal off the harbor area.

Johnny's face—as he drove up to East Smithfield Road and across Tower Bridge—was set. In the three years he had been working for Bally he had never seen him make one mistake. In bewilderment his thoughts flitted back and forth between the road, *The Ark*, the River Police, the crash, the immediate future and the limping fugitive in the gray overcoat.

"Would you," he said to the dog behind him, "have said that Bally's arms reach all the way to the ground when he stands up?"

Samson made no reply. But he stirred, affected by his master's unease.

Johnny had spent the past ten years of his life endeavoring to make himself invulnerable and he had almost succeeded. He had his work, with the van, and his home, again the van. He was mobile and dependent on no one. At his back he had Samson and via his radio transmitter he was in touch with ethereal friends throughout the civilized world. And yet here he sat behind the wheel, shaking. Because there was one chink in his armor that he had never succeeded in covering up: Johnny gambled on animals.

His was an anonymous, an almost invisible, weakness in a world where everything is a gamble. Bally was the first to detect something in Johnny's obsession other than dreams of winning and it was because of what he had seen there that he had taken him on.

Johnny did not play to win. He always placed the lowest possible bet and with a peculiar blindness in this betting, never knowing who the favorites might be and never giving or taking a tip. He gambled because of something he could not quite put his finger on but which had to do with being near the animals when they exploded into life. At the sight of six greyhounds all lunging as one after the mechanical hare, at the crack of the racing pigeon's wings as it takes to the air, at the Derby, at the trotting track, at Sedgefield or Pontefract races, at cockfights in the Indonesian neighborhoods, something indescribable happened to Johnny.

Bally had never said where his cargo came from, nor where it ended up, and their partnership had lasted this long—despite Johnny's awareness, from the outset, of the scale of the risk—because Bally had brought Johnny very close to that mysterious something for which he longed.

Behind him in the trailer section hooked up to his sleeping quarters, he had for Bally carried a Javanese rhinoceros with skin as cracked and hard as iron but a strangely gentle and querulous nature. He had carried two okapis; carried a saltwater crocodile measuring thirty feet in length in a crate that jutted out fifteen feet behind the truck. He had carried fifteen poisonous Amazonian frogs, blinking and perfect, like fifteen tiny cobalt-blue gems. He had carried eight rare giant angelfish in two thirteen-hundred-gallon aquariums. A half-grown elephant. Two Himalayan snow leopards with tails longer than their bodies. He had carried South American black saki monkeys and emperor tamarins. And on one unforgettable occasion, a family of tarsiers with two young ones which had swiveled their heads around 180 degrees and stared up at him from their box with their great eyes as though begging him to drive carefully.

He had not let them down, not them or any other creature. He had transported them with infinite tenderness and patience. He had adjusted the heating for them, fed and watered them, separated them if they fought. And the journey itself,

which he knew to be a dreadful experience for the animals—
hours and hours of disorienting darkness in a mobile prison—
had been smooth as a caress. Not one of Bally's animals had
ever died while being transported by Johnny.

During those hours on the road in the truck, with some
powerful or wondrous but always fragile creature in the back,
gliding over the bumps in the asphalt, Johnny had felt almost
happy.

Now it was over, he felt quite sure that something irrevo-
cable had occurred, that he would never again drive a con-
signment for Bally. That was why he was shaking.

Behind him the dog gave a hacking cough and Johnny
stretched back a hand to pat it reassuringly. Then he frowned.
Dobermans have dense, short-haired coats. What he felt under
his fingers was a shaggy rya rug.

Ahead of him the lights at the intersection of Southwark
Street and St. Thomas Street, diagonally below the railway
junction, changed to yellow. He brought the car to a halt and
looked in the rearview mirror.

The first thing the people in the cars sitting behind the
truck saw was the driver's door flying open. They saw Johnny
jump out and then begin to run away from the vehicle as fast
as his legs would carry him. Next they saw him stop in his
tracks, turn around and walk back. They saw him open the
door and peer into the cab. They could not tell what he was
looking for, but in his face when he saw that it was empty they
read disappointment, surprise and yearning. They saw him
drive the truck in to the curb, and as they drove past him, a
number of them saw that he was wearing earphones and holding something that might have been a street map. A few also
managed to read the whole of the text under the picture of the
dog on the truck door. It said: *This van is guarded by a Doberman. Fuck with it and find out.*

three

Immediately after Southwark Street the railway line splits into two. One branch carries on to Cannon Street Station on the north side of the Thames; the other runs on granite supports along a spur narrow as an animal track and high as a migratory route, through the fashionable district of Dulwich.

In Dulwich, at the foot of the railway embankment, stands a row of eighteenth-century town houses with large gardens in the rear. In one of these gardens, on the back steps of the house—now, in what was still early morning—a man lay, eyeing the ape through a telescopic sight mounted on a hunting rifle.

It was a Holland & Holland rifle with a hair trigger and it was loaded with a half-ounce bullet that could have slain an elephant with ease. All that had kept the ape alive up until now was the absence of a very slight touch of the man's index finger.

On the barbed-wire fence that marked the boundary between the bottom of the garden and the railway spur hung a sign bearing the words *No trespassing* and citing in true British style the law of Aggravated Trespass, and the man knew it made no difference that the ape could not read. He had the law on his side, and behind him—barricaded in on the second floor—he had his family to protect. And in his heart burned the old love of the chase.

But even though he had had the ape in his sights for forty-five minutes he had not yet pulled the trigger. And, what was worse, he knew now that he never would. Each time his finger had curled around the trigger the animal had made some move, a tiny, microscopic shift in position or a turn of its head that—for the first time in his life—had evoked in the man the overpowering feeling that were he to shoot this animal he would be committing murder.

Twenty minutes earlier, in desperation, he had gotten his wife to look up some telephone numbers and make several calls, and now he was waiting, waiting and hoping. Then the doorbell rang.

He had been expecting a commando unit, or at the very least a couple of armed men. Instead, the caller whom his wife ushered out onto the steps was a woman in her late thirties wearing a long dress and a hat.

The ape was sitting propped up against a tree, its chin sunk onto its chest. The woman walked right up to it. The man waited ten paces off. He held the rifle at the ready, but it was the woman and not the ape on whom his eyes were pinned.

Ever since, in his twenties, he had begun to earn money, he had been able to buy whatever he wanted—most recently this town house and the address that went with it—and it was his experience and his belief, generally speaking, that everything had a price tag. He had come across very few exceptions to this rule and had always felt both intrigued and puzzled when confronted by something for which no price had as yet been set. In the woman facing him he saw something he did not understand, a courage which he sensed eschewed the usual haggling.

"How come you didn't shoot it?" she said.

The man realized that, even though she had never met him before, she knew that under other circumstances he would willingly have paid ten thousand pounds and traveled halfway around the world for the chance, in different surroundings, to shoot an animal such as the one that had just shown up in his own garden free of charge. In vain he tried to come up with a plausible answer, only to find himself driven by the awkwardness of the situation to a new and unfamiliar honesty.

"I couldn't," he said.

Two men in brown coats came out onto the steps.

"We'll take it with us," said the woman. "Will you give us a hand?"

The man looked at her vacantly. The animal was as tall as a man and broader. And it was a long, long time since he had done any manual labor.

He had been under the impression that the woman was already standing up. But now, without any visible change in her stance, she grew an inch taller.

"It's dying," she said. "Would you be so kind as to help lift it."

The man bent down and grabbed hold.

From his window, a little later, he watched the ape being driven away in a black car that reminded him of a funeral cortege. He came to the conclusion that it probably would die and with that he dismissed the thought. But for a long while afterward he was bothered by pain in the small of his back from having lifted too heavy a weight and the unreal sensation of having lived through a dream.

The car was no hearse but an animal ambulance belonging to the Holland Park Veterinary Clinic, and the man who made the first cursory examination of the ape, as it lay on the ambulance cot, was Dr. Alexander Bowen, proprietor of that institution.

"Will it live?" asked the woman.

"We have to get it into the clinic."

An indiscernible nod from the woman sanctioned the implicit costs entailed by the ape's admission.

"I would rather it wasn't registered," she said.

The ambulance stopped, the woman climbed out. Halfway through the door she turned.

"If it lives," she said, "I'll see that you're well rewarded."

This promise prompted the doctor to give a little schoolboy bow.

"But if it dies you might as well fill one of your own syringes right there and then and put yourself to sleep."

four

In South Hill Park, alongside Hampstead Heath, outside the door of one of the vast rooms of a mansion that lay, hidden away, inside a garden as big as a park, Madelene Burden took a last swig from the water carafe in her hand, straightened the topknot into which her hair was drawn, pushed open the door and walked into the light.

"How do I look?" she asked.

Adam, her husband, drew himself up and took in the sight.

"Enchanting," he said.

Had he been closer he would have been able to catch a whiff of something else in addition to this enchanting vision—namely, the reek of ethyl alcohol emanating from his wife's pores and from the water carafe. But right now he was standing in the middle of the room and at that distance the illusion held.

With the exception of one large surgical lamp all of the furniture in the room had been pushed back against the walls and Madelene embarked upon an erratic progress along sofas, occasional tables and wing chairs.

"Is there going to be dancing?" she asked.

Adam Burden was fond of encapsulating any significant and complex phenomenon in a single, telling expression. For Madelene, on meeting her in Denmark, he had come up with the word "dewy." That had been just over a year and a half ago. At the time it had seemed to him to sum her up perfectly. Since then he had occasionally, as now, felt a twinge of doubt.

There was a knock at the door; their housekeeper opened it and stepped aside.

Out of the darkness and silence there came first footsteps and then a flash of white. Two men wheeled a hospital trolley into the room. They were followed by Alexander Bowen. Finally Andrea Burden, Adam's sister, stepped inside and closed the door.

The porters pushed the trolley into the center of the room. It was covered with a thin blue sheet, under which Madelene could discern the outline of a body. Only the deceased's head lay uncovered and, as yet, in shadow.

Andrea Burden trundled the surgical lamp over to the body, lowered the head and switched it on. The two porters removed the blue sheet.

The lamp blanked out the rest of the room. For a moment, within its golden sphere, the only thing that existed was the ape.

Like moths, Adam and Madelene were drawn toward the creature. Just for an instant Madelene forgot her tight skirt and high heels. She teetered dangerously, as though on stilts, regained her balance and positioned herself alongside the trolley.

She could hear the animal's breathing, thick with mucus, drugged. Behind her, in the darkness, she was aware of her husband circling around the light. Silence reigned in the room. But somewhere in that silence a secret dialogue had been struck up.

"Let's hear it," said Adam Burden.

"We pick it up the day before yesterday. In a garden in Dulwich. The owner looked in the Yellow Pages under Animal Protection Societies and worked his way down the list. At some point he gets through to Miss Burden, who calls me. There's been considerable blood loss, dehydration; it's suffering from delayed shock. General condition is critical. I operate as soon as it's admitted to the clinic."

With his forefinger the doctor traced a white bandage running around the animal's shoulder and upper arm.

"After administering a transfusion I remove forty pieces of number five shot from the area around the right scapula. The shot was fired from forty yards away, wounding superficially but causing pain and loss of blood. I sew up two gashes, in the medial and lateral gastrocnemius. Bite marks, possibly a dog."

He pointed to two dressings below the ape's knee.

"We took a fair amount of rust out of four vertical tears in the abdominal area. Where they back onto the railway embankment most of the houses have had barbed wire put up. Reinforced here and there by electric fencing."

He turned the palms of the ape's hands toward the light; the burn salve glistened like chalk.

"It came across the viaduct, saw the gardens and tried to climb down. The sides are sheer, concrete and granite, so it fell. Partially torn ligaments in both ankles."

He placed a hand on the ape's chest.

"London has etched a map of itself on this one," he said.

"How did it get to Southwark?" Adam asked.

"The Met and the River Police had cordoned off St. Katharine's Dock that day."

"But that's on the other side of the river."

The doctor motioned with his hand; the two porters rolled the ape onto its side. The bite mark was long, narrow, deep, every tooth having left a gouge that had either been stitched up or sealed by pus. The hair around the wound had been shaved off, exposing a third of the back. The skin was black and blue from bruising. Madelene turned around and began the journey back to the water carafe.

"A van left the area just before it was cordoned off. It has not been found. But they did find the Doberman which would appear to have been in the van. The ape must have had its back half turned to it when it climbed in."

Once more there was silence. Madelene located the table; under cover of the darkness she took a drink from the carafe.

"So," said Adam Burden, "everyone is now looking for a large ape covered with bite marks?"

"Everyone is looking for the skipper of a boat," said the doctor. "Some yacht rammed into the dock. There's been no mention of any animal."

Madelene felt how Adam became still, how—out of a range of unspoken options—he had reached a decision she did not understand.

"It can stay here," he said. "Wheel it down to the garden room."

The two porters drew the trolley out of the light.

Madelene's field of vision and her mental radius were now narrower and shorter than the room itself, and dwindling by the minute. She sensed rather than saw the meeting breaking up.

"But Mrs. Clapham baked some pastries," she said. "Cream horns. Oh well, I can always eat them with the baboon. When it wakes up."

A door closed. Madelene had no idea whether she was alone. She tried to drink, and failed. Then she rested her head on the tabletop. To Adam Burden, who had remained standing next to the surgical lamp, her heavy snores sounded exactly like the ape's.

part two

one

Each morning Madelene was resurrected. This resurrection occurred in front of her mirror and took between thirty and forty-five minutes. While it was under way she was totally absorbed; during that space of time, with uncompromising thoroughness, she did the one thing she knew herself to be truly good at: she re-created the myth which said that Madelene looks gorgeous.

The face that met her eyes when she seated herself at the dressing table was, in her own opinion, a dull face. Not a faded face or yet a face in decay—Madelene *was* only thirty years old. But it was—to her mind—a pale, nondescript face that looked as if it might at any minute disappear, not in some blazing inferno but simply because, being so drably mediocre, it might easily merge with its surroundings.

Onto this surface she now applied a mask that was at one and the same time sensual and reticent. Having first cleansed her face with skin lotion to create an oil-free base of tightly

closed pores, she then used a silk-matte foundation to erase
the past ten years of her life. The face in the mirror before
her might now, in all its smooth neutrality, have been twenty
or perhaps even fifteen or twelve years old.

With a concealing stick she eradicated the microscopic
lines around the eyes together with the gradually acquired
skepticism of a lifetime. She used a fine brush to raise her
eyebrows into the permanent wonder of youth.

It is in the dark areas of our faces that age and weariness
reside. Her eyes she enlarged with a pale eye shadow that
followed the line of her eyebrows before carefully outlining
them with liquid eyeliner. They were now wide, clear and
uncritically receptive. She then touched up her cheeks with
a delicate golden terra-cotta blush, accentuated the curve of
her mouth with a lip brush and enhanced the fullness of the
lips with a natural gloss. Last of all, with a sickly yet widening
red dot at the mouth of each tear duct she erased her iron
constitution. Her face now seemed childish, radiant and ever
so slightly delicate; so skillfully, so subtly reconstructed that
only an expert would be able to tell that cosmetics had been
used.

Madelene had learned the art of makeup from her mother.
Not by asking questions or being given any direct answers—
it was too sensitive a subject for that—but by watching her.

Madelene's mother's life had been one long succession of
panic-stricken but more often than not successful attempts at
beautification. First and foremost, the beautification of the
family's stylish and hectic day-to-day life in Vedbæk, north
of Copenhagen, where it was not only the dinner service that
was made of porcelain, where the very atmosphere was crys-
talline and under constant threat of shattering and no voice
was ever raised above a whisper for fear of starting an ava-
lanche of glass. But also, and in more exacting fashion, at the
receptions held by the family trust, at which the unresolved
tragedies of certain families were thrown together with the
calamities of other families and individuals to form an ele-

gantly turned-out, graciously served-up version of a modern-day hell on earth here, at the end of the twentieth century. On such occasions Madelene's mother managed to organize a repast that served as a form of social first aid; she could bid "A warm welcome to one and all!" in a voice that shut out emptiness as effectively as polyfiller. Not only that but, despite the force of both internal and external circumstances, she always looked wonderful. She could emerge from seeing to things in the kitchen enveloped in a cloud of steam and, when the air cleared, there she would be, looking décolleté, attractive, hospitable, attentive and girlish, to the point where even Madelene's father's features would momentarily soften into an expression of unmitigated pride of possession.

Around the turn of the century, by dint of a suicidal collective effort, Madelene's father's family had pulled themselves out of medieval poverty and accumulated the money that enabled Madelene's great-grandfather to study engineering. His two sons also went on to become engineers and—in the 1920s—uncommonly well-off. In a very low-key, Danish fashion and with a clear, inherited memory of the starvation and cholera epidemics of the previous century, the two brothers had used this sudden wealth to consolidate their position. They invested and reinvested, bought land, bred and made provision for their offspring, so that by now they were not so much a family as a clan—large, unremarkable, unobtrusive and exercising a direct influence on Danish foreign policy.

The family fortune had been founded on the building of cowsheds, a side of the empire that Madelene's father had kept up. These structures, though, were not half-timbered cottages down some leafy country lane, as featured in Danish Tourist Board brochures, but four-story, totally mechanized industrial plants for the manufacture of domestic animals. Madelene's father hated any kind of publicity and he had succeeded in remaining unknown to all but a select few. These few could, however, detect his personal thumbprint on Denmark's annual production figures—as quoted in the country's

Statistical Yearbook—of 20,650,000 pigs and 813,000 beef and veal cattle.

As is so often the case with people who attempt in their terror to put some distance between themselves and their poverty-stricken past, Madelene's father respected only people who had made their fortunes or who happened to be pioneering men of science and, until she ran away with Adam, Madelene had had to put up with her father referring to her—even, or perhaps especially, in her presence—as "Madelene, who is nothing really." While she had been given a token education, she and everyone else had always known the only thing that really mattered was that one day she would take her place by the right man's side, and in order to take that place it was not enough to be the heiress to a fortune; one also had to look good and looking good meant work, even now, this morning.

Madelene had never found the courage to stand up to her parents. With some defiance but unable to see any alternative, she had traveled down the smoothed and well-trodden paths marked out for her. But she had dreamt agonizingly, aimlessly, passionately of the chance of another kind of life. Into this dream stepped Adam Burden—a man, an amiable, attentive and not altogether harmless man, on the way up, and Madelene climbed aboard, both like the princess swept up behind the prince on his white horse and a castaway, all at sea and three-quarters drowned, clutching at the life belt that suddenly heaves into sight.

Madelene had had five hundred and twenty-nine days of marriage and each one had begun like this, in front of the mirror, just as what came next also followed a set pattern.

She would now get up and go down to the kitchen for a chat with Clapham's wife about the housekeeping. From there she would proceed to the terrace to exchange a few words with Clapham himself. After that she would go up to town to do some shopping, or play tennis, or go riding on Hampstead Heath. She would then take a stroll with a woman friend and be back home by five p.m. in order to welcome Adam home at seven.

Anyone whose days are all the same and free from want inhabits eternity of a sort and that was how Madelene looked upon her life. As though she had wished for, sought and found eternity.

She slipped into a short, pleated skirt and approved her reflection in the mirror. She looked like the oldest daughter of the family on her way to an early tennis lesson. Then she left the room.

In the doorway, as always, she paused for a moment.

Madelene had two rooms, a bedroom and a dressing room, which she left as an animal leaves its territory, tentatively and warily. The routine that lay ahead of her was familiar down to the last detail. Even so, it was not without its terrors.

She had personally taken care of the decoration of the two rooms she was now leaving behind. She never knew where she found the courage to insist on their pale wooden floors, clean-lined furniture and white walls. To her they represented the only piece of Denmark left to her. Over that threshold the Commonwealth began.

Adam Burden's parents had died while he was in his twenties but Madelene had heard his father's voice. One evening Adam had played her a recording from the BBC series *Tales from the Dark Continent* on which an assured and nonchalant voice described, warmly and wittily and with never a hem or a haw, the grand old days in India and British East Africa, and to Madelene it had seemed as though the house in which she lived were speaking.

This house had been built by Adam's parents on their return to England in the mid-fifties. They had built it as a memorial to their life by the Indian Ocean and named it Mombasa Manor. It was an L-shaped building with a tiled roof and vast parklike gardens planted with tropical trees and shrubs.

In its rooms lion skins were spread on wall-to-wall carpets and spears and shields hung next to the fireplaces, and Madelene knew that other people thought she led a very grand life, titillatingly exotic and much to be envied. She also knew that she was, ostensibly, the mistress of this house.

Nevertheless, every morning, including this one, she was brought momentarily to a halt in her doorway, checked by an instinctive sense of dread embodied in the thought that, since the British Commonwealth had subjugated everything else of an alien nature, might it not also devour her?

The pause was brief, this morning as on every other. Madelene shook her head, it was a crazy idea, she drove herself onward. And, as on all the other mornings, as she walked along the corridors, down the stairways and through the rooms, she left her fear behind her, a little of it in each room.

Clapham had a standard greeting for her. Whenever Madelene stepped out onto the terrace he would stand up, doff his cap, present her with a flower and offer her a cup of coffee.

He always made this offer in a whisper. The coffee was a token of their fraternization, the alliance—in a world that had never known anything coarser than Darjeeling first flush—between her, the foreigner, and him, the worker.

Up to a point Madelene trusted him. Like her, he was a part of the surroundings—and, like her, he was not one with them.

She walked through the door. Clapham clicked his heels together and handed her a lilac blossom. Smiling at him over the flower, she waited for his line. But it never came.

"Mr. Burden called," he said. "He's coming home early. To work."

Madelene put down the flower, grabbed hold of the chair and eased herself down into it. Adam had never worked at home before. She was not sure that he had ever spoken of his work at home. She had had the feeling that it was his intent—

and one that he had only ever declared to himself—not to so much as think about it once inside the walls of the park.

"Work," she repeated. "On what?"

Clapham's face closed, turning into that of a stranger.

"That you would have to ask Mr. Burden, madam."

Madelene looked away. Clapham had not called her madam since they had first been introduced.

He stood up and put down his cup.

"Duty calls," he said.

And he turned his back on her.

From the games pavilion, just below the terrace, Madelene fetched a racquet—the last part of her disguise.

The tennis court lay on the other side of the house, and it was in this direction that she headed with a lively spring in her step, but she did not go all the way there. The momentum and optimism in her gait lasted only as far as the corner, which, once rounded, hid her from view. From that point onward her movements became stealthy and feline. Leaving the gravel path, she walked through a door in the gable end of the house's other wing, and straight into the potting shed.

The room was warm and humid as a rain forest, half the roof was glazed, flowerpots and hotbeds held thousands of cuttings, water lilies in bloom floated in a large freshwater tank. Madelene caught sight of her own reflection in the door of a stainless-steel cabinet and smiled reassuringly at herself. Then she did as she always did.

She took a pipette from a wire shelf, a Pyrex flask from a cupboard, a little measuring glass from a drying rack. She removed the rubber cork from a demijohn packed in excelsior and drew off eight ounces of 99.6 percent alcohol for hospital and laboratory use. She then topped up the flask with distilled water from a plastic container. The resulting liquid was 55 percent alcohol. She knocked back the first half glass.

In her alcoholism, as in everything else, Madelene was pretty much on her own. She had no one to advise her, no companion and no experience. She was in the process of discovering alcohol, as a lone traveler explores a new continent. She did not know why she did it, nor did she want to know. But she sensed that 55 percent was the optimum. At 55 percent, just before the first rush, as the volatile vapor was absorbed into the mucous membrane of the throat, the destruction of the mouth cells brought an exquisite burning sensation. This burn was essential. In it there was clarity, in it Madelene discerned something of the spirit of abuse: the intense, all-consuming urge to self-destruct.

This was followed by the first wave of inebriation. She located herself in the cabinet door. Slowly, in the void within her, a hot pulsating spirit flame flared up. From having been nothing she was rapidly becoming something.

Mombasa Manor was hers, the park was hers, the world was hers. And she looked great. Not a fault to be found anywhere. She toasted herself, congratulated herself. Then she took a drink.

She swung a stylized backhand at the stainless-steel surroundings. A queen had a need for and a right to some space. She drew the racquet back over her shoulder and arched her body in a perfect fake smash at the door in front of her. The door into the garden room. She put down the racquet. The recollection of the ape struck her with the same force as the alcohol. She turned the door handle and went inside.

Mombasa Manor had been built with African rather than British conditions in mind: African wages for the servants, the African climate and the social round of the British colonial administration. When it proved too large, too expensive and too cold for London, the entire side wing—with the exception of Clapham's flat on the first floor and the workshops along the gable end—had been closed off. Madelene had passed through the room she now entered on only a handful of occasions. She recalled heavy tasseled curtains, plastic sheeting covering the carpets, bags around the chandeliers, dustcovers over the furniture and a heavy scent of something that was gone and would never come again.

The room was now in use.

It was a large room—more of a small hall really—extending, by means of a conservatory of glass and white-painted steel, fifteen feet into the park. The entrance to the conservatory had now been blocked by a metal grille. A tropical thicket of ferns, hardwoods and low bamboo had sprung up in front of this grille. And around the vegetation, splitting the room from floor to ceiling for two-thirds of its width, ran a glass partition. At the spot where Madelene entered the room the glass abutted on the wall. On the other side it came up against a white metal barrier topped by white bars that reached to the ceiling.

Next to the thicket grew a climbing tree of the type found in children's playgrounds. Next to the tree lay two tractor tires. Next to the tires stood a wheelbarrow filled with fruits and vegetables. Next to the wheelbarrow sat the ape.

With some effort Madelene succeeded in coming up with a sketchy log of the past two days. The ape had arrived the day before yesterday. She had spent yesterday in bed with her carafe and that dreadful migraine. The bulk of the setup in front of her must have been erected in less than a day.

The ape was asleep, sitting on its haunches, with its back against the wall.

Access to the cage was gained through a door in the metal wall. Affixed to this door were feeding and temperature charts and a vaccination checklist. There were two latches on the door. Madelene lifted both and stepped inside.

As soon as she crossed the raised doorsill she became aware of a subtle burning under her skin, as though her nervous system were overheating. The same sensation that she experienced when the alcohol seared the epithelium of her throat and mouth. That faint, almost cheerful call of the longing to go under.

She closed the door behind her.

"How do I look?" she said.

At the sound of her voice the ape opened its eyes. Madelene crossed over to the animal, one step at a time, until they were about ten feet apart, sat down on one of the tractor tires and placed the flask and glass at her feet.

The crossing of this boundary had rendered her all but sober. From a gentle, stupefying warmth radiating from her stomach she had moved into a state of crystal-clear hypersensitivity. She could hear them both breathing, her own breath coming twice as fast as the animal's. She filled the glass and drank.

"Cheers," she said.

There was a fleeting moment of pleasure in knowing that one could not be understood. Then she met the ape's gaze.

It was open, incalculable.

Madelene was overcome by a prickling sense of unease, as though she had sat on an anthill. She shifted position and still the ape kept its eyes on her. She had the feeling that she was being unmasked, spied on, scrutinized, as though it saw right through her, saw her naked, devoid of makeup, and, worse still, saw her pathetic inner self, her insecurity, her worthlessness.

Flustered, she started to get to her feet. It occurred to her that she too was an ape, for, while she might well be able to leave this cage, and this house, she would not get very far before running up against the financial, social and marital barriers that circumscribed *her* life.

Her hands were frozen, shaking. She had spilled some of her drink onto her wrist, and the chill of the liquid evaporating had turned it to ice. Up she got.

"Sorry," she said.

There was a peach dangling just in front of her. She followed the line of the branch on which it grew back to the trunk—the ape's arm. It had handed her a peach.

Very slowly and gingerly she took the sun-kissed, ripe and downy fruit from the gray hand. Then she inched her way backward.

"Thanks," she said. "As a matter of fact, I did forget to eat something this morning."

two

Madelene's bed measured six feet square; the bedclothes were of pink satin. To her it was both cocoon and kingdom and the only place where she could, on occasion, feel absolutely safe. Now she sat down in the center of it, legs crossed, with the carafe in one hand and a large medicine glass in the other.

Madelene liked to imagine that she inhabited a new age, one that had been ushered in by two more or less simultaneous events that had conspired to cancel out the past: her marriage and her discovery of B vitamins.

Whereas her marriage made it possible for her to escape from Denmark and her family, the large fifteen-milligram B_1 tablets, available over the counter from any pharmacist, had provided her with an ally in the fight against hangovers and helped her to carry on, seemingly unaffected, no matter how much she had drunk.

Now she felt all shook up, with no idea of why this should be. She poured the contents of the carafe over these feelings

like some soothing balm, and in order nevertheless to maintain
a clarity for what lay ahead, for every swig she took two tablets
and washed them down with half a glass of water.

What lay ahead was, like everything else in Madelene's
life, something that recurred at regular intervals, in this case
once a week. But whereas she kept all other appointments
with a blithe indifference, she approached this one full of
expectation.

The person she was going to meet was already present in
the room in the form of a dog-eared bus-pass photograph
propped up against the framed portrait of Adam on her bedside table. The face was that of a pale, freckled woman. Her
name was Susan and she was the only friend Madelene had
ever had.

When she was ten years old Madelene was enrolled at the
English school north of Copenhagen, an international boarding school and one of the last all-girls schools in Denmark. It
was run by the sisters of an Anglican lay order and attended
by the daughters of British businessmen and diplomats and
the daughters of Danish parents who wanted their children out
of the way and could afford to fulfill this wish in an academ-
ically defensible manner. Her first three years at the school
seemed to Madelene to be a period of deathly hibernation,
surrounded by teachers so distant as to be quite unreachable
and by classmates who looked upon one another not as individuals but as representatives of that gray uniformity of which
all were a part.

In her fourth year at the school a natural catastrophe occurred. Within just a few months sexuality broke out among
all thirty girls in Madelene's class.

The class had always been alarmingly quiet; in recent
years this silence had deepened and the sisters had made the
mistake of confusing restraint with apathy. In actual fact this
stasis was an illusion. From the outset the girls had constituted

a fluid which time had saturated with expectant, hormonal menace. Into this saturation there now fell a microscopic, never to be identified particle and around this sliver of the magic mirror the fluid crystallized. And then it exploded.

The catastrophe took various forms. None of the girls had known where they were headed and for some the change came as an incurable shock. On their bodies, which had until then been slender and boyish, swelled tumorous cushions of fat which held them back on the sports field, squeezed them out of their clothes and their familiar framework and exposed them to vitriolic masculine lust. Others were engulfed by the forces building up inside them. From a shy and tranquil childhood they were thrown—and threw themselves—straight into disproportionate, promiscuous prurience, first verbally, then physically.

It was like the end of a journey. They were like thirty lemmings all reaching the sea at once. And here they foundered in their convulsive attempts to stay in the world of childhood. If, that is, they did not throw themselves into the water and drown.

In the midst of this chaos Madelene and Susan caught sight of each other after years of unwittingly being an arm's length apart. They looked at one another, briefly and thoughtfully, and found that amid the general immersion they were both staying afloat. At that instant and without a word being said, they knew that they had both come to a secret understanding with the forces now shattering the world around them.

In tackling what was happening to their pupils the sisters had recourse not only to training and experience but also to a modicum of resolute brutality. But the force inherent in such synchronism caught them off guard and it took them the better part of two years to regain control. After that time, however, after a succession of abortions and cases of venereal disease and two successful suicide attempts and, in the end, open mutiny followed by the last, definitive purge, they were left—

on the face of it, at least—with nineteen well-adjusted, docile girls. Among them Susan and Madelene.

They had two more years at the school before disaster struck and during that time for the most part they went unnoticed. The people around them did not understand them and anything incomprehensible invariably remains invisible.

What they found in one another was a wantonness which, as far as their classmates and the sisters were concerned, went beyond the recordable range of the senses and into another, inaccessible dimension. They came to maturity like a couple of cubs. Bypassing the panic that struck their contemporaries, they quietly and undramatically grew toward an intense and certain knowledge of how it feels when it tickles. For most of the girls in the group to which they had belonged the journey ended here. For Madelene and Susan this was where the real journey began.

They were never in any doubt as to where it would lead them. Deep down in their neurological fundament they knew that what awaited them at the other end was a man. For whom as yet they had no name, face or even a body but whose nature they understood with instinctive assurance.

On this journey they helped one another. When the final grand expulsion left whole sections of the school deserted, they were given a room with four beds all to themselves and from this room they ventured out onto the high seas. The bed they shared was their ship, and the waters were first blue, then pink and finally dark red, and of the same delightful temperature as bath water.

During those two years they slept very little at night, nor was there any need to. Their love was like a game—leisurely, untouched by desperation and, for the most part, aimless. What they were trying to do was to surf for as long as possible over the torrid surface that spread beneath them.

They never spoke of what they were doing, not to others, not to each other, and not even to themselves. They knew that the fewer words one employs, the naughtier it becomes. No one ever saw one of them lay a finger on the other; in the life they shared with the rest of the school there was nothing to suggest that they were anything but very good schoolmates, chums and vaguely overlooked, quiet, fair-to-middling pupils at a good school. But alongside this sphere there lay another. And in that one a look, a flicker of a nostril, the way in which the tip of a tongue moistened the bow of the upper lip was enough to send a shaft of fire shooting from the inner thighs to the roots of the hair and on up into the blue sky.

Around this private, vivid, sensual orgy their everyday lives showed up, not surprisingly, in tones of charcoal-gray wretchedness. They were surrounded by teachers whom they feared, an overwhelming feeling of insecurity and schoolmates who were in much the same situation as themselves—having been handed over, at their fathers' expense, to insensitive women conducting a ludicrous curriculum.

Under these conditions the girls' friendship flourished, and it was there that they learned to love their bed.

At the end of two years Susan found her first lover outside the school. She was found out, given a warning, caught again and expelled, after which she was packed off back to London by her father, the British ambassador to Denmark, and consequently sucked out of Madelene's life.

Twelve years were to pass before they met again, in London. During those twelve years they had not been in touch with one another at all and yet the bond between them had never been severed. Just as they had, at the school, spent whole days each in her own corner of the bed, never exchanging a word, like fox cubs curled up and resting, safe in the knowledge of the other's presence in the room, so, throughout their twelve-year separation, they had sensed the whereabouts of the other. At that moment when they stood face to face once more, Madelene saw beyond Susan's two children and her husband and the nanny and Susan saw through Madelene's

makeup and the reek of alcohol and what they saw was that,

behind the guises they assumed, some parts of the world they had shared remained intact.

Since then, every Tuesday afternoon when Susan's children attended Danish lessons at the Danish church, they had gone for a walk together in Regent's Park. Whereas people will usually endeavor to reduce the gulf that separates them, one from another, through conversation, these two had once and for all accepted the differences between them and their walk was taken gently, lingeringly and often in silence.

But not today. Today Madelene arrived late and immediately started talking.

"You're on the board of the Royal Society for the Protection of Animals, aren't you?" she said.

Susan had to think for a minute. She was on the board of various charitable organizations. To please her husband, to embellish her idleness and to have plenty of excuses for not being where she was expected to be.

"Then you must know Adam's sister, Andrea?"

Susan shook her head.

"The Animal Welfare Foundation," she said.

"What's the difference?"

Susan fell silent. People interested her. First and foremost—besides Madelene and her own children—certain men. And farther out on the periphery of her awareness, the rest of the human race. For animals she felt a profound lack of interest.

And yet this question had conjured up, in her mind, an animal association. She remembered how she had always thought of Madelene as a cat, as loudly purring, electrified velvet or a sudden ball of fury with five switchblades on each hand. Now, within and behind her friend's urgent and vehement questioning, she glimpsed a number of other animals, less elegant but more stubborn: a sheep, a donkey, perhaps a cow.

"It has something to do with money," she said. "The Animal Welfare Foundation has something to do with money."

Between the two friends there existed an agreement which had never been voiced but of which both were aware—namely, that while Susan told Madelene everything, Madelene told Susan a good deal, but never more than that. Now Susan waited respectfully. But Madelene's face remained blank and withdrawn.

They headed toward the church, arm in arm. A tall, freckle-faced woman in whose abdomen the sperm of three different men were vainly trying to come to terms. And a gazelle of a girl with a blood-alcohol level that would never have passed a Breathalyzer test who stayed on her feet and relatively lucid thanks only to the support of her friend, B vitamins and her own curiosity.

three

The number of men whom Madelene had known, while too small to be statistically significant, had been large enough for her to deduce certain general rules of behavior. The most important of these was her discovery of the fact that the content and course of any love affair is revealed within the events of the first twenty-four hours.

Adam had called on her father on official business. He had met her at a party and, taking his time, as he always did with anything that mattered to him, he had begun to work his way through the crowd toward her. His whole being was contained, even then, in that one action. In his body resided his cricket, his javelin throwing and a succession of physical victories over other males; in his hide the requisite arrogance and essential resources and in his voice when he reached her a richness possessed only by those with a roar that comes from the gut, together with the kind of polish acquired only at the most expensive private schools and universities. Around him, like a mane or an aura, hung an awareness of having practically no natural enemies.

The rest of that first day served to confirm this impression, adding to it the observation that he seemed considerate and very, very interested.

In the course of those twenty-four hours, during which they never left one another's side, Adam Burden did not laugh once.

Not because he had no sense of humor. He commanded rich reserves of a fine-honed intellectual brand of sarcasm that might be triggered at any moment, especially if he felt professionally threatened. If anyone else were to question his knowledge, thereby encroaching on the cornerstone of his self-esteem, he could turn lethally witty. But at no point in the five hundred and twenty-nine days of their marriage, nor—presumably—at any time prior to it, nor—in all likelihood—at any time thereafter had it occurred or would it occur to Adam Burden that there might be anything funny about him. What his first move toward Madelene had shown and what all of his subsequent moves had confirmed was that he had all the monumental self-importance of the big beasts of prey and of the great dictators.

Not that Madelene looked for humor in her marriage. Laughter comes as an extra, a luxury item, and Madelene knew that Adam had saved her from certain familial ruin. For anyone who has survived by the skin of their teeth, the daily gratification of basic needs is a miracle and that is how Madelene viewed her marriage: as a daily, reciprocal and miraculous gratification of basic needs.

This mutual meeting of needs usually commenced at seven p.m., when Adam came home. But today he turned up two hours earlier; Madelene met him at the door at five p.m. Ten minutes later they were taking tea in the library.

———

The library was Adam Burden's den. It had all the murkiness, the snugness of a den, as well as its smell—a subtle whiff of Adam, of the tropical jungles from which the wood for the furniture had come and the leather of the book spines.

It also provided the restorative refuge of a den. By the time Adam arrived home his face was white with exhaustion. But the minute he sank into one of the armchairs in that room and put away his date book he began to revive. While one small fraction of his awareness drank tea and chatted, the rest of him was absorbing the security of his surroundings and the woman sitting across from him.

Madelene was well aware that during these ostensibly un-demanding three-quarters of an hour she administered the large feminine blood transfusion to the man in the chair opposite her.

Little by little during the course of this, Adam Burden dropped his defenses, becoming a weaker character than usual. Never before had Madelene taken advantage of this weakness to speak of anything of importance and now when she did so the question was thrown in casually, desultorily, one single element in a host of insignificant associations.

"And the ape?" she said.

Through half-closed, disinterested eyes Adam watched the question float past, like an insect, like steam from a teacup.

"It's in the garden room," he said. "Just for the time being."

"What kind of ape is it?"

There was silence. The borderland between them lay as yet unexplored. But Madelene sensed that she was verging on the demarcation zone.

"Some sort of dwarf chimpanzee."

"What's so special about it?"

Adam's face lay in shadow. Now, in this shadow, two yellow lights gleamed—as though some big cat were staring out at Madelene from the gloom.

"When a wild animal escapes from captivity it will either blunder around in panic or it will look for a place to hide. Animals are incapable of adjusting to unexpected freedom. The interesting thing about this one is that it got as far as it did."

Madelene bowed her head. A gesture of acceptance, of submission almost. Adam had not lied, that she knew. But he had divulged as little as possible of the truth. Behind his bone-china cup he curled himself around his prize with animal alertness.

She raised her face and smiled at him, the reassuring smile of a nurse. Then she poured tea for him, put sugar in his cup and stirred for a count of thirty, the exact number of stirs required to ensure the complete dissolution of the coarse, molasses-heavy tropical cane-sugar crystals.

That night she waited for Adam in his bedroom. It was two in the morning before he came up. But when he saw her on the bed his tiredness and tight-lipped exasperation were swept away with a smile and he began to undress.

Adam's date book was a little gray book to which he had, as people under great work-related pressure often do, committed his memory. It was date book and memo pad rolled into one; in it he made a note of everything from the most minor of errands to the heaviest of commitments and without it he could not remember a thing. It was a weapon in his self-defense, like the tea in the library, like his silence on the subject of his work.

Madelene had never looked inside this book before; she had never wanted to look inside it, for it had seemed to her both too trivial and too sacrosanct. But on this night she did take a look. When Adam went to the bathroom she swung her legs over the side of the bed and lifted the book from a drawer of his bedside table.

She had already abandoned any thought of deciphering the

main entries; Adam's notes were as cryptic and elliptical as bird footprints in the sand. Instead she concentrated on the loose sheets slipped in between the pages of the book.

There were five of these, a little larger than 8 × 11, held together by a paper clip and tucked in at that day's date. The first three pages were covered with an illegible scrawl; the last two contained drawings.

The drawings were of the ape. First some full-length sketches of the animal—in profile and head-on—not in any detail, merely capturing the posture and the relative length of the limbs.

Beneath these, several drawings of the animal's nostrils had been made one after the other, from different angles. Then came the hands, reproduced without hair or fingernails, leaving nothing but the outlines, resting on the animal's knees just as they had rested when she had sat facing it.

The last half page was impossible to make out. It showed a map, a group of islands shaped like two parabolas turned back to back, like a double-sided, inverted Polynesian atoll. This had been sketched out something like a dozen times, then again from the side, the islands seeming to rise up out of the water—some smooth, others rugged, or square, like circular towers, like planks of wood.

From the bathroom came the sound of Adam soaping his cheeks. She tore a blank white sheet from the back of the calendar. Using her eyeliner she copied out one of the maps, the only one where an attempt had been made at a polished drawing and one which Adam had also underlined. She drew it both from above and from the side, quickly and accurately. Anyone who has spent the whole of their adult life drawing on a face will find paper an accommodating medium.

Just as she was studying the relative heights of the islands above the surface of the water, just as she heard Adam patting his cheeks with after-shave, she realized what she had been copying. She had been drawing the creature's teeth. She opened the drawer and put the date book back.

In the drawer lay a strip of gray plastic. Some hazy recollection told her this was what the ape had been wearing
around its wrist when it was lying on the stretcher. She picked
it up. It was the type of thing used in hospitals to identify
corpses and the newborn. The band bore the word "Erasmus."

When Adam walked through the door she was lying back
against the pillows.

Now, as always, she was grateful for his careful prepara-
tions and his fastidiousness in lovemaking. She experienced
just one brief moment of secret, inner distraction before turning all her attention to him. She thought of the exasperated
look on his face and came to the conclusion that whatever he
had been looking for, the ape had not given it away. It had
not given anything away. Except to her. To her it had given a
peach.

four

Madelene woke up early and, as always, alone. She had never spent a whole night next to her husband. However passionate and intimate their lovemaking might have been, there came a time, often just before dawn, when Adam would turn in his sleep and brush against her and, registering the closeness of another human being, would be gripped by a kind of desperation. Asleep, but determined, he would get out of bed, gather up his sheets and retreat to the next room to bed down there. Madelene had never asked him why. Ten years in advance of other women of her age she had learned that there is no point in discussing matters that cannot be altered.

Usually she woke up to the feeling that the bed was an uninhabited island onto which she had been washed up during the night and only after she had made it to the mirror was the sense of impending doom dispelled. This morning was different. She awoke with the impression that she was floating. Without turning her head she stretched out her hand and located, under her clothes, the torn-out sheet with its drawing of an archipelago named Erasmus. Clutching this, she put on a kimono, returned to her own room and seated herself at her dressing table.

And here something strange happened. She got her coloring wrong.

Under normal circumstances Madelene could hit upon her pale, youthful base color with unerring accuracy. But this morning when she looked up from the brush and the section of her face reflected in the concave makeup mirror in front of her, she saw that she was way off the mark. While her face was indeed wrinkle-free it was still as colorlessly neutral as it had been ten minutes before.

She reached for the cleanser, then hesitated. She took a closer look at herself. She drew a line the width of a finger below each eye with the eyeliner, then gently rubbed this away, transforming it into a dark hollow, into five years of wear and tear. She took a lipstick and applied a hard, wide "proper madam's" mouth. She put on a pair of sunglasses. A scarf over her hair. She stood up. Tried affecting a slight stoop. She had quite forgotten herself. For the first time since she had, in a dim and distant past shed a child's delight in grown-up clothes, for the first time since then Madelene made herself look older than she was.

She positioned herself over by the window and felt the wind against her new disguise. She saw Clapham. He cut a rose from the bush next to the gate, let in a delivery van, turned away a gray man in a white car, walked back to the house. She was seized by the thought of the daily routine. She recalled that Adam was working at home that day, in the garden room, with the ape.

It was a disturbing thought. Madelene's was not only an emotional, legal and physical marriage. It was also a territorial one. Prior to this, until the end of the working day she had always known there was no risk of her bumping into her husband on her reserve.

She dealt with her unease in her usual fashion. She retrieved her carafe from beneath the bed and, standing by the window, she took the first little drink of the morning.

Her daring increased. She unearthed a thin duster coat and put it on, leaving it unbelted, shapeless as a sack. She found a pair of battered platform sandals. She looked at herself in the mirror. Her own mother would not have recognized her. Or at any rate would not have wanted to recognize her.

Into a little black bag she popped all the things a woman has need of: keys, money, lipstick, eyeliner, handkerchief, a drawing of an ape's teeth and a little plastic flask of alcohol. Then she left her rooms, swiftly, stealthily and without the usual pause in the doorway.

She went down the back stairs, through the kitchen garden and out through a little gate in the wall. It was the first time in a long while that she had gone anywhere on foot with no tinted car window coming between her and the outside world. She reveled in the sunlight, the sounds, the sharpness of the colors. She relished the anonymity of her new mask. She passed a truck with a picture of a dog on its door, the man inside the truck not sparing her a glance. She passed a maid walking Kasimir, the neighbor's borzoi, the girl and the dog looking at her with no sign of recognition. She walked past a white car in which sat the gray man whom Clapham had turned away, the man staring in the direction of Mombasa Manor and right through her. She came to an underground station and headed down.

On the platform she took fright.

Madelene had grown up in a singular and sheltered environment, in the domain of the well-to-do. For the greater part of her life she had been to some extent isolated from ordinary people; between her and the general public there had been filters, big houses, special schools, nannies and chauffeurs. Now, in the underground, she was brought face to face with the brutality of London, like a woman throwing herself out of her covered jeep in the middle of a game reserve to carry on alone and on foot.

Madelene was of course acquainted with tragedy, death, nausea and self-hate, every human being carries these things with them from birth. But she had had no practice in understanding overt misery, no words to explain it. The shell within which she had circulated had been very much of a linguistic nature. Not long after they met, Adam had presented her with a number of Debrett's publications, smiling as he showed her how here, in the twentieth century, you had a publishing house issuing—under a very thin veneer of self-irony—textbooks on the preservation of a feudalistic class supremacy. And Madelene had learned her lesson well. After only a year and a half she was speaking a slightly Latinized upper-class English with not a trace of an accent. But she lacked any kind of personal association with such words as bleeding gums, hunger, hard chancre, Wormwood Scrubs, knuckle-dusters, corns, the dole, foot drop, fractured skulls or delirium tremens. In the train she sat tensed, still and on the alert, shielded from the impressions that assaulted her only by what she sipped from her little flask.

She had no sense of time or space. Only after she had instinctively changed trains, gotten off, climbed up, gone around corners, dodged predatory animals and beggars, avoided being trampled underfoot and—finding herself in front of a long, low concrete building—realized that she had made it, did it transpire that she had any goal in mind. That she had been guided by a spatial law which was struggling to reestablish a balance. She had moved in the opposite direction from Adam. He had stayed at home; she had been led to where he ought to have been. She was standing outside the Institute of Animal Behavioral Research, one of the departments attached to the London Zoological Gardens. Adam was the director of this institute.

On Madelene's first visit to London, Adam had taken her

across to one of the Mombasa Manor outbuildings, closed the
door behind them and left her to stand there for a moment
surrounded by the darkness and the stench of moths, formaldehyde and barely suppressed decay. Then he had switched
on a dazzling electric light and recited his professional credo.

The shed was filled with his parents' hunting trophies.
With tusks, lion skins, shark jaws, bird of paradise plumage,
rhino horns, antlers, roebuck heads, python skins, whale
bones, a stuffed and mounted gorilla head and the skins of
two Komodo dragons grafted, by the new dermatoplasty
method, onto life-size models. Adam had steered her over to
a picture of his father and mother standing arm in arm atop a
mountain formed by the bodies of six elephants. In soft and
measured tones he had explained how his parents' object had
been to shoot, collect and exhibit—a task they had fulfilled
with panache. But the world had changed, now was the time
to study, present and preserve, and he had said this with the
gravity that comes from knowing that your family goes back
seven hundred years, that you have had splendid ancestors
and that you are yourself even better. Then he had told her
about the London Zoo.

"It's the oldest zoo in the world," he had said. "Once it
was the best in the world and it can be again. But, for that,
expansion is necessary. This is already under way, you've
heard about it, but it's going to be more far-reaching than
anyone imagines. Andrea and I are both involved in it."

He had run his fingers over a row of photographs and
stopped at one of the Last Night of the Proms showing the
composer Edward Elgar on the podium.

"A charity concert," he said, "for London Zoo."

His fingers had drummed a tattoo across the British upper-
class animal lovers. When he next spoke Madelene could tell
that he had forgotten her, that he was talking to his own class
and its ghosts.

"They did the work. Their children don't lift a finger; they
have control of a monopoly. When the London Zoo was

founded it was their own private property. These days it's all we can do to cover the day-to-day operating costs. They've lulled themselves to sleep but they're going to wake up to discover that it's too late."

This speech, which Madelene had remembered even though she did not understand a word of it, lay one and a half years in the past. Since then she had visited the Institute once, had been given a tour of the construction site and attended a dinner where the seating plan for the guests of honor had been arranged in strict pecking order, where she and Adam, as the director and his wife, had sat at the head, a dinner which she had gotten through only because she had been drinking before she got there and had continued to drink heavily throughout the evening.

Now, for the first time, she walked through the glass doors unaccompanied.

A woman darted out to a desk and barred her way, nippy as a terrier. For a split second Madelene was ready to turn and run. Then she remembered that today she was someone other than herself.

"I'm from the Meat Marketing Board Research Center," she said. "We have an inquiry regarding the arrangement of an animal's teeth."

The receptionist backed away. Behind her sunglasses Madelene understood her perfectly. They had both had too brief a schooling. They were surrounded by people who were cleverer than they and liked to flaunt their cleverness. And the words "research center" and "inquiry" acted upon them both like a command that could not be ignored.

The woman made a telephone call, then yelped out a name and a floor. No sooner had Madelene taken her first few steps toward the elevator than the woman had forgotten all about her, with the watchdog's instant indifference to anyone who has received its master's seal of approval.

The man who invited Madelene to take a seat at a large desk wore his white coat like a cloak, and it was by this way of carrying himself that Madelene recognized him. He had sat a little—but only a little—farther down the guests-of-honor table than she and Adam.

She placed the eyeliner sketch in front of him.

"We have a problem," she said. "We've been given this and they can't put a name to it, so they've sent me to you . . ."

"Why me?"

Madelene rapidly and judiciously surmised that this doctor's most prominent feature was his vanity.

"Back at the Center they say you're the best," she said.

"Do they indeed? Don't tell me they still remember my root-canal job on Roberto?"

"Not a day goes by without its being mentioned."

"It was the right tusk. I had to use two five-quart bucketfuls of chloramine just to clean it out."

"It has long been the stuff of legend," said Madelene.

The veterinary odontologist picked up her drawing, glanced at it and let it drop.

"I will not be made a fool of," he said.

Madelene removed her sunglasses and leaned toward him.

"It was sent to the Center," she said, "and they can't make head or tail of it."

Suspicion niggled at the doctor.

"You're not by any chance a vet yourself, are you? Or a dentist?"

Madelene smiled, warmly and dumbly.

"Office messenger," she said.

The doctor relaxed.

"Of course, one cannot be certain," he said. "Not with such a poor drawing."

His fingers drummed on the sheet of paper.

"Molars, small molars, conical canines, incisors and diastema. All of which points to a chimpanzee."

"But?" said Madelene.

"I could go along with there being four teeth too many. One extra small molar on each side. We're always coming across mutations. Even though evolution is tending toward fewer teeth. In a pinch I could even let the front teeth pass. But why the chiseled edges, like knife blades, rather than masticatory surfaces? And the dental arch, it's too rough, wouldn't you agree?"

Madelene nodded.

"That kind of curvature would be inconceivable in an ape; it's humanoid. I'll tell you one thing. You've been taken for a ride. Somebody has taken advantage of your ignorance. You've been sent the dental chart of a nonexistent creature."

Madelene sat back in her chair, took out her little bottle and sipped.

"Medicine," she said. "Asthma. I have all these allergies."

Slowly she got to her feet.

"Is any record kept of animals that have been stolen or kidnapped?"

"Newsletters. All zoos of any standing exchange a daily newsletter. Every theft is put on record."

The doctor was starting to freeze into the attitude in which she had found him.

"Doctor," she said, "what would you say if, even so, you were faced with an animal with just this set of teeth?"

"I would point out that there had to be some misunderstanding."

"And what if it was actually lying there with its mouth open and teeth like the set in that diagram?"

The brow above the desk creased, reluctant to budge, annoyed at being forced off its empirical pedestal.

"Until it was proved otherwise I would most certainly assume that there was talk of a hoax."

Madelene smoothed her skirt and smiled a wide, gummy
smile.

"Doctor," she said, "how many teeth does a human being
have?"

"Thirty-two."

"Well, I'm going to go back to the Center and have a look
at my teeth, just to make sure there's no talk of a hoax."

The doctor looked away.

"You can borrow a mirror from the toilet here. But there's
no need. I have already remarked on your dentition and oc-
clusion. They are quite normal."

Out in the corridor Madelene stood for a while tuning in to
the building. It had Adam's dynamism; it was young, intensely
businesslike, ambitiously efficient. It was a place where anyone with no good reason for being there might easily feel in
the way. In an attempt to stifle this feeling she took a drink
from the bottle. As she was wiping away her tears she noticed
Adam's name and title above her head. She had stopped outside his office.

She put on her sunglasses and walked in.

She entered the outer office. A woman in a swivel chair
whirled around to confront her.

Madelene had met Adam's secretary five or six times and
now she was struck by a fleeting sense of being in free fall.
Then she filled out her role from within.

"I have an appointment with Adam Burden," she said.

The secretary smiled—a pleasant, impersonal, pliant smile,
as much as to say there was absolutely no way Madelene could
have an appointment, since, if she had, it would have been made
through her, which was not the case, so there was no oversight
on her part, but this she could afford to gloss over.

"I'm afraid Mr. Burden is attending a lengthy and important meeting in town," she said.

"Is he somewhere where I could reach him by phone?"

The woman's face turned cold. Her civility, rationed from the start, had run out.

"I'm afraid that is quite out of the question. What was the name?"

Madelene stared at the woman in front of her in fascination. At the impeccability of her dress, her dismissive air of authority. Adam had once said that a great leader saw to it that the people around him never made mistakes. This woman looked incapable of making a mistake. Then she remembered Adam's dawn retreats, how he could not bear anyone close to him, the doors he erected between himself and the outside world. The woman facing her was just such a barrier. She leaned forward.

"I came to find out what happened to him last night," she whispered.

The secretary tried to get away by pushing her chair backward; Madelene followed her, closing further and further in until the woman could see her own reflection in the sunglasses and breathe the alcohol.

"And in the Meat Market no less," Madelene went on. "What d'you think of that?"

The secretary's back was pressed up against her word processor, all avenues of escape cut off. She had gripped the arm of her chair.

"You tell him," said Madelene, "that he'd better have one helluva good excuse, because otherwise I'm going to call his wife."

On the desk the woman's hand lighted on a slip of yellow paper with a note in Adam's handwriting. She held it out.

"Perhaps you would like to call him yourself and tell him," she said.

Madelene took the slip of paper and backed off.

"Four hours," she said. "Surrounded by frozen chickens and organic sausage skins. You just tell him that."

Even in such a tight spot the secretary could still summon up the strength for one last sally.

"And who shall I say called?"

"Priscilla," she said. "Priscilla from the Meat Marketing Board Research Center."

And she closed the door behind her.

Back in the corridor she stopped and gazed blindly into space. Madelene entertained many different feelings for her husband, not all of them unmixed. But her confidence in him had always been absolute. There were sides of Adam and of his life which she could not fathom. But she had always felt sure that, in time, she would get to the bottom of and learn to accept most of them. Now she found herself faced with the first downright lie of her marriage. Adam, she knew, was at home in the conservatory. But he had left a note for his secretary that said "Earp. Vet. Inst."

Madelene took a sip from her bottle. Then she made her way back along the corridor.

The veterinary odontologist was sitting just as she had left him. Madelene laid Adam's note in front of him.

"Doctor," she said, "there was one question I forgot to ask. The Center is considering doing some work with this institution. Can you tell me anything, in strictest confidence, about this place?"

The doctor looked out the window, across the covered construction site that was soon to become the New London Regent's Park Zoological Garden.

"I've more than enough to do just keeping people in line here," he said.

"I was so hoping you could help," said Madelene. "You're renowned for your contacts."

The doctor glanced at the paper, then looked out the window again.

"Drop it. Never heard of it. It's not in London, at any rate."

Madelene stood her ground. The doctor reached behind him and brought out a hefty-looking reference book.

"*The Royal College of Veterinary Surgeons' Annual Register and Directory*. Provides a list of all vets and veterinary colleges in the country. Comprehensive."

He looked something up, closed the book and put it away.

"You've been conned again. There is no institution by that name in Britain."

He regarded Madelene over his bifocals.

"Everywhere you go it's the same story. We're up to our eyes in inefficiency and incompetence. And a nice, polite girl like you too."

Madelene made a tentative attempt to let go of the desk, to see whether she could stand unaided.

"Thank you very, very much, Doctor," she said slowly. "And that comes both from me and from the Research Center."

Madelene walked across London for what might have been an hour before taking a taxi, stepping out as carefully and circumspectly as her condition would allow.

It was not herself she was endeavoring to protect, nor was it the fact that she had practiced one piece of deception and herself been witness to another that occupied her mind. What she was guarding was a new sense of inner worth. For the first time for as far back as she could remember she had stepped out and to one side of herself and become someone else. She was no longer just Madelene. On the fringes of her own being she glimpsed the silhouette of another woman who was also herself. It was this other woman she was shielding as she made her way across London.

———

Back in her rooms she removed her face with a cotton cloth and lay down on her back on the bed. She had been absent from Mombasa Manor with no explanation given and no one had noticed a thing. But elsewhere in the city three people had encountered a strange woman, different from Madelene and yet one and the same: Priscilla of the Meat Marketing Board Research Center.

five

When she woke, the clock showed midnight. The air in the room was heavy and humid. She groped around beneath the bed; her carafe was empty. She pulled on a dressing gown, the fabric hurting where it touched, and stuck the carafe in one deep pocket. Dizzy and weak, she embarked upon her journey to the source of the Nile.

The house tried to bar her way with its darkness, its menacing shadows, the sense of human breathing. The courtyard slabs burned the soles of her bare feet and the sky was black. But there was a bit of a nip in the air. She walked across the gravel and turned the handle of the door into the potting shed. It was locked.

Her first reaction was to freeze in the face of this strange new secretiveness. The outer perimeter of Mombasa Manor came under the aegis of the same security firm that guarded the rest of the houses on the road. But as a rule the house doors were never locked. Then she smiled. Like all expedition

leaders of foresight, on this her solitary journey she too had
laid down her caches.

The potting shed's large freshwater tank ran through the
wall into a trough and in this trough stood row upon row of
jars containing water specimens. Madelene shut her eyes, felt
around among the water plants and the goldfish and pulled
out a jar, apparently no different from all the rest. She un-
screwed the lid, took a cautious sip and let out her breath.
No chance of any tadpoles developing in this liquid. It was
crystal-clear 55 percent ethyl alcohol.

She settled herself on the rim of the stone trough. Above
her head the clouds parted and the Milky Way came into view.
From the basin came a murmur reminiscent of the fountains
and canals of Copenhagen. She drank to herself. She was
having a lovely time, what a delightful, cozy Danish-style evening this was, the perfect end to a perfect day.

She thought of the ape. Of how lonely it must be feeling
now, with no tiny helpers to sweeten its loneliness. Had anyone ever heard of an animal taking a drink? No. On the other
hand, no one had ever heard of Erasmus' tight dental arch
either. And it was never too late to learn to drink, was it? Not
when they could teach chimps sign language.

Madelene lay down in the trough. On her knees, with the
jar held well above any risk of dilution, she crawled through
into the potting shed. She crossed the threshold of the garden
room and switched on the light. The windows were masked by
inky blackout curtains. The cage looked just as she remembered. But the ape was gone.

She stayed where she was, beside the glass partition, until
she was quite certain. Then she unlatched the door and
stepped inside.

It is at the very moment of realizing that we are bereft,
when the loss bleeds and the awareness of it has not yet begun
to coagulate, that the significance of what has been lost strikes
us most forcefully. Advancing farther into the empty cage,
Madelene realized that she was going to miss the ape.

She had never had a pet. Without envy, without desiring anything of the kind for herself, she had viewed her friends' Shetland ponies, golden retrievers and hamsters and right from the start she had known that the horse between the legs, the puppy against the bosom and the guinea pig in the bed were substitutes for something else. In silence and feeling nothing but pity, time and again she had witnessed the collapse of a sentimental illusion, with an animal outgrowing its cuddly puppy stage to become large and tediously horny, at which point it was banished from the girl's bedroom to an outdoor run, there to develop—as a quite logical consequence of its isolation—a psychopathic savagery that would culminate in it biting the mailman and costing the family fifty thousand Danish kroner in damages plus seven hundred kroner to have it put down.

Now, standing in the cage, she saw that whereas those animals back then were supposed to remind one of something else—of children, of parents, of dolls, of men—the ape in its stoic helplessness had reminded her of herself.

Desolation washed over her. She drank from the specimen jar, in a ritual gesture of farewell, a funeral toast, like an exclusive little wake for a departed friend. As she drank, she wandered slowly across the cage and thus she arrived at the only spot in the room from which the ape was visible.

She parted the branches. It looked at first as though the plants had twined around one another to form a bed beneath the animal; then she saw that it was lying on a woven cradle. Without snapping or forcing them it had drawn branches and leaves together and plaited them into a hammock. The side of this hammock facing the glass was hidden by a screen of grayish brown, withered greenery which merged with the animal's fur, making it impossible to see the structure from the outside. At the only spot in the room where the vegetation formed a thicket capable of concealing it, the ape appeared to be hovering, around shoulder height, in a masterly piece of camouflage.

Madelene seated herself on a branch.

"You're even more invisible than you might think," she said. "You don't exist at all."

She pointed at the ape's teeth.

"Like the bumblebee. It can't fly; it's been proved. But it doesn't know that. So it does it anyway."

She drank a toast to the bumblebee.

"Would you mind opening your mouth?"

She opened her own mouth wide to demonstrate.

The ape's lips parted hesitantly; then its mouth opened.

Madelene saw the reddish white maw, the powerful gums, a palate ridged as a seabed, the glint of spittle under the tongue. She saw the two small molars on each side, the chiseled edges of the front teeth, the cone-shaped daggers of the canines, the tightly curved, humanoid dental arch. She saw the original of Adam's faithfully reproduced dental chart. But all of this she saw in passing, as it were, as one small part of something far more important.

At the moment when the ape opened its mouth it was not only its dental chart that was humanoid. For an instant its whole face seemed human, and not only human in the abstract sense but as human as her own face. And at that instant it imitated her movements, not like some sort of caricature, because there is always something unreal about a caricature, in the grossness of it. No, its imitation of her was totally true to life.

This impression lasted for a fraction of a second; it was like gazing down onto the surface of some fluid, pure alcohol for example, when all at once the surface becomes absolutely still and then you see your own reflection, and beyond it an abyss, and you feel yourself being sucked down into the abyss and there is a flash of not knowing whether the reflection is, in fact, the real you.

Then the reflection was erased, the animal sat back and Madelene pulled the carafe from her pocket. Using both hands, she filled it from the jar, took a swig, had to put down the carafe in order to catch her breath and would have lifted it again. Except that she could not, because some sort of plank had been placed on top of it. Her eye ran the length of the plank and met the ape's eye. It had put its hand over the carafe.

Madelene backed away.

"No," she said, "you're probably right."

Leaves and creepers dropped back into place in her wake, like waters converging. Soon only the ape's eyes were visible; then the thicket closed up and the animal was gone.

six

Madelene and Adam had been married for six months when Andrea Burden held a party at her home in Mayfair, the ostensible purpose of which was to welcome Madelene to the family. One minute after getting there Madelene had tried to make a run for it, but Adam had held her back.

Present had been twenty-odd members of the family, a cross section of the present and future British elite—men who had been fitted for their first dress suit at the age of five and women who had had servants to do their bidding from the cradle. And in Andrea Burden's company every one of them, regardless of age—from the youngest teenager to seventy-year-old Sir Toby, the government advisor on veterinary matters—had been as jumpy as a shoal of minnows sensing the shadow of the pike.

Drenched in champagne, the party had swum through a succession of rooms all opening off one another to end up in a dining room that looked for all the world like a gilded well, lit only by candelabra that were reflected over and over again in the burnished precious metals of the dinner service and with so many oil paintings on the walls that the wallpaper was only visible at those spots where a painting had been taken down and replaced by a small white card from Lloyd's stating to which special exhibition the picture was on loan.

In this room Andrea Burden had made a speech in which she thanked every one of those present—none of whom Madelene had laid eyes on before—for their support in setting up a "development corporation"—a term that Madelene was hearing for the first time here—for Primrose Hill, Albert Terrace and Gloucester Gate—places that lay Madelene knew not where. So Madelene did not, in fact, understand one word of the verbal side of this welcome, but while Andrea was speaking she kept her eyes on her and what she saw was that Adam's sister was neither a buxom queen bee nor a wiry, indefatigable she-spider but that she was slender, smooth, angelic and deadly and that one of her objectives in gathering all of these people together was to smite as many as possible with one blow. This blow was delivered by her speech and when it came to an end the company stayed down. Her guests had listened to it sitting bolt upright, eyes fixed on the tablecloth, with no hope of fleeing, transfixed by a blood tie of the sort which, beneath the seeming chaos on the surface, binds an anthill together through rigorous discipline. Afterward dessert was indeed served and a feeble conversation was even struck up and Madelene sensed that these guests must have felt the lash before now and developed a high threshold of pain. But the company as a whole was still reeling and one by one couples slipped away, seen to the door and kissed on the cheek by Andrea Burden, who graciously accepted their transparent excuses.

When only Adam and Madelene were left, the hostess sank into a capacious armchair across from them and eyed Madelene's wineglassful of cognac.

"She doesn't scare that easily, does she?" she said to Adam.

Madelene realized then that Adam's sister was driven by motives more complex than common malice. She had felt a twinge of curiosity, an urge to get to the bottom of the other woman.

Not long afterward Andrea Burden had shown them to the door. They had gone down just three of the front steps when she came after them.

"I'm sorry to have to tell you this, Adam, but they've been checking up in the kitchen; there's a fork missing."

Adam halted and stared wordlessly into the night.

"You two are, of course, above suspicion. I just thought I ought to mention it. It is C. J. Vander after all."

"I'll send you a replacement," said Adam, tight-lipped.

Then he and Madelene had leaned on one another—she reduced to a spineless jelly by drink and he rigid with suppressed fury—and together they had stalked off into the night.

Since then Madelene had seen Andrea Burden only briefly and in passing, until three days earlier when she had come with the ape. Now Madelene was on her way to see her again. For the second day running she was on the underground, heading this time for Aldgate and struggling, as she sat there, to reconstruct her ambiguous picture of Adam's sister.

Madelene had begun that day by changing her life.

She had woken up two hours earlier than usual, after a short but deep sleep, to the conviction that the past two days had been a bad dream, a hallucination, and that she was now going to make a fresh start. Even before she was fully awake she had perceived that the true meaning of life lay in love, that from now on she was going to live for Adam, unselfishly, following her mother's example, maybe even give up drinking.

And after a little concentrated effort in front of the mirror she raced down to the kitchen, still in her dressing gown, to persuade Mrs. Clapham to let her do the honors for Adam herself.

She brewed his tea, and made toast. She walked down to the garage with him, and once the car had turned the corner and driven out of sight she had a sudden urge to run, through the kitchen garden and out through the little door in the wall and out onto the pavement. There she would stand and wave, unexpected and stunning, as he drove past. She heard the buzz of the automatic gates and her hands were already in the air when it dawned on her that Adam's Aston Martin was retreating into the distance, that for the first morning ever he had turned right instead of left.

Right was the wrong way, eastward, in the opposite direction from Regent's Park and the Institute. To begin with, Madelene just stood there. Then she whipped off her slippers and ran.

She rounded the corner in time to catch a last glimpse of the car's rear end. She was still waving and shouting when a car pulled away from the curb a few yards ahead of her, and just as it occurred to Madelene that this was the same white car driven by the same gray man whom Clapham had turned away and whom she had seen again later, a truck with a picture of a dog on its door swung out and drove after the white car that was following Adam, and neither of the drivers in the two pursuing vehicles noticed Madelene, who was left standing there forlornly with no one to wave to, witness to a pattern she could not understand.

Back in her room, on her bed, with trembling hands she fished out her carafe, glanced fearfully about her like a deer on a riverbank, then knocked back two half glassfuls in quick succession.

She immediately grew calmer. Ordinarily, alcohol sparked off an amusement park inside Madelene, complete with a roller coaster in which, after climbing into it, there was no way of predicting in which direction you were likely to be catapulted. This time, however, she was not catapulted anywhere, this time the liquid immersed her in mellow, voluptuous sentimentality. She thought of Adam, of his iron will, his drive. She started to cry. Her tears watered the rose-pink satin and up sprang the desire for a grand reconciliation. She had to see him right away. She had to have him now, physically, inside her. Anywhere, in his office if necessary.

She grabbed the telephone and dialed his direct line, her longing for the sound of his voice so powerful that she had no chance to be surprised when the secretary answered.

"May I speak to Adam?" she said.

From the woman's voice and her reply Madelene gathered three things. That the secretary believed she was speaking to Priscilla, that she had already given up any idea of resistance and that Adam had managed to fool the world once again *and* to cover his tracks.

"Mr. Burden is working at home," she said. "Can I take a message?"

Madelene leaned back against the wall. Had she been alone, the conversation would have stopped there. But she was not alone. The secretary had summoned up a spirit, one that was now materializing. Priscilla took the receiver out of Madelene's hand.

"Write this down," she said. " 'Your body means more to me than all the streaky bacon in Smithfield Market.' "

Then she replaced the receiver.

She walked out into the corridor, down the stairs and through the house, not with any particular end in view but because she was too shaken to sit still. In the doorway to the terrace stood Clapham.

"Might I offer you a steaming-hot cup of freshly brewed mocha?" he said.

Madelene took the rose he held out to her.

"As long as it's strong," she said.

It was strong, black and thick as oil paint, and as she drank it, Madelene's eyes rested thoughtfully on Clapham. He seemed to be in good form, relaxed; everything was as normal. From his laid-back vantage point he could discharge his duty while at the same time exercising the control of an authoritative butler over the woman who was his superior in name only.

He thought they were alone on the terrace as always. Only Madelene detected the shadow of the other woman falling across the table.

"The car you turned away yesterday, I don't know whether that might have been any of my business?"

Clapham drained his cup and set it down, bottom up, in a definitive tradesman's gesture.

"Duty calls," he said.

Madelene's eyes clouded over. Right at this moment, more than ever before, she needed him to have remained in his seat. For him to have laid his head—metaphorically speaking—in her lap and shown her kindness and just a smidgen of respect. But instead here he was joining up with the caravan that had broken camp that morning, leaving her all alone in the British Sahara.

"Sit down!" she said.

Clapham froze.

"You do not get up when I am talking to you."

The man bowed his head. He felt the sting but could not see from which direction the blows had come. Madelene herself hardly knew. Priscilla alone was aware that the tone of voice she was now brandishing over Clapham's head came from Adam. That it was his master's voice the man in front of her was obeying.

"The white car, Clapham?"

"The veterinary authorities."

Neither of the two women had ever heard of such a body,

but they realized they were riding a wave that might break at any minute and there was no time to look back.

"On what business?"

"To see Mr. Burden."

"And you said?"

"That Mr. Burden was not at home."

Madelene paused, allowing events to build up to the final question.

"Where is Mr. Burden?"

Clapham's frame stiffened. Slowly Madelene and Priscilla got to their feet.

"Where is Mr. Burden?"

"Aldgate. The Animal Welfare Foundation."

Madelene followed through with her action, and Clapham ducked as though he really was expecting a blow.

But Madelene did not strike him. Gently she patted the uncooperative, unsympathetic, uncomprehending figure before her on the head.

"Thanks for the coffee," she said.

seven

You find them on the drab fringes of every European city: little offices where elderly ladies volunteer their time to discreet societies dedicated to genteelly, and quite inconspicuously, pleading the case for the preservation of the hedgehog or the gillyflower or the water shrew. And it was in such surroundings that Madelene had envisaged finding Andrea Burden. That, however, was not what she found.

The lobby on the thirteenth floor of the House of the Animals in Aldgate was not drab but actively gray and, standing before the polished tombstone on which the floor directory had been inscribed, Madelene began to suspect what was brought home to her in no uncertain terms once she had been let in by two steel-gray security guards—who then sent for a man in a gray suit—and had embarked on a long trek after said suit: that the Animal Welfare Foundation was not housed in one office or one section of some open-plan office floor but that this organization occupied a floating continent which took up one whole floor of the most expensive chunk of real estate in the world.

At journey's end sat two secretaries in a room as vast as the antechamber of a mausoleum. By now, under other circumstances, Madelene might well have felt overwhelmed by the weight of such surroundings. But not today. During the twenty minutes she had spent in the underground she had found some comfort. Not just in what she had drunk but also, and more especially, in a clear certitude as to her errand.

She had reviewed her previous meetings with Adam's sister, even though this severely taxed her powers of recall—she was by no means sober now and had been anything but sober then. This exercise had nevertheless had a calming effect on her, since she had eventually come to the conclusion that behind Andrea Burden's frosty demeanor there beat a warm and human heart. And if there was anything Madelene needed right now it was solace and human kindness. In Andrea's presence she would confront Adam, the other woman acting as a fond but firm intermediary, and everything would turn out just fine. Whereas Madelene had boarded the train like an animal fleeing a forest fire that has finally reached its own lair, she arrived at her destination like a lost chick seeking shelter under the mother hen's wing.

And there was in fact something rather maternal about Andrea Burden's smile as she entered the outer office, a warmth in the kiss she planted on Madelene's cheek, a protective air to the way in which she shepherded her into her office and closed the door behind them.

Then, softly, standing just inside the door, she delivered the first right straight to the chin.

"Madelene darling," she said, "what can I offer you this early in the day? A large gin?"

Alcohol was Madelene's most intimate secret, a deep-seated chamber of her heart, awash with liquid, which she could have sworn she had succeeded in hiding from the outside world. Until now.

In the gulf of suspended reality that now opened up, it occurred to Madelene that the one way above all in which animals differ from human beings is in the consistency of their thought processes. The most terrifying thing about the permanent uncertainty from which she herself suffered was its volatility. There were days when she mistrusted her body, others when she feared for her sanity and still others when she lost faith in her marriage, her hair, her financial situation, her actions, her smell, her senses. The possibilities were endless. Whenever she thought that she had now arrived at an albeit lengthy but at long last definitive index of all the forms taken by her self-hate, up it would pop in some hitherto unseen guise.

The face before her represented the antithesis of this inner imbalance. Andrea Burden eyed her with the cold, appraising curiosity of a reptile.

The room was empty; there was no sign of Adam. As things now stood, that was all for the best. Madelene sank down onto a chair.

"I just wanted to see this place," she said.

"A workplace must seem quite stimulating. To someone who doesn't actually do anything."

Madelene knew her time was up. She would find herself an elephants' graveyard to which she could drag herself off and die. If only she had the strength to get up out of the chair.

"A little drink would be lovely," she said.

A glass was placed in front of her.

"This place, why does it look the way it does?" she asked.

"The endangered species and the most popular pet animals attract very large sums of money. We distribute these funds."

"It looks like a crypt."

"Death is a great confidence inspirer. All banks are designed to look like burial vaults."

"Where's Adam?"

Andrea Burden made no reply. She had walked around behind the chair; Madelene could feel her hands on the chair back.

"You must see the view," she said. "Before you go."

The chair lurched under Madelene. The other woman had turned her and the chair around in a semicircle.

Madelene closed her eyes, smarting from the gin and surprised by the force of this maneuver. Then she opened them.

Three of the office walls were of plate glass. Beneath and before them stretched London, remote and unreal.

Andrea Burden had remained standing like a nurse behind a patient in a wheelchair.

"What are you thinking?" she asked.

London was not a city. Madelene could see that now. For a city has an end. There was no limit to the irregular, rippling expanse of stone below her. Even at the point where the curve of the earth formed the horizon, buildings reared up, out on the visible bounds of the universe.

She could see that it was too vast for just one sort of weather. Around them, over St. Katharine's Dock and the Thames, the sun was shining. The sky over the new City was cloudy and gray. To the east, over Docklands, it was raining. And on the south side of the river hung a yellow curtain of industrial fumes.

"How can anyone bear to live here?" she said.

"We adapt. Even to an existence such as this. The ability to adapt is the mark of a human being."

Andrea Burden stepped into the light, alongside the chair.

"20,500 chickens per day," she said. "To feed London. 5,800 pigs. 1,520 head of beef. 6,000 sheep. According to the Meat and Livestock Commission. Each day the city consumes four million pounds of animal protein. London could be regarded as a monstrous machine for the processing of domestic animals. That, however, is not how I see it. Because the slaughterhouses are only one small part of the story. If we look beyond basic sustenance, the first group we come to are the working animals. In Greater London there are at least 5,000 watchdogs registered with security firms. At least 5,000 horses in service as drays and hacks. 4,000 racehorses belonging to fifty different stables, 2,000 police and cavalry mounts, 3,000 greyhounds, 3,000 homing pigeons. Then there are the animals that satisfy other needs. The Office for National Statistics estimates that down below us there are a million dogs, one and a half million cats, five million cage birds (species unspecified), two million small rodents (guinea pigs and the like), and a number of reptiles and fish at which we can only hazard a guess. Not forgetting those animals in scientific research laboratories—private and public—and pharmaceutical plants, the livestock kept on city farms, at the veterinary colleges and so on. A group which, in the Greater London area, is estimated to amount to ten million animals, ranging in size from shrews to musk oxen. And all of this, all of these twenty million–plus living creatures are not even the half of it. The other half are what might be termed the animal lumpen proletariat of the city. The stray dogs, the wild cats, that band of semi-wild animals which strive to adapt to the city biotope: foxes, pigeons, house mice, seagulls, rats, insects. And we haven't even begun to talk about the zoos and aquariums."

Andrea Burden had moved across to the glass, her back to Madelene. Now she turned to face her.

"London is not just an organism that processes animals. There is far more to it than that. Our biologists calculate that this city contains more than thirty million nonhuman creatures, representing 10,000 separate species. They put the animal biomass at 350,000 pounds per square mile. Do you know what that tells us?"

Madelene shook her head.

"It means that not only are there more animals in London than in any British oak wood, or anywhere else in the British Isles for that matter. It means there is a greater incidence of animal life here than, for example, in Mato Grosso in the dry season. London is one of *the* largest habitats for nonhuman creatures on this earth."

Madelene looked out across the city, down into her now empty glass and out across the city again.

"So what?" she said.

She did not mean to be rude, but explicit politeness takes energy and Madelene was running on empty.

"Now let me see you out," said Andrea Burden.

She helped Madelene out of the chair. The carpet beneath her feet had acquired a muddy cast.

"But we humans," said Madelene, "we matter too, don't we?"

"We made a choice. Animals were brought here. It's the victims that concern me."

Andrea Burden put the gin bottle in a brown paper bag and handed it to Madelene.

"Take the bottle for the trip back. It was lovely to see you. Be an angel and call before you come next time."

Madelene steadied herself against the doorpost and scanned the face opposite her. It struck her that the other woman had set her a test. And that she had failed it, without ever having worked out on what question she was being examined.

"You forgot something," she said. "The animals the behavioral scientists work with."

Adam's sister gripped her arm, ready to throw her out. Already her gaze had grown distant.

In Madelene's mind five images converged on one another: London, the ape, Adam, Priscilla and the coldness of the face before her. They ran together and burst into flames.

"Actually, what I came to say was that I had a very strict upbringing," she said. "I've always had a terrible problem with any kind of wrongdoing. I can't sleep at night. Get throat infections. It's the ape. At our place. What with Adam's position. It was you who brought it. The boss of this splendid establishment. With never a word to the veterinary authorities. I might have to go to the police. That's what I came to say."

Prior to this, Andrea Burden's movements had been fluttery and spasmodic. The first time Madelene met her she had taken this for the mark of a ditherer, but she had since learned to liken it to a prizefighter bobbing and weaving around his opponent. Now she was still. She had no time to regain her balance before Madelene was on her again.

"Or maybe I should go straight to the papers. I haven't been able to eat for days. I kept hoping someone would give me an explanation."

They were back beside the window and there they stayed, on the brink of the urban abyss.

Andrea Burden lowered her head.

"I would like to invite you to London Zoo," she said. "Tomorrow. Before the workmen arrive. Would seven o'clock suit you?"

"I haven't been to a zoo since I was a child," said Madelene.

They walked back to the door. Andrea Burden opened it; the suit was waiting in the outer office.

"About the papers," said Andrea Burden, "and the police?"

Madelene kept her in suspense for a moment before answering.

"We'll have to talk about that tomorrow," she said. "At the Zoo."

eight

At first glance there was nothing remarkable about the way in which Adam Burden ate dinner. Closer inspection revealed that it adhered to a set of rules which represented the culmination of a four-hundred-year-long process of evolution in upper-class table manners. He received the food with a caress, parted it, conducted steaming-hot mouthfuls into his discreetly exposed innards, gently coerced corks out of slender bottle necks, dabbed his lips delicately with a napkin which materialized in his hand, then vanished without trace into his lap, that no meat juices would smear the gleaming glass held by the stem alone to prevent the throbbing pulse from affecting the temperature of the wine. When it was all over and Mrs. Clapham had taken away the dishes and laid bare the tablecloth, the white linen offered no clue as to what had gone before.

Madelene had known from the start that she would never be able to match this regular, daily balancing act. When she sat down to a meal she was hungry, usually extremely hungry, to the extent that the food occupied almost all of her thoughts, with whatever was left being focused on spilling as little as possible and—more and more often—on keeping herself from falling off the chair. So there was very little energy to spare for following Adam's animated conversation. Like a well-mannered season-ticket holder, she had long since learned to applaud in all the right places while her attention was somewhere else entirely.

But not this evening. This evening, though tired, she was all ears. Listening not to what Adam was saying but for the break in the flow of words that would facilitate her own entrance. Because this evening Madelene had devised a role for herself.

"There was a man here today," she said. "From the veterinary authorities. He was complaining that Clapham had refused to let him in. He wanted to talk to you."

Adam's face lost its air of preoccupation. First it went blank. Then a fine veil of fear settled over it.

"And then this woman rang."

Adam stood up and backed off toward the empty grate. It was a wintertime move, and futile—the fire had been out since April.

"Her name was . . . Priscilla something or other. She wanted to know whether there were any . . . animals here."

By the fireplace Adam froze.

"The birds, I told her. The ones we feed on the grounds. And Clapham's goldfish. But that's all."

Adam leaned his head back against the mantelpiece.

"I thought it best not to mention the ape. I mean maybe it hasn't been . . . what do you call it? Reported? If that's what you're supposed to do with animals? Or what? Could you tell me, please?"

It took some time for Adam to answer her and when he did his voice was hoarse.

"The Washington Convention lists all wild animals under

three different headings depending on how great the threat to each species is considered to be. Strictly speaking, animals that appear on these lists must be reported to the Ministry of Agriculture's CITE office—that's the body in this country which sees to it that the terms of the convention are observed."

"Which," said Madelene, "just hasn't happened in this case."

"More often than not the Ministry will contact us. So in a way I represent the controlling body."

"That's what scares me," said Madelene. "That's why I almost confided in this Priscilla woman, and said, 'Listen, what if these'—what were they called again?—'controlling bodies break the law themselves? What then?'"

What was running through Adam's mind during the long silence that now descended was not the connotation of what Madelene had said. Nor was it the painfulness of the situation. It was at Madelene as a person that he stared. Behind the woman across from him he was trying to catch a glimpse of the individual he had married only seventeen months earlier.

"Five days," he said. "It'll be here for another five days. Then it's gone."

Anyone who drinks tends to lose their natural, essential tiredness. In recent months Madelene had been having more and more difficulty in getting to sleep. Nonetheless, that night she took two caffeine tablets and drank three cups of black coffee, wanting to be quite sure she would stay awake. Then she sat down to wait.

At ten o'clock a car drove into the courtyard. From the window she watched Adam come out to meet two men, after which they and Clapham spent the next two hours carrying boxes of various sizes from the car into the garden room. Then the car drove away. At two in the morning Adam emerged and went up to his rooms. Madelene gave him five minutes, then followed him.

When she entered the room it was empty. Adam was in the bathroom. The long table that ran the length of one wall was covered with large sheets of paper and on top of the paper stood a jar containing a huge brain suspended in a clear fluid.

A good many hours had passed since Madelene had put her mind into neutral. Her actions were now guided by decisions taken at another time of day and so she did not stop to think before pulling out the large rubber cork and sniffing the fluid, with the instinctive curiosity that drives alcoholics to comb every new stretch of terrain for any potential reservoir.

The bouquet that rose to meet her nostrils was the repellent, sickly-sweet odor of formaldehyde.

She replaced the cork and straightened up. The feeling that washed over her was not disappointment that the brain had not been preserved in alcohol. It was the fear that this might be the ape's brain. That, having completed their examination, they had then cut open the skull and removed its brain.

The bathroom door opened and Adam came out. His face was gray with fatigue, his eyes red as an albino rabbit's.

He stopped dead. Saw Madelene's hand on the glass, read her thoughts and remembered dinner.

"It's the brain of a chimpanzee," he said. "From the Institute collection."

Remembering her mission, Madelene walked over to her husband and put her arms around him.

"I'm not quite myself," she said. "But I just wanted to touch you before I went to bed."

This close, convincing hug was what she had come to give. With it she wiped the exhaustion from his face. With it she erased the memory of that evening's discord. And with it, as the tips of her fingers ran up over his buttocks, from the clip on his belt she stole his keys.

She waited in her bedroom for twenty minutes. Then she snuck through the darkened rooms, found the key to the potting shed and garden room on Adam's key ring and let herself in.

A forest of boxes, lamps and instruments had sprung up around and in front of the cage and this she worked her way through, paying it no heed. She knew that these things were intended for use on the ape and that they would never have the chance to fulfill their purpose.

She unlocked the cage and remained in the doorway for a moment, looking at the animal. She was never going to see it again and so she tried to imprint its image on her memory, to take a mental farewell picture.

The ape was eating. It ate absorbedly, egoistically, as Madelene herself had always dreamed of eating, with every sense other than those of taste and smell suspended, stripped of all mannerliness and with that same lack of fear that had, from the beginning, seemed like a question aimed at her, a question that, she now realized, had been asking: How do you really want to be? And to this question her heart had answered: I want—in some way—to be like you.

"I've come to let you out," she said.

The ape rose. It placed its fists on the ground and pushed itself into a position which, while erect, still left it on all fours. From there it kept on going, relinquished its hold on the ground, straightened its back, lifted its head and clasped its hands across its chest.

Madelene had been aware that the ape had—to some degree and in a way she did not understand—been learning from the people and goings-on around it. Even so, she was staggered. For a moment they stood there, quite still, she and the ape face to face. Then she turned toward the grille and opened first it and then the conservatory door. They stepped out into the park.

The wind had risen. In a cold, midnight-blue sky it chased the clouds across the face of the man in the moon. The ape bent its head back, seeming to drink in the wind and the moonlight.

Madelene crossed to the wall, set her carafe on the top and clambered up after it. The ape materialized alongside her.

This was as far as Madelene had planned. She would now pick out an escape route for the ape, it would set out for home and she would be left standing in the moonlight, smiling, shedding a tear, looking wonderful and drinking one for the road.

She was, at this point, sitting a couple of yards above the ground. Suddenly, just as she raised her hand, she shot up another sixty yards. She grew to the height from which, in the House of the Animals, she had viewed London. She saw the city not with human eyes but with those of a bird. But this was by no means an objective view. It was a vision. And what she perceived was that the freedom she had been so eager to plot out for the ape no longer existed.

What she had seen from that building in Aldgate was a city that stretched to the ends of the earth. And even though she knew that to be impossible, that even this wilderness of inhabited stonework petered out somewhere or other, the principle of it went on forever. What mattered was not the city itself, since that too was only one small dot on the face of the earth. What mattered was the principle of the city—modern civilization per se. Madelene saw that there was no longer any end to that; it had totally enmeshed the globe. There was no longer any *outside* for the ape at her elbow. Any zoo, any game reserve, any safari park whatever was now contained within the bounds of civilization.

Everyone—even someone who has read as little as Madelene had done—takes for their own the dream of *terra incognita*, the unknown, unexplored world. For one painful moment this dream was bathed in the light of reality; then it dissolved. Madelene knew that this was now beyond her reach forever. From now on there was no quest for the Golden Fleece, or the jewels of Opar, the center of the earth, the

Promised Land, lost horizons, El Dorado, Atlantis, the Islands
of the Hesperides or simply the land of milk and honey.

She turned to face the ape.

"There's no such thing as *outside* now," she said. "If
there's any freedom to be found it'll have to be on the inside."

Over the past few days she had been reminded of her
childhood longing, not for some image of bliss, but for bliss
itself. Not for herself—her own sober common sense was, in
spite of everything, too strong for that—but for the ape. She
had grown more and more convinced that she could save it by
helping it to make the break for freedom.

Now she abandoned this last illusion.

There is nothing pleasant about abandoning the protection
afforded by hopes and daydreams and Madelene shrank from
it like a hermit crab forced to leave its whelk shell. There was
a hopelessness to her situation that would have prompted
stronger characters than she to contemplate a speedier form
of suicide than that offered by alcohol and Madelene was
struck, momentarily, by the thought of jumping to her death.

A split second and the thought was gone. Not only because
it dawned on her that she was not on the thirteenth floor but
only a couple of yards above the ground, but to a much greater
extent for another reason. Those alter egos who had taken their
place beside her over the last couple of days found the thought
that they should suddenly be snuffed out quite unacceptable.

It felt as though yet another woman had settled herself
beside her on the wall. Turning toward her, Madelene saw that
this was Responsibility. A figure both as neutral and as undeniably present as the moonlight and the wind and the smell
of earth.

Madelene slid down the wall, the woman followed her, then
the ape. They walked back the way they had come. Once
inside the cage Madelene locked the door behind them.

"It's not like when we were little," she said. "You can't
just run away from home. It's too complicated now. We need
more time."

She peered through the glass, across the electronic landscape. She saw the anesthetic apparatus, trolleys loaded with monitoring equipment, a white box on wheels resembling a twin-size coffin, a hydraulic chair connected to a huge machine that looked—with all its electronic purposefulness—like a domestic version of the electric chair.

"They're coming to get you," she said, "and it's going to be worse than it's ever been before."

She put out her hand and the ape took it. The palm of its hand was as big as a shovel but, contrary to what she had expected, it was soft as silk.

"I'm going now," she said. "But I'll be back for you."

This was not some ritual prognosis, like a wedding vow or a New Year's resolution. It was an oath of a kind to which Madelene had not been moved in twenty years. It was a fearless declaration of faith with no thought for the future, such as a child will make to an irreplaceable playmate.

nine

As a child Madelene had been dragged along, by people who thought they were doing a good deed, to Copenhagen Zoo. There she had seen ospreys in budgerigar cages, beasts of prey in menagerie box stalls, hippos in tiled bathrooms and anthropoid apes that flung first their excrement and then themselves against the bars surrounding them in mute protest. Since then she had never set foot inside any establishment in which animals were held captive. Now here she was, following Andrea Burden through the London Zoo, and on through a little door in the twenty-foot-high fence of wood and wire netting which had, for two years, encircled the construction work on the site overlooking Gloucester Gate. In less than two months, this site, together with the extension onto Primrose Hill and Albert Terrace, would be linked up to London Zoo for the inauguration of the New London Regent's Park Zoological Garden.

Madelene had been prepared for the worst. She had

brought along a cardboard tube which looked—and was meant to look—as though it might hold a student's, or perhaps an architect's, drawings—which, in a sense, it did—but which also contained a Pyrex flask filled by her on getting up that morning and now only two-thirds full. She had stepped through the door with eyes closed. Now, slowly, she opened them.

The light was golden, the shadows long and green, the air as fresh and cool as a fine spray of atomized spring water. Before them spread a grassy plain on the outskirts of which Madelene could make out a large lake with a llama grazing on its bank. In the middle of the lake was an island, on which an antelope bent to drink. Beyond the lake a forest reared up—one of the trees swayed back and forth, a group of gorillas having taken up residence in it like a flock of huge, lumbering black birds. To the west the forest ran out into a rocky outcrop atop which a pride of waking lions stretched languorously in the sunlight.

The memory Madelene had retained of the zoos of her childhood was of landscaped animal prisons. What she was confronted with here was a tropical scene, at the point where the savanna meets the jungle.

Only a distant skyline, the odd concrete barricade, a glass wall, an asphalt path betrayed the fact that the scene in front of them was man-made.

"At this hour of the day," said Andrea Burden, "I think I know how God must have felt walking through the Garden on the morning of the sixth day."

Madelene made a vain attempt to recall the chronology of the Creation.

"How did he feel?" she asked.

"There's a tranquillity to the early morning. One can think clearly. He would have been able to draw up his budget for the next day in peace and quiet."

They sat down on a stone balustrade. At their feet the ground plunged away to a ditch thirty feet below.

"But he didn't have the problems we've had with private landownership. Or free enterprise. Just as there were no such problems in the last century when Sir Stamford Raffles founded the London Zoo, for the edification of an exclusive, blue-blooded public and with a mere handful of specimens of the beasts of the field and the birds of the air. Things are different now. The land on which London is built, the ground on which we now sit is owned by the Crown. You cannot imagine—no outsider could possibly imagine—what we have had to go through to acquire the lease to this plot of land. Until the present government came into power all negotiations were channeled through the Royal Parks Agency. Now it's chaos. We eventually found ourselves dealing, on one side, with the Corporation of London and its representatives, the city of Westminster, the Borough of Camden, the London Boroughs' Association, the Common Council of London. On another with the Crown Estate Paying Commission, which handles the conveyancing of Crown property. On a third with the Department of National Heritage. And on a fourth with the developers who held the contract for Albert Terrace. Not to mention the agents of those residents who had to be bought out."

She took a deep breath.

"It's all settled now. We won the first round, now comes the semifinal. Once we're open, we'll be having to compete with the safari parks, and with every tourist attraction in the city. Both for visitors and for funding. We'll have to hold our own against six hundred zoos in the United States and Europe, eight hundred throughout the rest of the world. We will be required to keep a running record of results achieved within the fields of breeding, research and acquisitions. If we are to keep our place on the European Endangered Species Program and in the group that controls CBSG, which controls the allocation of all the most valuable wild animals in captivity and decides which zoo is to be in charge of the studbook for a particular species. We're banking on becoming studbook keepers for ten species within the first two years. And for ten more over the next ten. We've got our sights set on fifteen million visitors a year. We're budgeting fifteen million pounds for research. Two years ago we took over St. Francis Forest, for use as a breeding center. It's going to cost us ten million pounds per annum to run that and Whipsnade together."

Below them, in slow motion, a jaguar made its way across the rocks and down to the water and began to lap.

"Maybe you could get the animals to pay for their room and board," said Madelene.

"That's the name of the game if you want to create a zoo on this scale. If God were to take another crack at the Creation that couldn't be done from scratch either. Or for the benefit of two spectators in their birthday suits. Nowadays he'd have to get out there and raise the money first. And then he'd have to drum up a mass audience. And then . . ."

"Then maybe he'd just drop the whole idea and leave the animals in peace," said Madelene.

She could have kept her mouth shut. Only a week ago she would have said nothing. But behind her, on the stone balustrade, Priscilla had now perched herself. The jaguar alone had noticed and gazed intently at this third party to the conversation.

Andrea Burden stood up and closed in, making those small, slithery, semicircular movements that Madelene had learned to recognize.

"So she loves freedom, does she?" she said. "She loves the wide-open spaces. The true, the paradisiacal world of nature. The one she heard stories about as a child. So she could cope with the storybooks at home, then? And if not, no doubt there were always the cartoons."

She pointed at the jaguar.

"Do you know what lies in store for that in the swamp forests of western Brazil? Do you know what fate awaits those big cats? Those and all other wild animals? They're destined for the kind of suffering that can only be conceived of in statistical terms. Three out of four cubs die in infancy. Of those that survive the first year, one in two will reach sexual maturity, the others will perish. One in eight will go so far as to mate. Seldom more than once. After that they die of hunger. Or thirst. If they're not eaten by other jaguars. Or gored by warthogs, after which the wound becomes infected and infested with maggots that crawl up through the musculature and attack the brain, after which . . ."

"Stop," said Madelene.

"God knew nothing of this back then on the sixth morning, when he still believed that everything was just perfect. But eventually it must have dawned on him—like most behavioral scientists, he was probably a bit slow on the uptake—that what he had actually created was a factory for the manufacture of suffering. That the whole point of the jaguar is that by pushing itself to the breaking point it should be subjected to a certain number of afflictions which will keep it alive just long enough for it to mate."

"Well, at least it has a taste of love before it dies," Madelene said.

Andrea Burden drew her lips back from her teeth in a smile of sorts.

"You bet your life it does," she said. "And let me tell you how. You see, the jaguar goes through its life alone. Then one day it picks up a scent and follows it, driven by an innate biological urge it cannot understand. It follows this scent and all of a sudden it comes face to face with another big cat. It does not see it as a reflection of itself, because it has no concept of self. It sees it as a mortal threat. It wants to run—both animals want to run—but they cannot. They are pinned to the spot by a set of genetic stocks. She turns her back to him, prostrates herself, he jumps on top of her and digs his teeth into her neck. And do you know why? A sign of passion, perhaps? Of love? I'll tell you why. It is for a reason so glaringly obvious that even the zoologists could not miss it. It is because, if he did not hold her down, the female—terrified out of her wits—would turn on him and kill him. Then he couples with her. And just as he pulls out of her, just as he relinquishes his grip, all she-jaguars, all she-cheetahs, all she-tigers, all she-cats the world over make the same instinctive move. And do you know what that is? Do you know how they show their appreciation for this coupling? They stretch back their necks and swivel their heads around. And then they try to see whether they can get away with ripping his carotid arteries with their eyeteeth."

The two women circled around one another. The jaguar and Priscilla followed them with their eyes.

"None of you ever asked a jaguar," said Madelene. "It is quite possible to look as though you're suffering even when you're enjoying yourself."

"Every he-cat's penis is equipped with a number of barbs. As it withdraws, these barbs tear into the she-cat's flesh. The pain of this triggers ovulation. And that—through pain—is how nature guarantees the greatest possible likelihood of fertilization and the continuation of the species."

Madelene looked away.

"Even so," she said, "no one can know . . . how . . ."

Andrea Burden leaned on the balustrade and looked at the jaguar. Her face shone with the utter fulfillment of a mother watching her child.

"It is my firm belief," she said, "that the best zoos can provide animals with almost everything that nature could. Food, light, the right breeding conditions. While also to some extent lessening their suffering."

Priscilla motioned to Madelene.

"And the ape?" she said.

Andrea Burden did not answer her directly.

"Until a few years ago," she said slowly, "the polar bear enclosure was thought to be the most dangerous place in a zoo. Those thick, furry coats and brown eyes made people want to stick their hands in and scratch the animals' backs. If they did, one swat from a paw would tear the visitor's arm off at the elbow. I've been having second thoughts about that, though. The way I see it now, the most dangerous enclosures are . . . those ones over there."

Madelene followed her gaze. Above the ape jungle, on the other side of Prince Albert Road, towered the gray silhouette of the Institute of Animal Behavioral Research.

"The academic aviary."

She pointed up beyond Primrose Hill.

"Hampstead. Where the top-level civil servants—the decision makers—have their private residences. Right next door to the burghers of the financial world. The barnyard of political and financial power. With the most rigid pecking order in the animal kingdom. The most disproportionate relationship between body and brain size. Real peacocks throw themselves into a brief and bloody skirmish, after which they live in sly peace, with the victor as their leader. But out there there's no end to the lunacy of it, the infighting. Over there they give to the World Wildlife Fund with the one hand and sell weapons and trees from the rain forests with the other. Over there they had revoked London Zoo's funding and starved the place to the point where the animals were dying off in their cages. Until we embarked upon our . . . campaign. It is the members of these worthy bodies who will decide who is to be the new director, when London's two zoological gardens become one in two months from now."

Andrea Burden paused. Somewhere a bird screeched—a harsh, abrupt, primeval cry.

"This is going to be one of the most powerful posts in the zoological world. And I've made up my mind that they should appoint your husband to it. The ape will clinch his appointment. It will bring the last of the skeptics into the fold. You see, it's not enough that Adam is smarter than all of the others put together. Not enough that he has written forty papers and three books in five languages. Applications will be sent in from every corner of the globe. The ballot will be secret and thoroughly corrupt. But if he has a three-week start on the others, alone with the ape, no one else will be able to touch him. That is why it's being kept at your place. Under conditions that are in every way warrantable. And why we've strayed, very slightly, from the terms of the Convention. To ensure that much greater respect for it in the future."

"Adam says it's some kind of dwarf chimpanzee," said Madelene. "What do you think?"

Andrea Burden hesitated for a second.

"I'm not a zoologist," she said.

She took Madelene's arm and pulled her along. Madelene halted. Someone—herself or Priscilla—reached out a hand and grabbed the other woman by the arm.

"Why Adam?"

Andrea Burden tried to extricate herself. But via Madelene's hand Priscilla hung on to her arm with a grip accustomed to manhandling butcher's hooks and thousand-pound beef carcasses.

"Adam," said Madelene, "likes animals because . . . because they can't do him any harm. Because he's superior to them. But he doesn't trust them. He doesn't trust any living creature. Not even me."

A third woman had joined Madelene and Priscilla, invisible and as yet nameless, but quite distinct from Madelene herself. A person of a certain straightforward integrity. It was she who now spoke.

"Even at those times when we're really close, when you think that now everything is going to be different, he never lets go. He's afraid . . . that I'm going to turn my head around and rip his carotid arteries. And now it's worse than ever. It has something to do with the ape. He's very frightened. Very dangerous."

Andrea Burden lifted a face that was, for an instant, naked.

"Boarding schools," she said. "You're packed off to school somewhere between the ages of four and ten. That's quite usual for our class. It's considered to give one the best possible start in life. Sport, art and literature, four foreign languages. Courses on running a gracious establishment and household accounts for us girls. You get everything. Except love. For ten years. After that it's too late. For the rest of your life you're like a soldier at the front. Covering your back. Because no one else is going to. Like in Churchill's memoirs. The letter from Afghanistan. To his mother. In the break in his account of how they destroyed the irrigation network. About his time at Sandhurst. Where he calls himself a stunted tree. He didn't have the courage to say it straight out. That's why you make the choice not to have children. Because you know what they would have to go through."

The two women enjoyed a split second of intimacy, as people do when they stop insisting on their own private masks, if only for a moment. Then Andrea Burden shrugged off this weakness.

"You're a foreigner," she said. "You'll never understand. But, no matter what, Adam is a lion. He has style, ambition and the knack for dealing with the ministries, the boards of directors and the university. He has the capability to run the zoo without any internal wrangling. He knows how to cut the outside opposition down to size. He's tamed the environmentalists, the local action groups *and* the Royal Institute of British Architects. We have to respect him for that. You and I both."

"I'm married to him," said Madelene. "And a marriage is not a zoo."

The two women looked one another in the eye. Under different circumstances Madelene would have dropped her gaze. But that was before she had tried looking into the eyes of Erasmus the ape. And so it was Andrea who was forced to look away.

They had reached the door in the fence. They stepped back into London Zoo. The gardens were open, the first punters of the day had shown up.

"I'm going to stay here for a little while," said Madelene. "See if I can pick up what was running through God's head later on that day."

Andrea Burden stood still.

"What you said . . . about going to the papers . . . ?" she said.

Like all she-animals, Madelene cherished a powerful desire for everything to end well, for every leave-taking to be uncomplicated and warm and wistful. This one too looked set to go that way; Madelene was prepared for a reconciliation. But at her back were two other women and it was up to her to answer for all of them.

"It's been postponed," she said. "Indefinitely. But it hasn't been canceled."

Once alone she made her way through the Zoo until she came to a telephone booth. She sat herself down on the balustrade surrounding the enclosure that housed the anteaters, viscachas and guanacos, pulled out her flask, saluted the animals and took a swig. She looked up at the Institute windows and tried to pinpoint Adam's office.

She knew there was no time to lose. That she was in much the same situation as Eve would have been in the Garden of Eden if, as soon as she herself had been created, she had discovered that God was about to go too far and decided to stop him. She would have been every bit as bewildered and overtaxed as Madelene was now. Because whatever it was that Andrea and Adam were putting together it was close to completion.

She walked over to the telephone booth. Dialed the number for the direct line to his front office.

The secretary made herself known.

"It's me," said Madelene. "Is he there?"

"I'll put you through."

Madelene glanced up at the gray edifice. Her head spun. She had been so sure he would not be there, that today too he would have stayed at home, in the garden room.

"Yes?"

"It's me," said Madelene.

Even without being all that well acquainted with the secretary Madelene knew for a fact that she was listening in. The alcohol and the early hour made her voice rasp like gravel on the seashore. Beneath this surface racket Adam recognized his wife's voice. The voice his secretary heard was that of Priscilla from the Meat Market.

"I had to hear your voice," she said.

Adam growled seductively, flattered. Madelene tried to think. She had to get into the Institute. But without any risk of running into him. She had to make sure that he stayed in his office until she was back outside again.

"If only I could touch you," she said.

"Mm."

She knew Adam's sounds. She knew he now had an erection.

She glanced around her. A group of old people came past her carrying peanuts for the monkeys.

"I've got this urge to talk dirty to you," she rasped. "Can I call you back in fifteen minutes?"

She could hear his breathing growing heavier. Lust outweighs logic every time. It never occurred to Adam to ask why their conversation had to be cut short just then.

"I'll be glued to the phone," he said.

Madelene hung up.

Heading at a jog for the main entrance, she pinned up her hair, put on her sunglasses and unbelted her coat to let it hang loosely around her. Parked at the curb was a truck with a picture of a dog on the door. It was empty. She walked into the Institute foyer to find the driver of this vehicle standing at the reception desk, being treated to a snarling rebuff from the terrier. Madelene took the elevator up and hurried past the door behind which the secretary and Adam sat waiting for her call.

The vet's office was empty. Madelene sat down to wait. She had ten minutes.

He walked in after five. With a cup of tea and a muffin.

"Sorry about this," said Madelene.

The doctor sat down.

"Why don't you just move in," he said. "I can have a bed set up for you."

"I don't know who else to ask but you," said Madelene.

In her own voice, under the huskiness, she caught the sound of that new and somewhat honest side of herself, with which she was not yet quite at home.

The doctor waggled his head.

"I like a bit of company over my morning tea. And no one here talks to me anymore."

"Why not?"

He pondered this question.

"Maybe because I'm growing senile. Maybe because we're on the threshold of a new age. And I belong to the old one. Or maybe for some other reason. What can I offer you?"

Madelene removed her sunglasses.

"You wouldn't happen to have a beer?"

The doctor reached into a small refrigerator at his back, then set a bottle and a glass in front of her.

Madelene poured the beer and drank. She opened the cardboard tube, put her flask on the desk and shook out a small bundle of white papers—sketches of the equipment she had seen outside the ape's cage the day before. Drawn from memory, but not with eyeliner. With black ink, very early that morning while she was still sober.

She handed the vet the first sketch, of the twin-size coffin on wheels and the electric chair.

"Brain scanning," said the doctor. "Equipment for brain scanning."

"How does it work?"

He shook his head.

"That falls under the heading of this new age," he said.

Madelene handed him the next sketch.

"A sleep monitor. They have one like this right below where we're sitting. In the Institute for Sleep Research. This one is designed for larger animals. You hook the beast up to it and switch it on. When it falls asleep, the force of gravity will cause some part of the body, an arm, a trunk, the neck, to droop. At which point it will receive a shock and wake up. They measure the length of time they can keep the animals awake. It's a method that's been well used. They've proved that animals can do without sleep. They haven't managed to convince the animals of this, though."

Madelene held out two more drawings.

"Those collapsible boxes are part of an obstacle course. Those, as far as I can see, are checkerboards."

He took yet another sheet from her.

"A stimulation simulator. Straight out of the Institute for Neuroetiology, two floors below us. They've cast some doubt on the extent to which animals can feel pain. And suggested that until animals can tell us in proper English that they *are* in pain there is no reason to suppose that cruelty to animals is being practiced."

He looked at Madelene.

"This machine is designed to carry out an extensive test on a fair-sized animal. Have they started doing behavioral research at the slaughterhouses?"

"Testing for what? What type of behavior?"

"Intelligence tests, I would say. Problem solving. But we're looking at some pretty hardhanded methods here. That sleep monitor, for example. It's become extremely difficult to obtain permission from the Animal Procedure Committee for its use. But perhaps this research can't wait?"

Madelene gathered up her papers.

"Can I borrow your phone?" she asked.

The vet flung out a hand.

"It's all yours. Keep it if you want. I'll be retiring next year. And no one calls now anyway."

Madelene dialed Adam's number. It took the secretary a moment to compose herself sufficiently to put her through.

"Are you alone?" Adam asked.

"Completely."

"Are you wearing anything?"

Madelene eyed the vet.

"No," she said. "Not a thing."

Adam whistled under his breath.

"It's stiff as a poker," he said.

Madelene cast an eye around the room, looking for inspiration. This was a tricky situation. She considered a row of dental charts hanging on the wall behind the vet.

"Can it be felt with the tongue?" she asked softly.

A moan issued from the receiver.

"I'll be . . . coming soon," said Madelene. "So I'm going to have to hang up."

She hung up and picked up her sketches.

"How's that allergy of yours?" the doctor asked.

"Better, thanks."

"I rang the Meat Marketing Board Research Center. They'd never heard of you."

Madelene took a deep breath.

"They've forgotten all about me. No sooner am I out the door than people have forgotten me."

"I've gone through the newsletters. For six months back. No theft of any large ape or apelike creature has been reported."

"You're an angel," said Madelene.

"Of course, there are always rumors. Once or twice over the past ten years there's been the odd whisper of an unidentified species of ape, some sort of primate, being offered for sale. We, of course, do not deal on the black market. And such a thing is, of course, impossible. With the Vu Quang ox, the last of the big mammals was discovered and documented. It has to have been a cross between some known species of ape."

Madelene stepped into the corridor, pushed off and made an unsteady attempt at a run, wanting to get past Adam's office.

The office door swung open and out came the secretary. It was evident, even to Madelene, that while this woman would usually have the most precise and rational grounds for her actions, on this occasion she was driven solely by an overwhelming desire to get away and to give vent to her indignation. On being confronted with Priscilla in the corridor she flattened herself against the wall.

Madelene flashed her a big smile. A smile of relief at the fact that it was not Adam she was faced with and a smile that said: Just because we've had our occasional differences that doesn't mean we can't all get along. Then she went on her way.

The first button she pushed in the elevator took her to the basement but on her next attempt she made it to the foyer. Her senses told her she had enough in reserve for tying up one more loose end. She walked over to the reception desk.

"I'm expecting a car," she said. "That man who was here earlier, might he have been my driver?"

The terrier clenched her teeth.

Madelene placed her cardboard tube on the desktop. The woman regarded it coldly.

"These," said Madelene, "are urgent brain-scan results. Anxiously awaited by government ministers and princes. We're talking life or death. If you've let that car drive away without me, tomorrow you'll be so far out of a job you won't even be allowed to shovel the shit from under sea cows."

The woman considered the advantages and disadvantages of continued insolence.

"It was the street sweeper," she said at last. "He wanted the director's car moved. Wanted to know whom it belonged to. Wanted to sweep beneath it. Was naturally sent packing."

Madelene pulled herself up, swayed and winked.

"That's the way to treat them," she said.

She emerged into the sunshine and into the final, euphoric phase of her drunkenness. Singing a little song to herself, with no clear direction, she set out on her magical mystery tour through a benign and joyful world. Her mind seethed with thoughts of the zoological building site, Andrea Burden, potential and abandoned dreams, strange and unforeseen women friends, Adam's erection, a sketch of a sleep monitor and a drive that could not be explained away in purely chemical terms.

She passed the truck with the dog on the door. Up in the cab the ejected street sweeper sat staring into space, like the young man in the fairy tale just at the point when his strength and his spirits are at their lowest ebb, the point at which the witch comes to his aid.

Madelene reached up, opened the cab door and climbed aloft. She made herself comfortable next to Johnny, opened the cardboard tube, took out the flask containing her last few ounces of propellant and removed the cork.

Johnny did not move a muscle.

"Well?" he said.

"I have a street I want swept," said Madelene.

She drank from the flask and held it out to Johnny. He took a sniff and sipped cautiously. His eyes filled first with tears and then with respect.

"That's some booze."

Madelene took off her sunglasses. Only then did she notice the plaster-encased Samson in the bunk behind the driver's seat.

"You're his wife," said Johnny.

Madelene smiled. Halfway through the smile the downturn kicked in.

The effect was instantaneous. All reserves were exhausted;

the rocket decelerated, stalled and jettisoned its empty tanks. After which it plummeted earthward like a stone.

Madelene opened the door through which she had entered and hung out. Passersby on the pavement saw the look on her face and got out of the way. All except one. Adam's secretary, possibly on her way to lunch, still pale and shaken, stayed where she was. Madelene threw up. The secretary backed away.

Madelene would have fallen out if an arm that had in its time supported gnus and hippos had not wrapped itself around her and hauled her back into the cab. Johnny handed her a large, blue, freshly pressed and folded handkerchief and a thermos.

"Drink," he said. "It's water."

Madelene gulped greedily. In her coat pocket she found her vitamin B tablets, popped a handful in her mouth and took another gulp.

Johnny started the truck and pulled away from the curb.

Inside, Madelene was plunging downward at an ever-increasing rate. Off down the slope self-loathing lay in wait and, farther down, the corpse-filled catacombs referred to by the outside world, with inexcusable understatement, as a hangover. She had no energy left now for being enigmatic. At the same time she saw everything with the hysterical clarity that precedes utter collapse.

"That dog," she said. "It's the one Bowen was talking about. You had the ape in the van."

"It ran off," said Johnny. "First time it's ever happened. I didn't know it was there."

"How did you track it down again?"

Johnny tapped the radio.

"The police transmit on 148 MHz," he said. "The veterinary police on 146."

Madelene had never communicated with workers—skilled or unskilled—on anything other than a clearly defined set of prior conditions. They had furnished her with the material side of her existence and then they had carted off the garbage. She had engaged them, received them, let them in and out and treated them with an exaggerated friendliness born of the fact that she feared them without having any idea of what made them tick, and that—deep down—she was completely at their mercy, she herself being incapable of changing a fuse, digging a septic tank or baking a gâteau. In a taxi she always sat in the back. Now she was sitting up beside Johnny. On a drive that she herself had instigated. And for which no advance bid had been given.

When faced with a dilemma all living creatures will resort to the patterns of behavior they know best.

"You'll be looking for compensation," she said.

Johnny shook his head.

"How much?"

Johnny shook his head again.

Madelene looked at him with fresh eyes, the way one looks at some rare animal—a hornbill or a pygmy tapir. Or a person who is not on the make.

"What do you want, then?" she asked.

Through Johnny's limbs and across his face there swept a cavalcade of emotions, none of which found verbal expression. Madelene saw that beside her sat someone who, like her, did not know where he was headed but who, again like her, was positive that he was on the right track.

"I'd just like to see it again," he said.

They drove for a while in silence. Both of them were conscious of the fact that the ape had been there, in the cab in which they now sat.

"I've promised to help it," said Madelene.

Johnny nodded.

"I see."

"But I don't know how."

"I've driven the lot," said Johnny. "Rutting bull giraffes. Impalas. Which die if they so much as suspect they're no longer in Africa."

He stopped the truck. Only then did Madelene recognize the area. They were only a stone's throw from Mombasa Manor. Gingerly she climbed out.

"I could help you," said Johnny.

Madelene looked him in the eye. For her to trust a strange man from a different social stratum was an impossibility. But she was not alone. In her pain-wracked state of clarity she sensed that the hazy women behind her had taken a liking to Johnny.

"I'll park here from now on," he said. "I live in the van."

He passed the cardboard tube down to her.

"Tell it . . . say that me and Samson, we've forgiven it for what it did to him. It didn't have no choice."

Madelene shut the cab door, turned on her heel and started to fight her way homeward, with never a backward glance.

ten

She was woken by a light, the throb of an engine and a feeling of owing something to someone.

It was two in the morning but the noise was nothing new to her. Over the past few months, a six-lane highway had been run through her skull—a road on which traffic was especially heavy at night, at which time it was also lit by searchlights that played and flickered across the inside of her corneas. She had had time to get used to that particular inferno of light and sound. What bothered her this time was that these sensations were being picked up from the outside.

She positioned herself by the window. In the courtyard, by the light of dimmed floodlights, about a dozen men were hard at work securing and sealing off the garden room. During the two hours for which she stood there, they hung grilles over the windows, replaced the doors and built a little run that extended from the side wing into the yard out of fifteen-foot-high wire fencing topped off by three rows of electric cable stretched over insulators. That done, they drove away.

Madelene went back to bed but when sleep eluded her she got up once more. In the dawn light she saw Adam welcoming three men. Having pulled on lab coats, they all went through the door into the garden room. Not long afterward they were joined by Clapham.

As the day gradually grew lighter, Madelene fought the effects of the previous day's alcoholic poisoning with yet more alcohol. At first this looked like it was going to succeed.

Over the next three days Adam and his four assistants only came out to eat, to go to the lavatory or to catch an hour or two's sleep on a sofa or in an armchair. And through those three days Madelene drank steadily and without a break. Initially in order to take the edge off her confusion; later—when this failed—to put herself, if possible, to sleep. And when that too failed she drank to keep the hangover at bay and to save herself from sobering up.

In the course of those three days, the people living in that house acquired something of an animal air. The five men as well as Madelene. The first time they emerged they had bathed and changed their clothes. But by their second sortie, twelve hours later, they had already taken to sitting around the kitchen table in their gray overalls, eating in silence. After that mealtimes were canceled. The men forgot all about them or sent out for a sandwich or trooped into the kitchen in twos and threes, grabbed a slice of meat, flopped into a chair and fell asleep, slept for a couple of hours, then went back to work. The first twenty-four hours saw the eradication of all social differences between them. When they hissed at one another or sat slumped over the furniture, it would no longer have been possible for a stranger to figure out who was the workman, who the butler and who the future director of the most prestigious establishment the zoological world had ever seen.

They had set to work glowing with scientific optimism. And over those three days, through her own deepening alcoholic haze, Madelene had watched this optimism turn first to expectancy, then dogged determination, then depression and finally panic.

When Adam staggered upstairs to his bedroom at twenty-hour intervals, Madelene went with him and coupled with him and sometimes even nodded off for a few hours. It was here that she awoke, on the night of the third day, during the gap between one nightmare and the next to the certainty of her system's organic collapse.

The alcohol had drained her fluid reserves. It had drawn off serum from her cells to effect its breakdown, paralyzed the autoregulation function of her kidneys and contaminated the remaining ducts through its production of ammonium compounds. She was acutely aware of her fluttering heart, her overburdened liver, the deathly ineffectuality of her intestine. And above this internal catastrophe hovered the reptiles of her dreams, the great white venereal amphibians of alcoholic nightmare.

She struggled out of bed and over to the window. In the light of the waning moon she saw the ape. It made its way out into the pen, supervised by Clapham, and made one slow circuit. It was wrapped in a blanket, its face was in shadow, it was limping and its exhaustion was five times greater than that of all five men put together.

And yet Madelene could see that whatever it was they had been trying to get out of it they had drawn a blank.

The animal made just the one circuit, then disappeared into the building, and Clapham closed the door behind it.

Madelene looked at the window frame, the park and, beyond that, across the city. From conversations overheard in her childhood home she had retained a vague and repulsive impression of what conditions were like for domestic animals on factory farms. She knew the meaning of such terms as spontaneous fracture, tongue rolling, somatotropin, urine drinking, manger biting, neighbor pecking and monotonization of mating behavior. Now, in these terms, she observed herself. Swaying from side to side, she saw herself and the city reflected in the animal kingdom. She had been inwardly devastated, as though it were emptiness she had ingested, emptiness Adam had discharged into her. She thought of all the protests she had refrained from making, the chances she had wasted. Guilt assailed her. Not a bad conscience, not some petty, unpaid mental account, no nickel-and-dime debt, but a suicide's accumulated arrears. On the slippery slope that she herself had chosen she had slid to the level where lies remorse.

She thought of the ape. From her internal, alcoholic nature reserve to the reptiles of her hallucinations, across her family's stockpiled swine, cattle and poultry, a link was established with the incarcerated ape.

And so Madelene came to the realization that she was no longer a tourist traveling through a series of fascinating, alcohol-induced landscapes. She was—and had been for some time—a permanent resident, confined to a chemical prison.

The moonlight, which a moment before had seemed so pallid, now streamed into the room, stark as an X ray. In this light Madelene saw her own weakness, saw it clearly, saw herself as the ape had seen her and then she gave up. She gave up hope, she gave up her role as a drunk, gave up the gentle, spirituous tailwind that had blown her through the events of the past few weeks. She gave up her martyrdom to the hard stuff, her alcoholic identity. She gave up drinking.

eleven

She woke to find that she was not alone. Beside her—in that spot from which Adam had fled during the night—lay the previous day's acknowledgment of her own frailty.

Madelene sized it up. It seemed alarmingly undiminished and yet alien to her.

She got up. Shaking, she took the first steps across the room, turned around and walked back.

She seemed to be heading back toward the bed and the comfort of her carafe. But these she passed by, making for Adam's worktable. There she rolled up a selection of the hundreds of large printed sheets he had carried upstairs from the garden room and slid them into her cardboard tube. From the top drawer of the desk she took two bundles of banknotes. Then she walked across the room and out. And with this action—modest in physical terms though it was—she put a part of her life behind her.

In the hall she cast a fleeting glance at the telephone, but
all the phones in the house were connected to a switchboard
in Clapham's office. She forged on—out into the garden,
through the little door in the wall and onto the pavement.

Before she had quite reached it, Johnny had the rear door
of the van open.

Madelene had never resided at any address that did not boast
at least eight thousand square feet of living accommodation
plus full basement facilities plus grounds. Johnny's mobile
home contained a bed, a desk, a television, a minibar, a telephone, kitchen, hi-fi system, rugs, plush wall covering, lamps
and built-in cupboards—all in an area measuring eight by ten
feet. In the thirty seconds it took her to clamber in, collapse
into a chair and drink the glass of water held out to her by
Johnny, she formed a number of what were to be lifelong impressions regarding the relationship between social standing
and territorial limits.

"I've stopped drinking," she said.

From his childhood and from his own personal experience
Johnny knew the power of the rush to be had from alcohol.
He looked at Madelene with respect.

She drew the sheets out of the tube and spread them out
on the table.

"Have you any idea what this is?" she asked.

Confronted by a mass of symbols Johnny froze.

"I had five years at school."

Madelene nodded. Much the same as herself. Once you
deducted all the absences.

She reached for the telephone and dialed a number.

Adam's secretary had abandoned all thought of resistance,
her voice was subdued, her tone resigned.

"He's out of town. He'll be back the day after tomorrow.
Can I give him a message?"

Madelene hung up. Johnny watched her, blank-faced. She made another call. Was transferred twice before getting through, to Andrea Burden.

"Now that we're confidantes," said Madelene, "and have no secrets from one another, could you please tell me how much longer that thing's going to be staying with us."

"He hasn't told you?"

"He's trying to protect me."

"They'll be winding up tomorrow."

"And where do you suppose it will go from here?"

Her response was all too snappy, all too slick.

"Oh, but the Institute has St. Francis Forest. Well out of the way and delightfully secluded."

"That sounds wonderful," said Madelene. "I feel much happier now."

She hung up.

"We've got twenty-four hours," she said. "Before they move it. How do you move animals?"

"It'll be put in an ape box."

"Where do they find those?"

"Bowen makes them. Bally always said, when it came to boxes Bowen was one of the best."

"Bowen?" said Madelene. "And Bally?"

"The one who brought in the ape."

Madelene looked at Johnny. At the cardboard tube. At the graphs. At Samson and his bandages. She looked out the window. At the morning light. At the man in the gray suit strolling down the street with a perky little cappuccino-colored wire-haired fox terrier on a leash, a man she was now sighting outside Mombasa Manor for the third time. She became aware of a vibration deep inside her body, apart from and different than the shakes of withdrawal. This sensation grew into a tremor that ran through her from top to toe, as if she had just had her first drink of the morning. But there had been no drink. What she was experiencing was something else again. It was the materialization, out of the blue, of the galaxy of intoxicating possibilities which present themselves to someone who has made up their mind to be creative and left all their options open.

She lifted Samson's leash from a hook, clipped it to his collar, opened the van door and climbed down, with the dog, onto the pavement.

At the sight of Madelene the gray man tensed imperceptibly, wheeled about and began to walk away.

Madelene could have let him go. But a nasty migraine had started spreading throughout her body, working downward from the back of her head. Where there had always been a volatile energy—readily ignited and quick to burn out—to be derived from drink, she now found there was a destructive, brazen power in coming off it. She and Samson caught up with the man and his terrier.

"So how's everything down at veterinary police headquarters?" she asked.

Until this moment she had only seen him sitting down, in the white car that time when Clapham had turned him away at the gate and on those occasions when he had been parked outside the grounds. On his feet and close at hand he proved to be tall, lean and tough, every inch of him born, raised and trained to be nobody's fool.

He took his time, letting the dogs have a sniff at one another before replying.

"Well, of course, it's quite a big place now. There used to be just four or five of us. Now we have the race meets, all the doping cases to see to. And the petnappings. We have twenty men checking the pet shops alone. With vets and blank search warrants."

Madelene's upbringing and her interest in men had taught her how to distinguish unerringly between those people, like Adam, who had stepped into the station to which they had been born and those, like the man facing her, who had worked their way up.

"Why," she asked, "would a man armed with search warrants tolerate being turned away by our doorman?"

The man had given up following the dogs with his eyes. He now focused only on Madelene.

"Search warrants are fine for pet shops and small apartments where people keep protected reptiles in shoe boxes. But among the upper levels of society they can be risky bits of paper."

People who had pulled themselves up by their bootstraps fell, Madelene knew, into two subcategories: those, like her father, who had striven all their lives to distance themselves from their origins and those, like this man, who had found it simplest to adopt a white car, a suit and a mustache but who had remained steadfastly working-class.

"You wanted to ask about the ape?" she said.

The man did not answer.

"We could trade," said Madelene. "I tell you where it is. You tell me why you find it so fascinating."

The man said not a word.

"It's in one of the wings," said Madelene. "With a truckload of machinery. They've been studying it. They're looking for something. Something they haven't found yet. It's worn out, but alive. Now keep your part of the deal."

In the space that elapsed before he answered, Madelene was struck by a rare flash of inexplicable, intuitive insight into the character of another human being. All at once she knew that the man opposite her had gotten as far as he had through being hard-nosed and intelligent and that, in addition to these traits, he also possessed a formidable sense of justice—which explained why he had not risen any further.

"We're not so much interested in the animal," he said. "Our prime interest is in the skipper of the boat that brought it here."

"Bally," said Madelene.

The man nodded.

"If there's such a place as an animal hell, then, when his time comes, Bally will make chief demon down there."

"Deputy chief," said Madelene. "The chief demon, that's my father."

The man extended an arm. Madelene thought he wanted to shake her hand, but it was his card he gave her.

"Smailes," he said. "We fished Mr. Bally out of the Thames and are keeping him in custody. But we've nothing to go on. We'll have to let him go soon. We had been wondering whether we should obtain a warrant anyway and just barge our way in and demand an explanation."

"Give me twenty-four hours," said Madelene.

"What do we get in return?"

"The evidence to nail Bally."

Smailes started to lead the terrier away.

"Where did the boat come from?" Madelene asked.

"From Denmark. Like you."

"What a lot you know. Considering you didn't make it past the gate."

"I've been taking the dog for walks in the neighborhood."

Madelene looked down at Samson.

"I've always been a believer in that myself," she murmured.

Smailes was almost out of earshot when he turned around one last time.

"Twenty-four hours," he called softly. "And not a minute more."

twelve

The Holland Park Veterinary Clinic invited unconditional surrender. Not only was it the most expensive, most up-to-date private animal hospital in London; it was also known as "the Smiling Clinic" because the people who worked there all wore a smile. The affable doorman smiled, the charming nurse in reception smiled, the helpful porter smiled and the clinic supervisor who lifted Samson up onto a low table smiled warmly and compliantly.

"I'd like to speak to Alexander Bowen," Madelene said.

The woman's smile was apologetic.

"You'd have to make an appointment," she said.

Madelene plucked a scrap of white paper and a ballpoint pen from the desk, scribbled a line on the card, wrapped it in a fifty-pound note from Adam's bankroll and handed it to the porter.

"The operation was touch and go," she said. "Alex begged

me to be sure and send for him. So he could see Samson personally."

Three minutes later Alexander Bowen walked in, wearing a white coat and a smile.

It was a halfhearted smile. Despite his powerful position the vet's life was a life spent on the edge and the situation he had just walked into was even more of a cliff-hanger than most.

On the paper Madelene had written "£1,000 as arranged. Lady Mortensen." Alexander Bowen knew *Debrett's Peerage* inside out, he could recall every animal he had ever treated and by far the greater majority of invoices written in connection with said treatment and he knew that he had never heard of Lady Mortensen or come across the woman in sunglasses and a duster coat with whom he was now confronted. But he also knew that this dog was the Doberman he had not dared to put down, out of fear of that driver—what was his name again?—the one who had done the carrying for Bally.

What had prompted him to come was the reference to the thousand pounds. What held him there was part fear, part curiosity.

In the prevailing behavioral vacuum he opted for an approach that was forceful but noncommittal. Briskly and solicitously he approached the dog.

"How is he?" he asked.

"Better," said Madelene.

She held out the big sheets from her cardboard tube. In the same move she slid ten one-hundred-pound notes from her bundle onto the desk.

"I brought his X rays," she said.

Madelene had grown up in a home where the women purchased the men with sex, the adults bribed the children with toys, the children procured concessions by means of tantrums or caresses and the whole clan had bought its way to a position in high society and a place in Danish history. From infancy she had been trained in the virtuoso techniques called for in the art of bribery. Had the vet's face displayed the merest hint of resentment she could have placed a hand over the notes and blotted out this tiny slip-up. But his face evinced no suspicion. On the contrary, his features cleared and became more composed.

"These aren't X rays," he said. "They're MRI scans. And that's no dog."

"Our chimpanzee," said Madelene. "I must have picked up the wrong ones."

The doctor shook his head.

"See that frontal lobe?" he said. "Seat of the higher cognitive functions. That's a human being. Although obviously a very large human."

He ran his finger out to a column of figures to the right of the picture.

"A volume of 2,700 cubic centimeters. Abnormally large."

He flicked through the sheets and stopped at one particular frame. The colors were dazzling—ruby red, shimmering gold, royal blue.

"Him again. An EEG superimposed on PET. Not many people in Europe can do that. Where did you say these were from?"

"What's PET?" Madelene asked.

"Positron-Emission Tomography. He's been injected with radioactive water, which causes the brain to increase the cerebral blood flow. Then it's just a matter of monitoring the level of radioactivity."

Treading warily, Madelene fingered the bankroll and sneaked one more of Adam's notes onto the desk.

"At least let me reimburse you for your time," she said.

The doctor's eyes clouded over. An insidious stream of distractedness, boyhood memories and titillated vanity had taken hold of him and swept him along in its wake.

"PET," he said. "Excellent spatial resolution. Accurate to between three and five millimeters. But poor time resolution.

Takes as much as ninety seconds. Which is why you super-impose it on an encephalogram. That way you can see every-thing that's going on in the brain, down to the last millisecond. It's fantastic. And when you think that this is a piece of mobile equipment. They've put a helmet on him. That's the latest thing. I didn't think there was anyone but us who could do that."

His finger slid down the column of figures.

"They've sent him around an obstacle course. Is there something wrong with his motor functions? Language tests, eye tests, various practical exercises. Anatomical localization, extremely detailed, thirty cross sections from all four angles."

"What were they looking for?" Madelene asked.

She threw down yet another note. The doctor's face had a faraway look, like that of someone in a hypnotic trance. Madelene knew she had him anesthetized. Now it was a matter of keeping his suspicions dormant but his mental faculties intact.

"Ah, yes, what are we looking for?" he said. "Can anyone answer that?"

"We?"

"I too have sought."

"Did you find what you were looking for?"

The doctor's eyes were fixed on some distant point, visible only to himself.

"Does one ever?"

"These pictures, did you take them?"

He shook his head.

"I think back on the old days," he said. "Those golden days. Barely ten years ago. When one still dared to hope."

Madelene stroked the arm of his white coat, probing.

"I think of them," he said. "But I don't speak of them. It's better that way. As things stand."

"Just say it," Madelene urged gently. "The dog won't un-derstand a word anyway."

Alexander Bowen was aware of a pleasant lack of clarity.

His surroundings put him in mind of his own hospital, the scans implied that he was a speaker at a scientific symposium, the listening woman might have suggested a board meeting, the money pointed to an appointment with his lawyer. This situation seemed to reconcile all of the deeply incompatible sides of his character in the most delightful manner.

"Massachusetts," he said. "The question of the nature of intelligence. Pioneering research—nothing to touch it. So far in front that the rest of the field was nowhere to be seen. We believed we were so close. You must understand. We were actually inside the brain itself. As far in as you can go. You don't get any closer. It was so . . . staggeringly intimate. Even if they were only apes. We came so close. To becoming one. With an unknown intelligence. Picture the disappointment. When everything suddenly melts into thin air. Comes to nothing. There you are, left with that awful emptiness. While everyone around you is still living in hope. But *you* know it's all over. *Horror vacui.*"

"Like a love affair," said Madelene.

The vet stared at her.

"Were you there too?"

"I know how it feels."

"You understand me," the vet said. "Like a marriage. That's exactly how it was. You felt cheated. Because in fact, even though I would never admit it, not to anyone, not even to you. If we had succeeded in getting to the bottom of the mind, the soul, the intellect, in decoding the brain. And if one could have placed a woman on the table. And run her into the spool . . ."

"Spool?"

"MRI produces a huge magnetic field. You lay people on a trolley and push them into a spool. They don't feel a thing. She wouldn't have felt a thing. There's a fan heater inside it. And a mirror. And they can put on headphones. And listen to sweet music. *Rosenkavalier*, or some other wonderful piece. And then you would talk to her over the headphones, and say,

'Alexander—what do you think of when you hear the name Alexander?' And then it would be possible to stand outside and see her thoughts as they occurred; they would show up as computer images, like *pixels*. Penetrating further into any woman than any man has ever done. To the heart of the female psyche. She would have no chance of lying. And if there were someone else, if she had someone else, or merely thought of anyone else, it would be spotted straightaway."

Madelene handed him her handkerchief.

"You're sweating," she said.

The vet mopped his brow.

"Then one might have managed to save one's marriage," he said.

Madelene surveyed him pityingly.

"I think it would take more than magnetic scanning to do that," she said.

"I know, but it doesn't stop you from hoping. It's only human, isn't it? Right to the last we kept on hoping. But in the end it just couldn't be done. Because what is being measured is the oxygen consumption. And there is no formula for the relationship between oxygen consumption and cerebral activity. Nor will there ever be. No objective measurement of intelligence, no way of pinpointing thought. So we reverted to the old methods. Well, we had over eighty million dollars invested in equipment alone. And the sponsors were looking for results. So back we went to the needles."

"Needles?"

"You know, the way it had always been done. You strap them down. The apes, that is. And remove the brainpan. The top half of the cranium. To expose the brain. And then you have these needles. Terrifically precise. Single Neuron Recording. You can pick up a single neuron. See how often it pulsates. See just exactly when a given signal passes through it. Then, of course, there are clusters of needles. Multiple Neuron Recording. We should never have dropped that system. Even though it too has its drawbacks. In order to get at any spot farther in, the needle has to be worked through the overlying tissue. And chimpanzees are getting harder to come by . . ."

Madelene said nothing. The doctor detected an unaccountable shift in mood but could not get a fix on it, could not catch what was being thought of him.

"The limited staying power of the big apes also posed a problem. Three weeks was the most you could count on. After that they began to deteriorate and gradually ceased to function."

"Do you still . . . do that?" Madelene asked. "With the needles, I mean."

Somewhere within the stupor into which the vet had sunk a warning light flashed, harsh and prolonged. He stopped dead.

Madelene grabbed the lapel of his white coat and drove him back toward the wall.

"Go on," she said.

"I believe I have answered your questions."

A low trolley caught Alexander Bowen behind the knees and he toppled backward. Madelene knelt over him.

"I have one last question," she said.

The vet stared at her vacantly. As with every awakening from an anesthetic, this one too was nauseating and painful. And yet there was also something mysterious and deliciously illicit about this moment.

As deep down and as far back as he could go—as a boy, in the country, on Jersey—Alexander Bowen had been a genuine animal lover. He had grown up taking a delight in being close to a cat or dog, savoring the smell of a stable and deriving from the presence of cattle a peace of mind that required no explanation. He had made up his mind to become a vet and had then gone to university. And there he had learned that animals are machines. Delicate machines, to be sure, with an ingenious biological mechanism, but still—when all was said and done—machines. And faced with this revelation, his mind had, for the first time, split in two. Alongside the original Alexander, he developed a scientific alter ego. Now, when he stroked a dog's head, this onlooker would think: What is happening here, the feelings of warmth and kindness I am experiencing, are but illusions, emergent phenomena made up of millions of processes all of which, taken singly, are quite banal and fully explained. By the time he finished his studies his nascent reductionism was fully developed and for the next thirty years he had borne the ever greater burden of that test-tube monstrosity, that inner homunculus. He had come home from the United States with the very best references and a severe case of depression. All actions—whether physical or mental—were, he knew, fundamentally chemical in nature and thus quantum electrical and hence causal and hence deterministic and all, therefore, preordained—if not haphazardly random—and so free will was an illusion, which meant that it made no difference what he did since the solution to what would happen in his life would make itself known of its own accord anyway. Which it did. One gray morning he woke up to the realization that since there is, after all, nothing behind the physical universe except a handful of elementary particles and a standard formula for explaining the interplay between the forces of nature, one might as well go all the way, and this he did—that is to say, all the way into a world which is a little—but not much—simpler than that of physics, namely the world of finance, founded upon a few basic monetary units and the four arithmetical operations. And in this environment he had stayed ever since.

Now, sprawled on the floor, he found himself being momentarily dragged out of that world, something which came as a relief. As with all of those who inhabit a purely scientific or purely financial universe, Alexander Bowen dreamt of deliverance and right now Madelene's face was speaking to him of another sort of reality.

"The last question," she said, "is what it would cost to be allowed to remove your brainpan and look for compassion. To see if there is any."

For a second the vet thought he was lying in his father's meadow, on Jersey, under the blue sky.

"More," he said. "Do it again."

Madelene released her hold and fished a card out of her duster-coat pocket. The blend of fatalistic resolve, self-loathing and physical discomfort produced by her withdrawal symptoms honed her actions and her choice of words to a razor edge.

"Read this," she said. "And I'll promise to kick you in the stomach afterward."

It was Inspector Smailes' card. The doctor read it slowly and with difficulty. Then the hunger, the pain and the confusion cleared from his face and it grew sober.

"He's waiting outside."

She took off her sunglasses.

"Mrs. Burden," said the doctor.

Until this moment he had been convinced that this situation, like all others in his life, would ultimately prove to be under control. That any minute now two porters would come rushing in and take this madwoman away and see to it that she paid a substantial sum in recompense for pain and suffering, in return for which the hospital would agree not to press charges and he himself would return to the meeting he had left fifteen minutes earlier. And the only reminder of what had taken place would be the hematoma he had just been dealt by the linoleum floor. Now he saw that the situation had slipped through his fingers.

Madelene pointed to the scans.

"That's the ape, isn't it?"

"It's a human being."

"Is this where it's supposed to have the top of its skull removed? Now that Adam has given up?"

Alexander Bowen's face had turned white, only a shade darker than the tiles on the wall.

"The Washington Convention," Madelene said. "It's a prison sentence for you. And a whopping great fine. And you'll be forbidden to practice."

The doctor moistened his lips.

"It's a minor operation. A lot has happened in ten years. It won't feel a thing. It will survive and be none the worse for it."

"You examine all Bally's animals?"

The doctor did not answer.

Madelene gathered up the banknotes and slipped them back into her coat pocket.

"I'll have to owe you for Samson," she said.

The dog jumped down from the table.

"You'll call me if you change your mind?" Madelene said.

The doctor looked at her blankly.

"I mean, if on closer reflection you should decide to let me lift off the top of your skull. It would just be a minor operation. You would function quite normally afterward."

Johnny's truck was parked by the curb. Madelene and Samson climbed in.

"Do animals think?" asked Madelene.

They were halfway to South Hill Park before Johnny answered.

"Pit ponies," he said. "I used to look after them, as a lad. In Morton. The mine shaft ran out for six miles under the Atlantic. You got out there by diesel train. But out by the coal face the tunnels were so narrow that only men and horses could get through. The last bit not even the ponies. There you had to crawl along on your stomach. With a lamp and a hydraulic hand drill. Six miles out and a half mile under the seabed. You couldn't get your mind off the props. Holding up the roof. So spindly. But when you started thinking like that, that's when you looked back. At the horse. They catch any sign of shifting long before a man would. Sense if the air supply is starting to give out. Or if there's a leak. And they can give signals. Like people. But more subtle. If the horse was calm, everything was okay."

"Why didn't you leave?"

"Where would I go?"

Madelene gestured vaguely at the light, the trees, the affluence surrounding them.

Johnny gazed out the windshield. At the walls around the houses, at the closely guarded iron gates, at the fence encircling Parliament Hill.

"Would that have been any better?" he said.

For the third time in less than a week Madelene's notions of freedom listed to one side; then they keeled over and started to break up.

"You got used to the heat. To working lying down. To the air. To the fact that there's no room to move. The hard bit was being alone. Because there wasn't a sound to be heard. It's dead quiet. And suddenly you feel that you've been deserted. That you're the last person alive on earth. A half mile down. That was when you shoved the lamp back and looked at the horse. Its muzzle was all black. Like your own face. Its eyes glittered. Like your own. It was the same as you. But perfectly calm. Not because it was stupid. But because it wasn't thinking unnecessary thoughts. It wasn't thinking about yesterday, or tomorrow. Nor closing time or the Third World War. It was thinking about here and now. And looking at it, you began to feel the way it did. And then you grew quite calm. And sometimes . . . almost happy. Like when I drove the animals. Most of the time your thoughts flit about all over the place. Yesterday. Tomorrow. Problems, problems. But transporting Bally's animals you didn't think about anything but the driving. No loneliness. And behind you in the dark, their eyes glittering, you could feel them. Fine, powerful, strange. To be protected.

You couldn't make the slightest mistake. Or there would be a cave-in. Your mind was one hundred percent on the job, and there, on the road, you were . . . you became . . ."

"Almost happy," said Madelene.

They sat there, saying nothing.

At last Madelene opened the door.

"Tomorrow," she said. "We have to get it out before tomorrow. If it's to have any brain left for not thinking unnecessary thoughts."

She looked up at Johnny and the dog.

"You two will be here this evening?" she said. "Won't you? You're not suddenly going to take off back to Morton?"

"They closed down the pit in '85. That was all there was to Morton, the pit. There's nothing to go back to."

thirteen

That evening Adam ate with Madelene for the first time in five days and, seen from a distance, he seemed loving and attentive.

But Madelene was not seeing him from a distance. She was seeing him at very close range, and, closer still, she was also seeing him from the inside, from a mistress's point of view, and what she saw was his absence. Even though he was sitting opposite her, Adam had not put in a personal appearance at the table. His mind had stayed behind in the laboratory with the ape.

This was not a new state of affairs for Madelene. What *was* new was that she found it less than satisfactory. After the first few minutes she was in no condition to eat or talk and she did not utter one word until the point when they climbed the stairs together and stood outside the door to his rooms and he reached out for her and she pushed his hand away.

"No way," she said.

Then Adam Burden reentered his body.

Before he met Madelene, Adam had had a number of relationships which, in retrospect, he either could not or did not wish to tell apart. It seemed to him that all of those girls—despite being in their twenties and thirties—had had babyish voices and bedrooms full of cuddly toys, that they dreamt of his turning out to be yet another teddy bear, and that—once he had afforded them a glimpse of the mere shadow of his desire—they had been smitten by mystified panic.

Madelene had been different. The very first time he reached out for her, she had taken on an air of languorous, slack-limbed menace. With half-closed eyes she had watched him dancing closer and when at long last she had chosen to respond to him her response had been wholehearted. Adam had had no antibodies to combat these moments of female lust, so suddenly aroused only, afterward, to sink without a trace. Madelene had invaded his bloodstream like a fleeting attack of blood poisoning. By the end of their first whole day together he was a sick man. When she spurned him for the first time his sickness was rendered incurable.

For an instant, there on the landing, his face glowed with the sort of hate that moves people to commit murder. But it never found an outlet. The emotion flared up for a split second, then it was doused and his figure hardened into an excruciating encapsulation of the situation thus presented.

It was then that Madelene was struck, for the first time, by the thought that she was too much for her husband. If one is to survive an attack of desire of the kind by which Adam had been struck, one must be able to cope with rejection. For every time that Madelene said yes to him there were three more when she turned her back on him, and she now had a suspicion that he could not bear this, and never had been able to. He was a winner, a born winner, who had in her come up against the trouncing of his life and, what is more, a trouncing which was not to be suffered once and once only, but had to be played out again and again like some cyclically recurring annihilation.

For a moment Adam just stood there. Then he turned around, slowly and stiffly, and went into his room.

Once the door had slammed behind him he walked over to the window, opened it and—as was his habit in situations such as this—committed the first of a series of murders.

From the moment he first laid eyes on Madelene, Adam had been dazed, shell-shocked by jealousy. He was convinced that she was a danger not just to himself but that she constituted a threat to mankind as a whole, that any man would give his life to get inside her. Consequently he had appointed himself to be not only her husband but also her bodyguard and eunuch and if he could have infiltrated her soul he would have been her thought police too.

Now, standing by the window, he fantasized that he had been caught napping and that she had succeeded in taking a lover and smuggled him into her room. Lingeringly, he grilled his imagination over the spectacle of their undressing and the opening moves in their lovemaking, at which point he himself stepped in armed with his father's double-barreled Purdy and discharged both barrels, three hundred and fifty pieces of lead shot at a range of ten feet. This done, he then wallowed in his own despair over all that was left of Madelene.

This first killing mollified him slightly, and so he committed another, and yet another—feeling a little better with each one. In his normal, pragmatic state of mind he would, with some pride, have described himself as totally lacking in imagination, but during the half hour he spent by the window like a lone executioner his fantasies acquired an artistic lifelikeness that made it hard to separate them from reality. When he spied Madelene gliding across the lawn, light-footed as an elf maid, he thought at first that he was gazing upon his own, inner stage. Not until she opened the little gate in the wall around the grounds and let in a man did Adam observe that

this fantasy did not have the same liberating effect as the
others.

The moon was on the wane, the sky somewhat overcast. In
such a light it was impossible to make out any details. Although, in his present condition, even broad daylight would
hardly have been strong enough for that. He could not see
Johnny clearly, did not see the collapsible wheelchair he carried. All he saw were the contours of a short, thickset gnome
with a hunchback.

In Adam's fantasies of a moment earlier Madelene's lovers
had been members of the royal family, or godlike figures; her
infidelity had been upwardly mobile, thus acting as an indirect
social leg up for himself. Now, in this fickle light, he saw a
male figure dredged from the sewers of London.

He stood there, rooted to the spot, a quarter of an hour
elapsing before he was once more capable of thought, half an
hour going by before he could come to a decision. He would
go straight to Madelene's room, kick the door in and lay this
lover low. And then, with a screaming Madelene kneeling at
his feet, he would consider his next move.

He was on the point of turning away when the last act of
the evening's drama passed in front of his windows.

In the lead came the hunchback. Behind him, closely en-
twined, came Madelene and a new male character.

Adam had never seen the ape walking on two legs and he
had, of course, never seen it wearing a long coat and a trilby.
So he had not the faintest notion of the humanizing effect
clothes and an upright gait can have on an animal. Nevertheless, had he been in possession of just some of his senses, his
thoughts would have turned to Erasmus. But all his senses
had deserted him, he was completely cut off from the realities
of everyday life, he was off somewhere where the ape did not
exist. Dwelling in the fiendish realms of jealousy. What his
eyes beheld was his wife and her two lovers, two creatures
radiating a total want of finesse, and through his mind paraded

the vast number of sexual degradations made possible by this new, third person.

Not wanting to see any more, he took two steps back into the room. And so he did not see Erasmus, Madelene and Johnny exit from the grounds through the door in the wall, saw nothing at all, in fact, outside of himself. All his attention was driven inward and there he found that the Adam Burden he thought he knew had been given his marching orders. Over him and through him and out into the night thundered herds of runaway elephants and enchanted swine. He was incapable of moving a muscle, and not until day began to break, and his inward bellowing died down to be replaced by a kind of lethargy, was he able to drag himself across the floor and lift the telephone receiver.

fourteen

The Danish Society in London is located in Knightsbridge,
backing onto Hyde Park. It was here, at eleven in the morning,
that Madelene presented herself, and she was not alone. In
front of her she pushed a wheelchair in which sat an elderly
lady enveloped in a voluminous traveling blanket, her head
shielded from the sun by a black hat complete with veil.

Madelene's presence here of all places had come about in
the following manner: That same morning, early, after a night
spent in Johnny's mobile home in a parking lot in the far-flung
suburb of Hemel Hempstead, northwest of London, Madelene
had heard herself being reported as missing on the radio.

Not one of the truck's four passengers had slept a wink
that night. With not a word being said, not a move made—
apart from Johnny getting up twice to make tea—in silence
they had felt the night float by, for all the world as though
they were a crew and the van a ship steaming across the ocean,
sure of making landfall by dawn. At sunrise, as on every other

morning, Johnny had tuned his receiver in to the police wave band. The minute he heard Madelene's name mentioned he had curled up into a ball in a corner of the bed like a game bird sensing the approach of the beaters.

Madelene, on the other hand, showed no sign of surprise or alarm. The all-points bulletin was broadcast just as she was shaving the hair off Erasmus' face and she kept at this task while her description was being read out. She was, this morning, brimming with confidence.

She was not putting her trust in any overt form of justice—since she had never been able to ascertain that such a thing existed—but on something better. Madelene had her hopes pinned on the law of the jungle. Those environments in which Madelene had grown up, her family, her schools, her marriage, had all been controlled by a social order which, far from being one big, bloody free-for-all—any more than the biological jungle law was—involved a subtle pecking order that kept the individual in his or her place with a minimum of outward conflict. Social legislation was an integral part of this structure and the Washington Convention an integral part of this legislation, and Madelene's plan was quite simply to get a vet to testify that the ape was covered by this convention. Then she would take this attestation to Inspector Smailes, whereupon the convention would come into play and the old order restored.

She had no idea what would happen to her personally thereafter. But she harbored no illusions. She had lived a pigeonhole existence—biologically speaking, a highly specialized life, a state of being fitted to a life of wedded idleness, life as a decorative appendage. As with all specialists, in the animal world as in the human, this way of life was extremely sensitive to change. Her confidence in the early hours of this morning was for her companions. As far as she herself was concerned she held out no hopes. Impassively she heard the bulletin out. Then she reached for the telephone.

The veterinary odontologist did not announce himself. He merely grunted into the telephone and from that sound alone Madelene could tell something was up.

"I have the ape here," she said.

"There's a hunt on for you."

"You're the only one who can do it . . ."

"There are twenty vets in London who could do it. Almost as well."

"At the Meat Market they're always talking about how brave you are."

There was silence at the other end. When the doctor did reply his voice was so faint that Madelene thought for a moment she was speaking to someone else.

"It's my job that's on the line here."

Madelene had been brought up to take no for an answer. Only a few weeks ago she would have bade him a pleasant good day and acknowledged defeat, then gone over and curled up beside Johnny and left the inevitable and disastrous chain of events to run their course. Or rather: A couple of weeks ago this conversation would never have taken place. But the Madelene who was now on the phone no longer had any clear memory of that time, and the thought of giving up never crossed her mind.

"You've only got one year to go anyway," she said.

The odontologist's silence was fraught with uncertainty. Madelene could sense that he was teetering on the brink. She moved in and gave him one last nudge.

"And then there's your reputation as a scientist," she said.

"What about it?"

"When word gets out about this conversation. How you refused to help. After seeing that dental chart. I don't know what the Institute will have to say. But at the Meat Market they'll be dining out on it for years to come."

"You don't work at the Meat Market. You're Burden's wife."

Madelene said nothing. She knew she had penetrated, she had won through.

"Mrs. Burden," said the doctor, "strictly between ourselves, are you never scared?"

"Always."

"You do realize that your husband has had you reported missing?"

"A misunderstanding. Happens to the best of families. And please call me Madelene."

"Thank you," said the doctor. "My name is Firkin. Where's it to be?"

Prior to this, London had always struck Madelene as being as barren and bereft of possibilities as a desert. Now that she had forfeited her usual routine and her rights, now that she no longer had any place in the day-to-day life of the city, it seemed to abound in chaotic eventualities. She shut her eyes and tilted her face upward, opened up her mind to those veins of inspiration that are always there for those who seek and a moment later she caught the scent of water.

"You know the Danish Society," she said, "in Knightsbridge . . ."

fifteen

To Danes abroad the thought of Denmark changing in their absence is not to be borne. On our return we want to find that country not merely as we left it but as it ought to have been. The desire to meet this wish led, in London, to the setting up of the Danish Society—an institution which, on its founding at the beginning of this century by a group of Danish diplomats and businessmen, was already more retroactively sentimental than Denmark had ever been. Since then, true to the law which says that time, in patriotic societies of any description, will always run backward, things had gone from bad to worse.

Madelene had been there once, dispatched by Adam to enroll them both as members, and she had never been back. On that one visit she had been filled—instantly, the minute she crossed the threshold, and before that even, on seeing the building from the outside—with terror, and what had frightened her was her own acquiescent fascination: She loved the lions in the Danish coat of arms on the door. She loved the animal painter Philipsen's red-and-white cows in the sunset. She loved the elephant on the Order of the Elephant around the neck of absolute monarch Christian VII's English-born wife, Caroline Matilda. She loved the seagulls on the dinner service in the library and the stylized plum-tree branches on the plates in the restaurant. She loved the porcelain polar bears on the mantelpiece, the poster of city traffic being held up to let a mother duck and her ugly ducklings cross the road and the photos of the lifelong feathered pairing of a stork couple in Ribe. She loved the bearskins on the heads of Guards changing the guard before the statue of Frederick V on horseback on the square at Amalienborg Palace. She loved the pictures of black grouse on moors that were no more. Faced with this whole image of Denmark as a social and zoological paradise which she knew had never existed, she had been irretrievably lost.

Had it been possible, had there been even the slightest chance of getting away with it, back then, on that first visit, Madelene would have scrambled up into the case containing Denmark's best-known butterflies and taken her place among the most unassuming of these—the cabbage white, for instance, and the small tortoiseshell—and mounted herself there with a pin through her chest and, lastly—prior to her full and final surrender—at her feet in her best copperplate she would have written: "Madelene Burden, née Mortensen. Widespread and quite, quite common."

Sadly, she knew that such a venture was doomed to failure, because she had already had a go at it, long before. She had tried to be a good daughter, a good pupil and a breathtaking young girl but all of these attempts had miscarried. She seemed to have been born not to flutter elegantly hither and thither but to cause trouble. Her first conscious memory was of the leaden, yet crisp sound of shattering faience overlaid by the word "clumsy" uttered coolly and dispassionately in an adult voice which might have been her mother's, or perhaps the Queen's, or God's.

But she had never given up hope altogether. Even though she had bowed her head and tiptoed away from her family and into marriage and out of Denmark, deep down she had always felt that maybe one day, in spite of everything, a reconciliation would be reached, and now, as she pushed the wheelchair toward the front steps of the Society and the front door opened and two men came hurrying out to greet her, her past seemed suddenly to stretch out a hand and give her another chance.

The two men who had come down to meet her were the Society's doorman and its manager. The latter grasped her hand, shook it, then looked at the lady in the wheelchair with an expression that did not so much ask for as expect an explanation.

"My grandmother," said Madelene. "Mrs. Mortensen."

The manager tried to peek under the brim of the hat but could make out nothing behind the veil other than the outline of a large, dark face.

"We are honored," he said.

The two men took hold of the wheelchair, one on each side and heaved.

Nothing happened.

Smiling still, not batting an eyelid, the manager took a look around the back of the chair to see whether it might have got caught between the paving stones, or was perhaps electrically operated and hence weighed down by both a motor and batteries. This, however, was not the case. It was a flimsy, collapsible model. The two men heaved again. And succeeded in lifting the chair four inches off the ground. Then they eased it down again.

It was hard to comment on such a state of affairs and so Madelene kept her mouth shut. But she was seized by a number of urges, strong among them the temptation to do what she usually did, what she had done so often before, to run away. Nonetheless, she stayed put. She could not leave the wheelchair. Added to which, several times during the past week or two she had found herself in painful situations and she was starting to discover that, if one bided one's time, something usually turned up.

This something turned up at that very moment in the shape of a third person: Sir Toby, Madelene's late father-in-law's brother, joined the group.

On the surface Madelene gave nothing away; dutifully she put out her hand and had it kissed. But inside her an alarm bell rang, as yet faint and far-off, at the sight of Her Majesty's Government's consultant on veterinary matters.

The three men grabbed hold of the wheelchair and lugged it up the steps, through the doors and into the elevator—the door of which closed, whereupon it began to ascend.

The men were desperately gasping for breath. Madelene had the feeling that an explanation was in order.

"Comfort eating," she whispered. "Ever since Granddad died. She weighs over three hundred pounds."

The three men regarded the figure beneath the hat, the veil and the traveling blanket with sympathy and fascination. The manager alone still felt a faint twinge of unease. Each and every trade tends to develop a form of recall unique to its own field and after forty years of running the Danish Society this man had perfected a memory worthy of the most chauvinistic butler. In it he had filed away data cards on every Dane with whom he had ever come into contact in the United Kingdom. Right now his need to enter the old lady into this file outweighed his oxygen debt and so he leaned toward Madelene.

"Her feet," he gasped.

Madelene looked down. The ape's feet had crept out from beneath the blanket. Admittedly they were encased in a pair of Johnny's woolen socks but in the tiny elevator, perched on the wheelchair footrest, they still seemed unduly large.

"Fluid," she said, "fluid retention in her feet."

The manager's features exuded palpable sorrow.

"And her head?" he whispered.

In order to get Mrs. Clapham's hat over Erasmus' head it

had been necessary for Madelene to take the scissors to it. This headgear had now slipped, and through the crown peeped the ape's skull—brown, smooth-shaven and enormous.

"Fluid," said Madelene. "In her head too."

The elevator came to a halt; the door opened and Madelene pushed the chair out. And there, walking toward her from the far end of the corridor, was Susan.

It did not seem at all odd to Madelene that she should bump into her friend here. She knew that she had stepped into some sort of alembic. Not an open-necked Pyrex flask like the one in which she had mixed her drink, but a sealed laboratory alembic, a retort containing a goodly proportion of her essential elements. She was also aware that she had now lit the burner under this flask, and to this mixture, from the outside, she had added the ape and it was her dream that finally, at long last, if not gold then at least some sort of equilibrium would now manifest itself.

Susan was an intrinsic part of this alloy and Madelene greeted her with a warm smile. But deep inside her the peal of the alarm grew in intensity.

Susan had, so she thought, taken in the situation at a glance, but even though she saw things more clearly than the three men in the elevator, nevertheless—as always when people come up against the incomprehensible—first and foremost she was seeing herself.

"Madelene . . . !" she said.

"It's not what you think," said Madelene.

Susan licked her lips. Then her face took on a worried look.

"We're having a meeting," she said. "Of the Royal Society for the Protection of Animals. We always have our lunchtime meetings here. Because of the cakes. Adam will be here any minute."

Madelene braced herself against the wheelchair. Susan took her by the arm.

"Let me help you two," she said. "I keep a little flat. For just this sort of thing."

Madelene shook her head. At Susan's back a door opened. Dr. Firkin stuck out his head. Madelene drove the wheelchair forward.

Susan gave her arm a squeeze.

"Well, if nothing else I can keep him out on the patio," she said. "Enjoy yourselves!"

Dr. Firkin was terrified. Not only was he clad in a broad-shouldered wool jacket, over this he also wore a bulky over-coat and a felt hat, and when he divested himself of the hat and coat it was plain to see that he was freezing, in spite of the summer heat. His eyes were trained on the floor and he kept them downcast as Madelene pushed the wheelchair into the room. Only after she had brought it to a standstill and removed the traveling blanket, the hat, the veil, the gloves and the socks did he lift his head to look at the figure in the chair. Slowly, never taking his eyes off the ape's face, he walked over to it, gently stroked the hair on its arm, measured the length of its forearm with his outstretched palm, turned its hand back and forth several times, circled it, surveying its ears from all angles, ran his fingers over the smooth-shaven cranium, studied its epidermis at some length, delicately parted its lips to disclose its teeth. Finally he knelt down and took one of its feet in his hands, lifted it and gazed long and hard at the sole of the foot. And throughout all of this he kept up a soft, soothing stream of baby talk. When he was done, he stood up and plodded slowly back across to his coat.

"Is he drugged?" he asked.

Madelene shook her head.

"I'm sorry," he said. "But there's nothing I can do."

He avoided looking directly at Madelene.

"It doesn't belong to any known species. So it must be a crossbreed. There were a lot of those produced in the twenties and thirties. But it's rare now. And strictly forbidden. There are one hundred and fifty species of ape. A hundred and eighty if we count the prosimians. I can't say which species have been crossed here. I would suggest you take it along to the Veterinary School of London. They'll prepare a detailed description of it there. And send tissue samples to the genetics laboratory at the Institute for Population Biology."

Neither Madelene nor the ape stirred. Hesitantly the doctor looked up at Madelene. When he spoke his voice was very hoarse.

"Nothing fits," he said. "The body bears a faint resemblance to that of the dwarf chimpanzee but it's too tall and too heavy and the facial skin is too pale. The cranium is as big as a gorilla's but gorillas have a sagittal suture running across their skulls, serving as a linchpin for the masticatory muscles, and this one here's skull is quite smooth. This coat is a summer pelt with vestiges of a winter one, but we know of no primates from a temperate climate. The hands and feet have the retentive grip found in humans but the prehensile musculature is formed like that of a gibbon. Had there been no more to it than that, I would go along with it, I would sign on the dotted line and report Burden, I would say to myself, 'Well, even if we *are* going to hell in a handbasket at least we're doing it in style.' But that's *not* all."

He got into his coat.

"Apes can be trained to do the most amazing things. If they are hand-reared. And it goes without saying they end up a mess. Demonstrate abnormal behavior, become incapable of mating. But they can be tamed. Were we to assume that this fellow here has been brought up among humans, then that might explain his docility. And if we were less fussy about the scientific details, we could perhaps put his appearance down to his being some sort of crossbreed. But what we cannot explain away is the look in his eyes. Even the most psychologically twisted performing chimp cannot tolerate eye contact. It's the ultimate challenge of the animal kingdom.

What sets us apart from the animals is not language or intelligence. What sets us apart is the fact that we can look each other straight in the eye."

He donned his hat.

"This thing is too big for me. It was your husband who started it. And his sister."

Madelene said nothing.

"My pension," said the doctor. "Have you any idea what it's like to be a seventy-year-old living in Britain without a pension?"

"The veterinary police?" said Madelene.

"They're supposed to hand over wild animals to the London Zoo. Which means Burden. A report has to be filled out, and this the Home Office will countersign once it has been ratified by the Animal Procedure Committee. Which again means your husband. And his sister."

He bent his head.

"I'm sorry about this," he said. "That's why I've always got on best with animals. I was always almost as afraid as they were."

"I must remember to tell Erasmus that," said Madelene. "It'll give him something to console himself with when they're pulling him limb from limb."

The doctor turned on his heel, opened the door and was gone.

Madelene stood by the window. Her eye fell on Adam down on the street, standing next to a white car. Out of the car climbed Inspector Smailes and three other men. Out of four other white cars climbed almost a score more, in no great hurry, dressed in pale, lightweight summer clothes. Parked farther down the street was a closed van with the initials RSPCA painted on its side. A collection van from the Royal Society for the Prevention of Cruelty to Animals. It was a tranquil scene, bathed in sunlight. And yet it represented, beyond a shadow of a doubt, the final phase of a hunt.

The men fanned out around the building. Madelene turned

back into the room. The ape and the wheelchair were gone.
She walked out of the room into the corridor. Some way down
by a window stood the ape, looking out. In the walled garden
backing onto Hyde Park the committee of the Royal Society
for the Protection of Animals was gathered around a table
loaded with Danish cakes and pastries, a sight that stopped
Madelene in her tracks.

This table called to mind a birth. It smelled of milk, it ran
with strawberry-marbled whipped cream, buttercream and
confectioner's custard, so perfectly formed that no one could
have told from looking at it that within the past eight hours it
had been both killed off and brought back to life.

The original idea behind this table had been that over this
spread Adam would advise the committee of an extraordinary
zoological subject that had come into his possession, going on
to ask them for their support in keeping this hidden from both
the public at large and the Animal Procedure Committee for
a few weeks longer.

The table reservation had been canceled at four in the
morning when Adam called his sister to tell her that his wife
had run off along with the ape. It had been rebooked that very
morning when he had rung to assure himself that Smailes had
located the truck and that it was in the process of being surrounded.

Twenty minutes later he had called again to say that the
van had been taken by storm and the driver arrested. But that
Madelene and the ape were nowhere to be found.

Adam had lost two pounds in weight for every one of the
past ten days, a fact borne out by the sound of his voice. Not
only had he lost his wife and his ape, not only did he now
have to watch the most crucial offensive of his career brought
to a grinding halt or called off completely, but beneath all this
there lay a more profound exhaustion. For three almost sleepless days and nights he had, for the first time in his life, been
confronted with a zoological phenomenon that was not open
to investigation.

This situation had led to the following conversation between him and Andrea.

"The papers," said Adam. "She'll go to the papers. And the police. That driver is the one who worked for Bally. We're sunk. I've been considering suicide."

"The newspapers," said Andrea Burden, "know nothing about apes. But everything about the law of libel. Before printing so much as a line they will check back with the experts. With the Institute, that is. And that, little brother mine, means you. You will examine the ape and conclude that it is a chimpanzee. Of a rare but not unknown species."

"They'll confront me with Madelene."

"And you will reveal—reluctantly, but constrained by circumstances—that your wife is an alcoholic. You won't be spared the front pages. But the headlines will read: 'Zoo director's drunken wife steals rare chimpanzee.' "

"This will ruin my prospects."

"It will give them a boost. You will not only have the support of the scientists and politicians. You will be buoyed up by the sympathy of the man in the street."

Andrea Burden paused.

"What it will do to your marriage," she then said airily, "is another matter."

Adam shut his eyes, and came to a decision. Not a personal one, not a subjective or an emotional decision. What he did was to set up an imaginary chemical balance. In the one pan he placed Madelene, her drinking, her mystery, the now exhilarating, now depressing attraction she held for him. In the other pan he placed his future. His infinite potential, both professional and sexual.

It was not he who wrote off Madelene. It was the law of gravity.

"And this evening," he said, "you and Bowen will appear on *Newsnight* and back me up."

And so it was that this cornucopia of cake had been let off with its life, and now here it was, reminding Madelene that she had eaten nothing in more than sixteen hours or more.

The ape had not had anything to eat either and it was now on the move, making its way down the stairway, tripping lightly as a ballerina with the wheelchair under its arm. Madelene thought at first that it had got wind of what was afoot and was making one last, desperate bid for freedom. But at the foot of the stairs it stopped, swathed itself in the traveling blanket, slapped the hat down over its head, seated itself in the wheelchair, drew the veil down into place and bowled through the doorway, heading straight for the party around the table.

The meeting had not been formally called to order and so the circle opened up accommodatingly and with no surprise to admit the elderly lady in the wheelchair. Then silence fell, to be broken eventually by Sir Toby. He was related to this new arrival, he had ridden with her in the elevator, his back still ached from carrying her.

"Mrs. Mortensen," he said, "Mrs. Burden's grandmother."

Everyone bowed politely toward the veiled face. The committee members were twelve in number and these Sir Toby now proceeded to introduce one at a time.

He was halfway around the table when the old woman made a move. An arm shot out from the blanket, an inordinately long arm in a dressing-gown sleeve—like a crane at the end of which hung a grab in a workman's glove. With care and exactitude this hand worked its way under an entire chocolate-coated Othello layer cake, lifted it and guided it underneath the veil.

Knowing, as he did, of the old woman's deep sorrow and terrible problem, Sir Toby completed his introductions, his expression deadpan. The dowager's other hand darted out, hovered in midair for a moment, then snatched up three jugs of cream in rapid succession.

Madelene emerged from the stairway. She crossed the patio, treading slowly and with dignity. She did not acknowledge the committee, did no more than nod at Susan, who registered the clarity and hopelessness in her friend's face. Madelene took hold of the wheelchair, turned it around and pushed it the few yards to the bottom of the garden, down by the high wall adjoining Hyde Park. All she wanted was one last moment away from other people and in physical proximity to Erasmus.

She placed her hands on the ape's shoulders. Then she closed her eyes and measured the full extent of her defeat.

She had believed that the law of the land would protect the ape and she had been wrong. She had expected social convention to allow her at least a breathing space and here too she had been wrong. She had pinned her hopes on her own triumphant feeling of being on the right track and this feeling had proved to be an illusion. Now she took stock of the universe and could discern no trace—not even out on the farthest reaches of her experience—of supreme justice. She was being driven, unresisting, toward conceding that the world is a machine in which men and animals are merely components or, at most, minuscule self-contained machines—in other words, lifeless—or worse still, a lifelessness that is life-like in action, the tiny *perpetuum mobile* of death.

The door to the garden swung open and Adam, Inspector Smailes, the two vets from the RSPCA and a bunch of easy-does-it white men issued onto the patio. They split up into two groups, to skirt each side of the table.

Madelene lowered her head.

"I'm sorry I couldn't do better," she murmured.

A short distance in front of the wheelchair the men halted for a moment. One of the vets cocked his rifle, the other unfurled a net. Madelene looked back, the wall behind them was yellow, the sun and shadows dancing across its face had a merciless look about them, as though this were the wall before the firing squad, and more than that, a metaphysical wall, a definitive blockade against any hope of a meaning to life.

Then the ape got to its feet. It pulled off the hat, pulled

off the blanket, the dressing gown, and let them drop. In the sunlight it faced up to the men: tall, short-legged, grotesque, with arms that hung down to the ground and a whipped-cream clown grin on its clean-shaven face.

The men instinctively took a pace backward. The ape wrapped its arm around Madelene's waist.

"Let's go," it said.

It leapt like a cat, with no visible preparation, did an about-face in midair and ran, carrying Madelene, up the vertical face of the wall.

It perched for a second on top of the wall. Then it took off and to the people on the patio it seemed to spring straight up into the blue sky with Madelene and disappear.

part three

one

London is a troubled city. Its stock exchange and banks form the financial heart of the world; its mass media constitute the eyes and ears of the English-speaking world; its libraries, museums and archives stand anxious guard over the most comprehensive historical memory in Europe; it is the seat of government, it houses both the Lords and the royal family and, hence, the world's largest repository of aristocratic genetic material. And through the University of London and that institution's neural links with Oxford and Cambridge it is responsible for the inhabited world's greatest accumulation of civilized intelligence, for the biggest brain on earth. With the result that this city is a hypochondriac; it frets to the point of distraction over its health and therefore boasts one of our planet's most extensive and most paranoid immune systems. It was this monstrous, yet timorous piece of surveillance equipment that was activated minutes after the ape's and Madelene's vanishing act.

When Erasmus leaped from the wall, Andrea Burden turned on her heel and disappeared. She was gone for only a minute or two—a time frame so short that those who stayed behind in the garden did not even notice its passing but at the same time a flash of eternity insofar as, staring at the top of the wall, they felt that they were gazing up into infinity. But for Andrea Burden it was just enough time to walk to the nearest telephone and dial a number which bypassed the duty officers and put her straight through to someone in authority.

The man at the other end took down the details.

"Should we try to take it alive?" he asked.

It took Andrea Burden less than a second to weigh a number of complex considerations.

"There's no reason to take any risks," she said. "The experts consider it to be dangerous."

This done, she returned to the patio, from which Inspector Smailes and his white men had already slipped away, whispered something to Adam, asked the committee to be seated and proceeded to present the first public—more or less—and not untruthful—at least not in all particulars—report on Erasmus the ape.

Within five minutes of her call Hyde Park had been cordoned off. Five minutes later the first helicopter from the Scotland Yard heliport on Thornhill Road flew over the park. Five minutes thereafter the first dog patrols went in. And five minutes after that sentry posts were set up at fifty-yard intervals around the entire perimeter of the park.

None of those who knew of or were involved in the search were in any doubt that the runaways would be tracked down within the hour. It is possible, under certain circumstances, for a person to evade detection in London. But not an anthropoid ape. Which happens to be holding a woman captive. And which has already been hemmed in.

———

Madelene and the ape observed the manner in which they were cut off from the outside world from the top of a lime tree situated next to Speke's Monument by the Long Water in the northern section of Hyde Park. They were not readily visible, the ape having twined branches and leaves into a little cupola that screened them on all sides. But obviously it never occurred to Madelene to cherish any kind of hope. The police were everywhere, the nearest dog patrol was less than thirty yards away, diagonally below the tree in which they sat. Wherever she looked she saw men with walkie-talkies, with television cameras, telescopes and rifles with telescopic sights. She knew nothing of Andrea Burden's telephone call. But she could hazard a guess at what the world around them was gearing up for—as far as the ape was concerned, at any rate. Not capture but execution.

Even so, her main feeling was not one of fear. More than anything else, she was filled—in this state of absolute hopelessness—with that curiosity which goes on growing in all living things, like hair and nails after death. She viewed the people and things around her with fresh clarity, freed from any interest in where they had come from and unconcerned as to where they might be going—distinctly, like after the first drink—acutely, like being in the midst of a diabolical but miraculously painless hangover.

She looked at the ape. It was following the course of the hunt, absorbed but unmoving, apart from the odd time when it stopped up a gap in an effort to perfect the leafy cupola. Madelene saw how much it resembled a little boy.

All at once she felt at home. She recognized the green universe that surrounded her; here were the hideouts of her childhood, in the trees of her childhood, with her childhood playmates. Although actually it was more than that, since in her childhood there had, in fact, been no trees. Her nursemaids had discouraged her from climbing aloft for fear that she would fall, in which case they would be fired; her mother had begged her not to because of a fear of heights so severe that it also embraced everyone else around her; and her father had forbidden it on the basis of a vague aversion to the thought that his daughter might climb out of sight and into the heavens while in the company of some boy. So the hideout that now arched over her head was not something which she had ever experienced. It was like a dream that was only now coming true. She and the ape were bandits and down below them on the ground there were not only soldiers but a consolidation of all the gangs of boys from strange streets and unknown neighborhoods whom Madelene had never fought against, and she followed them with eyes that were agog with excitement and yet totally serene.

She knew of course, as did the ape, that beneath them they had, not real live children, but something better, Death itself, and without giving any thought to it they both smiled the same smile. Contrary to what adults believe the joy of children at play comes not from having no knowledge of Death—every living creature has that. It comes from their divining what the grown-ups have lost sight of; that even though Death makes a fierce opponent, it is not invincible. The ape and Madelene laughed, soundlessly and convulsively, holding one another up, because they knew that tomorrow too they would be alive.

At sunset the guard on the outer wall of the park was doubled and at nightfall stands rigged up with searchlights were erected at hundred-yard intervals, lighting up the park like a football stadium. At the gates, patrols from London Fire Brigade's Pioneer Squad armed with ladders and accompanied by the antiterrorist corps prepared to institute a systematic search of the treetops come daybreak.

Even by London standards this was an impressive display of force. Prompted—as only a very few, including Andrea Burden, knew—by the fact that an action was being mounted against an unequivocal enemy.

Having once exceeded a certain critical size, every organism develops a number of self-destructive traits, and in London's gigantic mycelium of police, military and intelligence units, departmental rivalry, hole-in-the-corner intrigue and bureaucratic jealousy had long since borne fruit in the form of well-advanced, tumorous growths. And what a tumor craves, of course, is neither an internal purge nor its own liquidation. What it wants is a good external foe. Erasmus the ape was not just good, he was wonderful, seemingly heaven-sent—like the Falklands War, only on a smaller scale, a dragon, an economy-size King Kong tailor-made for taking the public's mind off such insoluble problems as the general deterioration and impoverishment of the city, race riots and widespread organized crime. Besides which it was completely apolitical. And to top it all it had kidnapped a princess. Hyde Park had been floodlit to create an arena into which St. George of the System might ride.

An hour after nightfall the ape rose, wrapped an arm around Madelene, parted the screen of leaves at a shadowed spot and leapt, almost horizontally, into what seemed to Madelene to be a pitch-black void.

Their glide lasted long enough for her to note the hissing drag of the cool night air, the warmth of the ape's body, its stillness in the air after takeoff and its gradual preparation for landing. It lighted upon a branch eight yards farther on with the muffled weight of a tawny owl swooping down into the undergrowth, and then it began to run.

Heading away from the wall of the Danish Society toward the center of the park, it had propelled itself forward by means of its long arms, in great pendulous swings. Now it had forsaken this sweeping movement, forging ahead instead by means of both feet and its one free hand, and where the trees were too far apart it jumped.

Not once did it get caught in the light. They made the park

wall as if through a tunnel of shadow. A few yards above one of the lookout posts the ape paused. The moment it was waiting for came half a minute later: those few seconds of inattention among the men beneath them which resulted not from negligence or loafing or any other reason unique to these men, but because it is in the nature of human consciousness to switch on and off, on and off. In that second when it was disconnected, while the men were swapping places and exchanging a brief word or two, the ape jumped.

Its jump carried them into a light so bright that they might have been leaping from the wings onto a stage and Madelene shut her eyes. She waited for the shot, or the cry that would give them away, but it never arrived. The only sound came from the traffic beneath them and the wind whistling in the trees along which the ape was traveling. Madelene opened her eyes. She saw that the creature was running. Straight ahead—parallel with the street but high above it—it ran, along cables, across scaffolding and buttresses. Its physical and sensory faculties could pick out a path invisible to human eyes, cutting across the city at third-floor level.

Madelene saw the vehicles below them, she saw people on the pavement, people in cars—saw them quite clearly. She saw the backs of the men patrolling the park. She saw the fire engines with their extension ladders and their crews waiting for the dawn and—directly beneath her, on a low roof—she saw two of the police snipers, saw their faces, their eyes, their night glasses. But they did not see her and they did not see the ape, even though she and it were fully visible, bathed in the light.

The ape was climbing higher now, up drainpipes, over balconies and fire escapes, then up another story to a heart-stoppingly haphazard network of flagpoles, cornices and balustrades. Then farther up still, to the lowest unbroken run of rooftops in London.

They passed by windows beyond which families huddled

around the television. They ran across verandas on which people were taking in washing. They came past men and women in elevators and stairwells, people on balconies who looked straight at and past them.

No one noticed them. This progress of theirs was not just a journey through space; it also constituted a passage through the civilized consciousness, and for the first time ever Madelene had the feeling that this watchfulness was not something omnipresent but that it was, in fact, concentrated. She saw how people on the street only took in what was happening at street level. She saw how those who were searching for her had forgotten themselves and everything else in the outside world other than the spot where they believed their quarry to be. She saw how people sitting in front of a television became oblivious to everything except the tiny patch of flickering unreality before their eyes; how, when engaged in any sort of activity, people paid no heed to anything other than the job at hand.

Carrying Madelene, the ape ran straight across a glass roof beneath which children played; they passed a dinner party on a roof terrace just an arm's length away; they raced around and past a young couple who looked straight through them and up at the stars and no one noticed them. And having come within spitting distance of them, Madelene understood why. It was because these people did not expect to see them. Faced by the mass of stimuli and information generated by London, its inhabitants had closed their minds, quite categorically, to the possibility of anything truly miraculous.

Until this moment, Madelene had always pictured the British capital as the city liked to think of itself, as a nerve center of sleepless, hyperactive vitality. Now she discerned a truer picture. Looking into these faces, devoid of all suspicion, she saw that the city had its head in the clouds; that—despite its seven million people, its telephones, its never-ending supply of energy, its feverish activity, its streams of nutrients and effluent—its mind was quite simply elsewhere; that it hung suspended in a permanent and only spasmodically interrupted absence.

Through this gigantic urban daydream the ape moved like a circus performer high above a stunned audience. Whereas a human being, pulling up short, would be caught off balance just for an instant, it could stiffen—even when running, even halfway through a turn—and hold itself still as a statue. If a figure suddenly appeared in a doorway, if a face behind a window was turned in their direction, the ape would freeze into inertness, and always, in such situations, some escape route would present itself—a ledge behind which to duck, or a power cable to drop onto—as though the animal itself were creating the world through which it moved. Eyes blank with concentration, it executed a sequence of movements for which the city provided a backdrop, while at the same time it was capable, quite suddenly, of becoming one with a gray wall, a ventilation shaft or a chimney pot.

But no illusion is ever perfect, and the ape's were no exception. There were times when a section of drainpipe came away from the wall in its hand and plummeted clattering into the abyss. Times when a sudden, unexpected breeze wafted its burnt-rubber odor across a dinner table; when a woman in a kitchen suddenly pulled back a curtain and peered out at their vulnerable joint silhouette—exposed, backlit, swinging from three washing lines suspended eighty feet above a backyard.

But no one took any notice of them, no one sensed their presence, no one saw them or smelled them or heard them. Until that moment Madelene had never known any form of unconsciousness other than sleep. Now she realized that even when they are awake people may be asleep. Oblivious to space, they slept, their sense of smell slept, their hearing, their vision and their sense of touch. And their imagination slept— their ability to conjure up images, which might have kept a channel open to the unknown—that too slept.

In that hour a hush fell over the city. It closed its eyes, its lights went out, its streets emptied, it abandoned the last semblance of vigilance. Its televisions shut down, its traffic came to a standstill. Even around Hyde Park, far behind Erasmus and Madelene, the men on watch withdrew into themselves. During that hour there was something moving about London, as if it had cast aside all pretension and revealed its true nature: it was not, after all, some superior life form since no living organism ever grinds to such a complete halt. Nor was it a forest or urban jungle, since no jungle sinks into such a torpor at night. What it in fact now proved to be was a machine. A sorry machine—worn out, dilapidated, to some extent faulty, full of blind spots and flat points, and crisscrossed by the forgotten tracks along which the woman and the ape were now traveling.

two

On a flat roof high above the city the ape set Madelene down then dropped over the rim like a falcon diving. It seemed to pitch headlong from ledge to ledge, disappearing from view to return seconds later carrying a crate full of bananas and oranges. It put the crate down and began to eat as quickly and methodically as a migrating bird breaking its journey to rest, knowing as it does so that the longest stretch still lies ahead.

It dawned on Madelene that the ape still did not know her name. She placed her hand on her chest.

"Madelene," she said.

"Madelene," repeated the ape.

Its voice was dark, darker than any human being's, but its pronunciation was distinct, accentless, perfect.

The feeling of all rules being waived went to Madelene's head like an injection of alcohol and she took a step backward. Even before this action was effected the ape had anticipated it, risen and stretched out an arm, but Madelene was not about to fall. She was on the point of lifting off. Only an hour earlier she had been awaiting her execution and before that she had been a suicidal alcoholic caught in a breakneck downward spiral. Now she had ascended out of this pit, it had taken her less than an hour to rise up and she was still climbing.

"I don't know when you . . . that is, animals . . . I mean apes, grow up," she said. "But I've often wondered when humans do. And now I know."

In all the time she had known the ape, she had heard it say a total of two words, but it never occurred to her that it would not be able to understand her. What she now had to say was, she felt, of universal importance, comprehensible to all living creatures.

"I've often thought: Now I'm no longer a child. I thought it when I married Adam. And at our high school graduation parties. And with my first boyfriends. But I see now that this was wrong."

"Wrong," repeated the ape, its mouth full of banana.

"Grown up," she said, "is something you become only once you are free."

"Free," the ape said, and peeled an orange.

The eyes above the steadily working jaws rested on her, and Madelene experienced the uplift that comes from talking and being listened to, felt it like a warm, soaring thermal airstream, and she spread her wings and took to the air.

"Something else has happened too," she said. "I think I know who I am now. I'm a sort of princess."

This was a sudden promotion, one that took even Madelene by surprise, and for one brief moment she threatened to metamorphose from a bird into a balloon. Then she felt the ape's hand take her arm in a grip that gently but firmly anchored her to the roof.

"It's got nothing to do with being royal," she said. "It has something to do with being chosen for something important."

The ape moved a few paces away from her and straddled a low parapet.

"Bowel movement," it said in explanation.

It defecated with the horse-dropping weight of the herbivore, like an earthquake in a compost heap. Then it was by her side once more, put its arm around her, took a few rapidly accelerating strides and leapt into the night.

Two full days had passed since Madelene had last had a drink, and even though her liver had had nothing like enough time to clean out the alcohol residue in her body, nevertheless in one sense she was more sober now than she had been for two years. In another sense, however, she was more heavily under the influence than ever before.

She let her head fall back against the ape's shoulder. Like one of those birds that fly at night, a wild duck or a nightingale, she looked up at the stars to get her bearings and what met her eyes were more than just tiny, gleaming pinpoints; what she saw shining in the heavens were the images of femininity by which she had steered up till now, those sophisticated, rapidly burned-out personalities: Billie Holiday, Marlene Dietrich's Lola-Lola in *The Blue Angel*, Judy Garland, Janis Joplin, Julie Christie—the supernovas of female alcoholism. But now these fixed points paled, now their place was taken by a fierce self-confidence.

Under such conditions London acquired a certain beauty. Madelene viewed the skyscrapers she passed as sleeping cathedrals of solidified lava. She felt in no way irritated by the city's slumbering inhabitants, felt only kindness and pity because these people could not see her, Madelene, demigoddess, in the moonlight, riding on an ape, heading toward something tremendous. It was as though the Lord God Almighty had made himself known, like a kind of talent scout whose eye, on this night, had at long last fallen on her, Princess Madelene, and he and she had come to an arrangement, a sort of contract, the first clause of which stated that Madelene was never again to be unhappy.

Reality struck without any warning. She had been aware that they were no longer as high up and that they were now moving through gardens and parks but in the dark, seen from above, looking down on it from treetops and tiled roofs, she had not recognized the landscape. Until the ape slid carefully down a roof and deposited her on the balcony outside her room at Mombasa Manor.

At first she was incapable of movement. The ape had already straightened up, it was ready to take off, in a moment it was going to disappear over the edge of the balcony and leave her here, the way men had always left women, except that this was a hundred times worse because the animal was only an ape, or more horrid still, a talking ape—in other words, not even a proper animal.

Madelene blushed, but not out of embarrassment. Out of hate. It had taken her a whole life filled with a long succession of privations plus a fortnight of upheaval plus these past hours of dramatic flight to come to a point where she could feel the fleeting, magnanimous sense of empathy with the people of London of a moment before. Now it took her one second to turn into a demon in female form.

She pulled herself up to her full height, she walked over to the ape, she smiled. The paralysis had lifted, she seemed herself again. But she was no longer herself. Every trace of humanity had gone from her. Although the ape did not know it, across from him now stood the figure of pure, smiling feminine ruthlessness.

She laid her hands on its shoulders.

"Wait a minute," she said. "There's a dear."

The ape's eyes searched her face.

"Dear," it said.

Madelene turned around and walked into the house. She walked through her rooms looking neither to right nor to left, touched by no memories of the time she had spent in them. She walked out into the corridor, walked down the stairs and through the public rooms of the house as she had never walked through them before, at speed, paying them no heed, feeling no fear, feeling in fact nothing at all. She climbed more stairs, walked along the corridor and into her husband's room, for the first time ever without knocking first.

Adam Burden was lying on the left side of the bed, on his back, with the telephone on the bedside table right next to his head in order that he could, any minute now, receive the call with the message that the ape Erasmus had been put down and his wife taken into custody. When Madelene crossed the threshold he was in the middle of a bad dream.

Twelve hours earlier he had taken his leave—silently, in his head—of Madelene. He had excised her from his mind and it was with the feeling that he would soon recover from this operation—or, no, that he was in fact already well again—that he had turned in for the night. Nonetheless, her image had come to him in his sleep, pursued him, caught up with him and fallen upon him like the phantom pain of an amputated limb. He had dreamt that she stood before him and that he had stretched out a hand to her but could not reach her.

It was a nightmare of the kind in which, even while it is happening, one begs to be wakened and when the bedroom door opened the first thing he felt was gratitude. Then, in the moonlight, he recognized Madelene, let out a roar of terror, sat up in bed alive to the fact that his nightmare had been elevated to a higher and more merciless level of reality and pressed himself back against the wall.

Madelene put out a hand and switched on the light.

"It's out on the balcony," she said. "You have to do something."

Adam saw her lips move but he did not hear her words. Standing there in front of him, determined and desperate, she radiated a corona that penetrated his sleepiness and firm decisions that insinuated themselves under his quilt and down into his pajama trousers, causing his entire being to stretch out to her—this woman whom, in the same breath, he also hated—to hold on to her.

Madelene stepped one pace backward.

"You'd better bring a gun," she said.

Adam swung his legs out of bed, grabbed a rifle from the back of the wardrobe and followed Madelene, befuddled, clad in a dressing gown, pajamas and flip-flops and with an erection that refused to subside.

The ape had not moved. It was standing in the position and on the spot in which Madelene had left it and they could see it silhouetted through the French doors when they entered Madelene's room. Adam had left his sandals outside the door, they moved in absolute silence with the whole house on their side, not a door hinge or a floorboard uttering a sound. But still the ape detected their presence. It drew itself erect and tried to peer through the darkness before it. Madelene pushed Adam forward; they stepped out onto the balcony.

Adam Burden was not a doubter, he was the inexorable man of action. Even so, under other circumstances the situation with which he was here faced might well have cracked and broken him, involving as it did all the conflicting forces and considerations in his life. It involved his career, his marriage, his home, his past and his future, not to mention a number of incalculable legal and political considerations. But he was not aware of these conflicts. For him, the instant he saw Madelene standing opposite his bed, the situation had become very, very simple. It revolved around one thing: how he could hold on to her. Right at this minute he could not have cared less about the ape, the outside world, in a way he could not even have cared less about himself. There was one person who mattered and that was Madelene.

When they trod out of the darkness the ape glanced briefly at Adam and at the rifle. After that its eyes never left Madelene.

"Why?" it said.

Adam stared at its mouth, at the point from which the

word had issued. For a second or so the lover in him gave way to the scientist. Then he shook his head.

"This is some kind of hoax," he said.

Madelene was not listening to her husband.

"I don't want to be left here," she said.

A deep furrow appeared in the creature's broad, smooth-shaven brow. It searched—frantically, fruitlessly—through the useless technical glossary it had gleaned from its keepers in a vain attempt to say something so convoluted that precious few would ever be able to articulate it.

It gave up, pointed around, in a gesture that embraced the whole house. Then it nodded at Adam and looked quizzically at Madelene.

"He let me down," she said.

Adam moistened his lips.

"It was a mistake," he said. "Everything's going to be all right."

The ape looked out across the park, and beyond, toward Hampstead Heath, which Madelene knew would be its escape route.

"Shoot it in the legs," she said.

Adam lowered the rifle and took aim. The ape ignored him. In its face, a face that Madelene was very gradually getting to know, she saw something new, something quite inconceivable in an animal, nestling like a shadow in the corner of its eye. It was not fear, it was not animal ignorance as to the impending danger of the situation. It was sadness, or possibly despair.

She stepped into the line of fire.

"Wait just a moment," she said.

Adam looked from her to the ape and back again.

She walked over to Erasmus.

"I've just had a thought," she said.

"Move," said Adam.

Madelene did not hear him.

"You know," she said, "what I've been chosen for."

The ape regarded Madelene intently. Both it and she had

forgotten everything else around them. And so they did not see Adam raise the rifle. He was no longer aiming at the ape's thigh. He was aiming at its head.

"To go with you," said Madelene. "That's what I was meant to do. Observe your behavior. Like a zoological experiment."

She said it very softly, but there was something in her voice, something heard only occasionally, very rarely, in a woman's voice when something is vitally important to her and she reaches for it—never forcing it—a kind of music, the music of the spheres, an ultrasonic signal directed straight at a man's central nervous system. And so too it struck both the ape's and Adam's. For a split second they both stood there, vibrating like a couple of tuning forks.

The next instant a surge of murderous jealousy shot through Adam and out of his index finger, and he pressed the trigger.

Too late. The white-hot projectile sped out into the world never to find its target. It flew whistling across Hampstead Heath and then, over the Vale of Heath, it began to waver and rotate and lose height, before falling impotently to earth. For by the time Adam fired the ape had already, a moment before, wrapped an arm around Madelene, lifted her off her feet and leapt off the balcony.

three

Seven days they were under way.

The first night brought them to the outskirts of Greater London and after that they traveled during the daytime. To begin with through parks and housing developments, later along ditches and hedgerows and later still along the banks of rivers and through orchards and woods. No human set eyes on them, and even the wild animals they passed, even the pheasants, foxes, badgers and deer, had no time to register them before they were off again, leaving no trace of themselves other than the scent, baffling to animals, of anthropoid ape with a dash of perfume.

The only living creatures in a position to observe them long enough to see which way they went were the birds of prey that overtook them, dropped out of the skies, drew closer and hovered for a moment in the air. Madelene waved when she saw them, as two motorcyclists or two nuns passing one another will signal to say that while everyone else may be tied down they are free.

If she could have flown and taken wing with the birds and followed them she would have seen that every single bird was part of a pattern, one among millions of birds all crossing, at one and the same time all over Europe, the same parallel and all with the same purpose in mind: to mate, build nests and have young, and set against this greater design each and every unique and free-as-air bird was fettered and anonymous. But Madelene could not fly and at this point her thoughts barely left the ground, far too taken up was she with being able for the first time in her life to do, brilliantly, exactly as she pleased. She never watched the birds for long and she never guessed that the reason they hung over her and the ape only for a very little while was not because they gave them up as potential prey or gave up trying to understand them. Not at all. It was because the birds had seen that this at once shaggy and smooth-skinned, multiheaded creature was neither hunter nor hunted. It was making its way toward a definite geographical and psychic location. It was migrating, just as they were.

It might have looked as though it was the ape who chose their route and it may even have seemed that way to the creature itself. But in fact—as is so often the case—it was Madelene, the woman, who with the minimum of almost passive, but nonetheless unremitting, intuitive obstinacy dictated their course.

That first night, in the still dusky light of dawn, while she waited, the ape had broken into a department store, with practiced ease, and helped itself to two air mattresses, two sleeping mats, two extra long goose-down quilts, two sets of bed linen and a large backpack in which to carry all this comfortably. The first time it made up beds for them on the mats, in a tall oak on the edge of suburban St. Albans' botanic gardens, Madelene—noticing that it had had the nerve in the gloom of the department store to grope its way to bedclothes of especially soft, long-fibered Egyptian cotton—realized that besides being a large anthropoid ape it was also an arrant freeloader and from that moment on she steered them in one particular direction.

At a crossroads, having divined the wording on a road sign from some distance away, she made an imperceptible decision. When they left the shadow of a forest and had to choose which way to go next, she came up with an all but invisible suggestion based on a tenuous understanding of the four points of the compass. She compared—virtually without herself being aware of it—the names of the villages they passed with a cartographical snippet in her head.

Erasmus ate, she discovered, between twenty and twenty-five pounds of fresh fruit a day, preferably supplemented by nuts and raisins, hopefully by honey, better still by three quarts of heavy cream. And preferably these provisions should be easily obtainable, within easy reach—in a refrigerated warehouse, for instance, or a parked long-distance truck. And it did not care for cold water. Like Madelene, it had a profound and possibly neurological, genetic need for a hot bath every day.

Having once grasped this fact, Madelene understood also that they would have to keep to the outskirts of villages and other built-up areas. On that first night of their journey she had felt that they had the whole of England at their feet. Now she took yet another step toward understanding the nature of freedom. She realized that they would have to walk a line, a tightrope, between, on the one hand, the destructiveness of technological civilization and, on the other, Mother Nature's exasperating lack of creature comforts. That right from the start there had been only one course for them to take: to a place where one could stay under cover and have one's food served up, a place that could accommodate both their congenital yearning for freedom and their congenital laziness. She had spent eighteen months caught up in a torrent of zoological information. She knew that in the whole of Britain there was only one such place.

When, on the sixth day, they reached the fringes of the town of Chatteris, she made the crucial choice. Had they turned east, as any *Homo ferus* or any honest-to-goodness wild animal would have done, they would have ended up in the most out-of-the-way, the most desolate, the most isolated spot in England, in the impenetrable marshlands of Bedford Levels. Instead Madelene led them northward. Toward St. Francis Forest, the London Zoo's private wildlife reserve, the largest zoological breeding and research center in Europe.

Throughout their journey Madelene had given Erasmus lessons in both English and Danish and the ape had learned fast—not as a child learns, since children learn under great pressure from the need to express themselves, but playfully, effortlessly. On the seventh day they traveled in silence, with no language lessons, no behavioral studying, no waving to birds. Late in the afternoon they crossed a high wall, exactly like so many others and yet significantly different, and on the edge of a wood, overlooking a grassy plain, they halted. Madelene's inner compass was now spinning wildly and erratically. They had arrived.

A gray boulder meandered across the plain, coming their way.

"That thing there," the ape asked, "climb trees?"

Madelene shook her head.

"Eat people?"

Madelene had been brought up in the suburbs of a large city and for a moment there was some doubt in her mind. Then she shook her head once more.

"That's an elephant," she said.

———

When darkness fell they lit a fire in the fork of a tree and watched it flare up before dying down into glowing embers as fires are wont to do when the wood is dry and piled on top of half a dozen fire-starting blocks. After that they propped themselves up against one another on the two air mattresses, which were spread on a flat, solid and comfortable base of spruce branches. The twilight hour, the teaching hour, was upon them.

Like their journey, their language lessons had followed—without their being altogether aware of it—a quite specific route. From the personal pronouns they had sallied forth into the surrounding world's forest of nouns, moving on from there into ever more abstract linguistic territory. But just at this juncture Madelene woke up to the fact that there was something they lacked, something important which they had come to quite naturally in a roundabout way. What they lacked was the body, the human anatomy.

· She ran the tips of her fingers along the sole of one of Erasmus' feet.

"Foot," she said.

The animal jumped and they both laughed. A little and near-soundless laugh, much like people giggling before the altar—the last brief burst of self-consciousness before the moment of truth.

Madelene slid her hand up to the ape's knee.

"Calf," she said.

Erasmus did not answer. She placed her outstretched palm on its chest and ran it downward. The creature's body remained motionless. But directly below its navel its member rose to meet her. Madelene wrapped her fingers around it. It was white and at first sight almost unreal. It had the smoothness of ice, or of a cool breeze against a cheek, but at the same time, beneath this elusive softness, there was a rigidity as substantial as fired granite.

Madelene looked up. She placed her other hand on the ape's face and felt the same thing there. The skin was pale, quite fine, transparent. Beneath and across it she could sense the microscopic, fast alternating surges of feeling, the thready, capillary trees of blood. And underlying this fragility was something else—its pulse, the solid urgency of its arousal.

She nodded in the direction of its penis.

"Cock," she said.

The ape stretched out an arm, laid the back of one hand on her leg, then eased it under her dress. Madelene felt the warmth of its hand in her crotch but it did not touch her. It looked at her inquisitively.

"Pussy," she said hoarsely, enlightening him.

Without taking her eyes off the ape's she lifted up her dress until her breasts broke free. Slowly the ape leaned forward, bent his head as if in some ritual salute and took a nipple between his teeth.

It straightened up and they looked into one another's eyes as no living creatures are ever given to looking at one another. Then it took hold of her panties—very gently with hands that had no difficulty differentiating, even in the pitch dark, between satin-weave cotton and plain mercerized—and pulled them off. Madelene slid backward, still in slow motion, and the ape came after her.

They kissed one another only fleetingly. The potential lip-smacking, familial quality of a kiss would in this case have been but a digression. Madelene was very soft, very warm and very ready to clench him between her thighs. But just at this point Erasmus stopped and for a second Madelene thought it was a misunderstanding.

"Come on," she said.

Nothing happened; impatiently she pushed herself up onto her elbows and looked at the ape.

The combination of the flickering light from the embers and the dense shadows made it hard to read the ape's expression accurately. Nonetheless, as far as Madelene was concerned there could be no doubt. What she saw in its eyes was not simply lust, not merely the beast in him, not only naïveté.

Peter Høeg

There was something else there too, the subtle sadism of the street-wise kid. The animal had not stopped because of some misapprehension. It was holding her at bay.

She tried to get out of it, of course she tried to get out of it. She waited for disgust to flood through her from top to toe. But it never came. Something else came instead—more desire, a need, pressing, beyond all question of pride and submission.

"Please," she said.

Erasmus entered her with a kind of sensitive ruthlessness, along the golden mean between pain and sensual delight, and as he did so, she bit his earlobe, gently but deeply, until on the tip of her tongue she felt the first metallic hint of blood and her nostrils were filled with a scent, a savanna of scent, a continent of scent, of animal, man, stars, glowing embers, air mattresses and burnt rubber.

four

St. Francis Forest was established by the first Duke of Bedford in the seventeenth century in an attempt to re-create the Garden of Eden. The duke was a devout man; he named his park after the patron saint of animals and laid it out in strict accordance with the few, vague directions afforded in Genesis and the detailed description given in the *Divine Comedy*—in the twenty-eighth canto of the *Purgatorio*—of the garden outside which Virgil leaves Dante and in which he meets Beatrice. Like all the great gardens in European history, it was founded on the idea that nothing, and especially not nature, is good enough as it stands. What the duke and his successors had in mind was not a mild adjustment of the landscape; what they had wanted to construct was a machine, a horticultural machine designed to seize the awareness of the visitor and turn his thoughts to God. It had been their wish to create a *drug* of a garden, a landscaped hallucinogen.

This was, of course, a preposterous idea, not to say blasphemous, since any god whose work is deemed to leave that much room for improvement obviously cannot be omnipotent, at best he may be a great—though not infallible—landscape gardener, and, as one might expect, this scheme failed. In an endeavor to stick as closely as possible to the Bible, in which we are told that the effect of Paradise is so elevating that the lion and the lamb graze there side by side, the duke introduced a number of wild animals to the park. Just when it seemed that his enterprise was to be crowned with success, at the point where he had been hand-feeding fourteen Judaean lions with roast potatoes for thirty-one days and was about to declare these wild beasts to be tamed and converted to vegetarianism, they betrayed the trust shown in them and ate him. Over the next four centuries the park underwent numerous changes of ownership and extensive restructuring—under the supervision, in the latter half of the nineteenth century, of the renowned landscape gardener "Capability" Jones—and at the time of its purchase by the Royal Zoological Society in the early 1970s it epitomized quite perfectly—with its rolling luxuriance, its lakes and streams, its groves, its exotic flowers and trees, its rockeries and perfumed Persian rose gardens— what people look for in a Paradise.

It had, by that time, a reputation so bad that for two hundred years its owners had found it impossible to recruit workers locally. It had been hit by so many floods, droughts, lightning bolts, forest fires, cases of Dutch elm disease, fire blight, attacks of red admiral caterpillars and heart-rot fungus and the park's owners were similarly plagued by such an endless succession of human natural catastrophes that the very earth seemed to be against them. It was as though the land itself were an enormous creature, a buried whale which, when people scratched its back, shook itself to throw them off. Just as there are children who are extremely difficult to raise, and areas of the human psyche which are very hard to control, so intractable was St. Francis Forest that some inexplicable form of geographical and biological anarchy appeared to reign

there. The last owner managed, shortly after the Second World
War, to see the gardens completed and for a few fleeting moments he thought that he had gotten the better of the place.
Neither his wife running off with the gardener nor his daughter
running off with the gardener's son could make him give up.
Not until the whippet his wife had left behind them had a
litter of mongrel pups by the gardener's mongrel dog did he
perceive that what he had been experiencing was not a lasting
victory but merely the momentary check of the pendulum at
the outermost point of its swing and that ahead of him lay the
downturn. The following day he put the park up for sale.

St. Francis Forest met with success for the first time as a
game reserve. It became the first breeding ground outside of
Africa of the mountain gorilla, the first breeding ground outside of the Russian taiga of the Siberian tiger, the first hatch-
ing ground outside of Australia of the penduline owl. During
the seventies and eighties it boasted the most impressive results ever of any zoo or wildlife park in the breeding of certain
endangered species. These results were reported to the general public, which formed the impression that the wild animals
in St. Francis Forest had found an Eden, a place even better
than their place of origin, that they lived a life of mild-
mannered zoological ease. This too was the reason given pub-
licly by Adam Burden, on his appointment as head of the
Institute of Animal Behavioral Research—under whose aus-
pices St. Francis Forest came—for the park to remain a re-
stricted area. The reason no outsiders were allowed access,
explained Adam—no representatives from animal protection
agencies, no research scientists who had not first been approved and sworn in and, under no circumstances, journalists
or representatives of the public at large—was so as not to
disturb the park's distinctive air of high zoological spirits.

In actual fact this was not merely an embellished rewrite
of the truth, it was a downright, but necessary, lie. St. Francis
Forest was one of the first research centers to have been arranged according to the modern-day cognizance of the fact

that the more animals are left to themselves, the better they will thrive. The place was run with the minimum of interference and consequently a balance of sorts came into play, not a divine harmony, however, but the unfolding of the animal kingdom's own unsentimental brutality.

Adam knew that what the public want to see in a zoo are lovable tiger cubs, cuddly old bears, garrulous seals, communicative baboons, child-loving elephants and an all-pervading sense of positive control. What they would have been presented with in St. Francis Forest was the animal kingdom's volatile ruthlessness toward the small, the old, the sick and the misfit. They would have seen spotted woodpeckers stealing fledgling tits from the nest, anteaters sucking the entrails out of baby maras, lions serving up cheetah kittens to their cubs, zebras safeguarding their territory by slaughtering waterbuck kids, squirrels demolishing goshawk nests and eating the goshawk's young, pike clearing a riverbank of ducklings. They would have seen what only the zoologists at this point understood: that what really vitalized the animals and caused them to thrive and grow and breed was the opposite of indolence and protection. It was the fact that their days were fully taken up with the struggle simply to stay alive.

What Madelene and Erasmus had arrived in was the first garden in Europe ever truly to come to resemble its ideal. Not some nice cozy Paradise but the game reserve that Adam and Eve must have beheld, with its mixture of the fascinating, the thought-provoking, the appalling and the utterly catastrophic ways in which the animal world can develop when left to its own devices.

All this they saw. And they also grasped something else, something that none of the biologists, the gardeners or any of the park's four centuries of workers and owners had grasped. They discerned the essence of the place, its topographical soul.

Madelene saw it first, that first morning. She woke up; Erasmus was gone. She sat up and her eye fell on him. He was squatting on the riverbank, drinking as he always drank by sticking his whole hand into the stream, then licking off the water soaked up by the mat of hair on its back. Sitting there, in the sun, his hairless buttocks looked like two halves of a honeydew melon, only twice as large. At that moment Madelene realized where they had landed. That it was to the pornographic Garden of Eden they had come.

five

They stayed in St. Francis Forest for seven weeks and during
that time the place posed them three questions, the first of
which was put that very first morning just after Madelene had
woken up. She was making her way across the meadow at the
time, toward the ape, she was naked, she was strolling along
and she had the feeling that she was shining. Her face shone,
her breasts, her genitals, the palms of her hands. In a moment
Erasmus would turn around and be dazzled.

The ape had his back to her. When they were five paces
apart it turned.

"Morningsleepwell?" it said.

Madelene froze in her tracks. The ape's face looked
open, rested and full of pride at having remembered the correct form of greeting. But of the gratitude she had expected,
to which she was entitled, there was no sign. Yesterday
was gone, the night was gone, leaving not the slightest
trace.

At that moment Madelene grew afraid.

Madelene lived by love; she had always done so. Or rather:
she lived by dependence. The few times in her life when she
had taken a risk, the few independent steps she had taken in
her thirty years—up until three weeks before—she had ventured only because she knew that beneath her there hung a
safety net. A net formed by the conviction that the men who
loved her would go into a decline and die were she to leave
them. This certainty constituted the essential amino acids of
her character. What was not in evidence in the ape, as it stood
there facing her, was fear. There ought to have been a touch,
just the faintest hint, of meekness and dread. But there was
none, the animal was totally fearless.

It was then that the garden posed her the first question, as
distinctly as if it had been voiced by a narrator, and the question was this: Who has made the decisions in the love affairs
in your life? And even as she heard it uttered, before it was
finished, she knew that she did not see herself as staying there
long enough to hear the answer.

For the next three days she kept her distance from Erasmus.
Together they patched up their nest in the trees, they tracked
down one of the park's feeding sites, where fruit was put out
each day, and they ascertained at what times the site was not
under surveillance. And throughout all of this Madelene
treated the animal with quiet friendliness; on the face of it she
was a happy and contented girl of summer.

But in her heart winter had set in. Her eyes took in the
ape with a new scrutiny. She used it to get her bearings in the
garden, to discover the location of the closest point of the outer
wall, to calculate the risk of going on foot; she used it to gather
provisions. She was preparing for her breakout, her attempt
at escape from Paradise.

———

The third day was warmer than the previous two. On the grassy plain running down to the river bloomed three enormous rhododendron bushes and in the shade of these Madelene and the ape lay resting. The bushes floated like green and violet mountains on a sea of grass. Madelene had barely slept at all over the past three bitterly cold nights. Now she had dozed off.

She was woken by the ape licking her, here and there, working from her knees up the length of her thighs, its tongue possessing the same superficial softness and underlying insistence as its penis. It took Madelene some time to come to; sleep had disarmed her and by the time she was fully conscious it was too late. Desire bore down upon her slowly; like a ship, it came sailing across the plain, and when it drew close enough and she saw that she herself was on board and that there was no chance of getting off, she was struck by a sudden clarity. In a flash of erotic satori she saw that even that last vestige of her freedom of movement had been an illusion. She had been led to this place and the tongue now sliding over her belly. And not only she; the ape too had been led there, for, even if there was something importunate about its mouth at this moment, there was also an entreaty, it was begging her to surrender. Mutely Erasmus pleaded, because he too was a victim.

The last thing Madelene heard before she yielded was the answer to the garden's first question. She answered it herself, and the answer was: Whoever made the decision it was neither he nor I.

What happened to Erasmus and Madelene was what happens to all of those who pass through Paradise, either of their own free will or ostensibly by chance: love took possession of them and did with them as it pleased. But unlike so many others, they did not fight it. They had no time to prepare themselves, no time to build up hopes or develop prejudices, and when it

hit them they had nowhere to run to and no one from whom
to seek help. They simply gave in, they abandoned themselves
to the fundamental uncertainty of this unpredictable situation.

At no point, while they were in the garden, did Erasmus
make Madelene any promises whatsoever. To begin with, she
persuaded herself—half in anger, half in panic—that the animal was retarded or at any rate that its language skills were
at too low a level for it to understand all the subtle little ways
in which human lovers are constantly reassuring one another
that they and their love are alive and well and that they are
still bound together by a warm umbilical cord. But after a day
or two it dawned on her that this was not because Erasmus
could not. It was just that it never occurred to him. And what
was more, *she* did not want it either. She felt the fantasies with
which she had comforted herself dying out; she noted how she
had rejected her own promises before they could be put into
words. For the first time in her life she walked along a tightrope without looking down. For the first time she began to lose
interest in the future.

They were heading into a variant of eternity. One night while
Madelene was sitting astride Erasmus she realized that they
were not alone. She was not only with him but with two men,
one of whom she had inside her while the other caressed her,
and with eyes closed she sensed who that other was, it was
Death. She dropped her head back, looked up at the heavens,
gave up offering any resistance and saw that, when time ceases
to exist, the present moment then engendered is not without
its dark side, not even in Paradise.

six

Their life in the garden revolved around three distinct occu-
pations—hunting for food, sleeping and attending to their love
and their language lessons. Imperceptibly the barrier between
them was lifted. They experienced a didactic breakthrough
when Madelene reached the section dealing with the bawdy
element in language. She had him inside her at the time and
she said, "Lie still and tell me what I'm doing to you. What
am I doing now? And now? Describe that!" Or she would shift
Erasmus' hands and say, "No, look me in the eye, don't do a
thing, just tell me what you feel like doing," and then Erasmus
would speak without thinking first, then language broke
through to him, and at that moment in the shade of the
rhododendron bushes they were joined by the ghosts of
Denmark's world-famous language teachers: Diderichsen,
Hjelmslev, the glossematicians and the entire Copenhagen
School of Linguistics.

They frequently forgot to eat, with the result that they experienced real hunger, experienced being weak from starvation—experiences indistinguishable from the intimacy they shared. When they had gone for a night, for several days, for a week without laying hands on one another Madelene was filled with yearning, and then it struck her that not since she was a child had she been truly hungry. Whenever the animal inside her had growled she had tossed a meal down to it—a pound of chocolates, a caress, a cocktail, a glass of pure alcohol—not out of hunger but as a means of repression, to quell the fear and the horrid noises.

Now she was becoming acquainted with want. She was treated to the experience of watching Erasmus move across the meadow, sometimes on two legs, sometimes on four, and had the feeling that it was not only she who wanted him; it was the grass that stretched out after him, the air that longed to stroke him, the water that wished to straddle him.

Little by little they lost interest in consummation, in bringing their lovemaking to a conclusion. They wanted to be wide awake, and on one such night of famished, crystal-clear wakefulness Madelene caught Erasmus unawares. She had dozed off, she opened her eyes, the ape was sitting looking at her. Thinking itself unobserved. Gone was its alertness, gone its brute strength, its indifference. It was engrossed in the sight of her, the look on its face was one of profound joy. It caught on to the fact that it was being watched but it did not alter its expression, it could not, what it was feeling held it transfixed.

"Lovely," it said.

And a moment later it formulated—quietly, wonderingly, despairingly, chiefly for its own benefit, as it placed its hand on its chest—the empirical law which says that there is no light without darkness.

"Hurts," it said. "In heart."

———

That same night, later, Madelene awoke and perceived how the world is ordered.

The ape was sleeping a little ways off from her, its body stretched along a branch and its arms dangling in midair. She got up and through a gap in the treetops she saw the sky and the stars, saw too that what the grand scheme of things amounted to was a perpetual act of unconsummated, uninterrupted coitus between heaven and earth. Then she lay down again and went back to sleep.

Early in the morning of that same night the garden posed them the second question. This presented itself as a sharp pain which made Madelene sit up with a start.

"It's not enough," she said.

The ape never passed through any sort of waking-up phase, moving instead—this time too—straight from deep sleep into total readiness. It sat up and looked at her.

What Madelene was trying to say was something she could only feel, because now, for the first time since her childhood, she was living her life without an anesthetic. What she wanted to say was that she had seen, half in a dream, how right at the heart of the ultimate in sensual intoxication and ecstasy lies a spot stricken by famine. What she was trying to explain was that even while she was experiencing the most intense erotic hunger and the most lavish sexual feast of her life, it had suddenly struck her that one can never eat one's fill.

The ape grasped her meaning immediately.

"Never enough," it said.

Then it was that the garden posed them the second question. Madelene was the one who put it into words and it was the question concerning the course of love.

"What's going to happen to us then?" she said. "Where is all this leading?"

It was Erasmus who provided the answer, later that same day. They were sitting with their backs against a tree gazing out across the river where it divided into two around a long, narrow islet.

"What's the word," asked the ape, "for when there's water all the way around?"

"Island," said Madelene. "An island."

"Erasmus comes from an island," said the ape.

Something chill breathed on Madelene. It was time, a reminder that something else did exist apart from the two of them, that the universe went on turning beyond the garden wall.

"How big is it?"

"From the top of the tallest trees you can see the water on the one side and on the other side and behind. But not ahead."

"Is there fruit?"

The ape nodded.

"On the trees?"

The ape considered this.

"It's easier in the shops," it said.

"Are there people living there? Like me?"

The ape took her hand.

"Lots," it said. "But none like you."

It was the first compliment Erasmus had ever paid and under other circumstances it might have been hard to swallow. But at this time and in this place Madelene shut her eyes and relished its honeyed sweetness. When she opened them again the ape's face was nose to nose with her own. It rested the palm of its hand on her abdomen.

"Couldn't there be a child?"

Madelene had always regarded children with indifference. Whenever she had seen them on the street or in playgrounds they had seemed so helpless to her and she had thought with pity about how they were now covering the same bleak distance that she herself had once, miraculously, completed. Once they left her field of vision she forgot all about them.

Not so with Adam Burden. To him children were not irrelevant and it had not been with pity that he regarded them. It had been with positive distaste.

Madelene had read in books that one can expect to become one with the person one loves. But she had never become one with Adam. She had become two. She had split into two people—one viewed the world as Madelene had always done, the other learned to view it from Adam's point of view and this other Madelene had looked at children through his eyes.

She had seen how children evoked the animal in people. She had perceived—still with Adam's eyes—that children are themselves animals. Cubs is what they are, ungainly, attention-grabbing, bumptious, raw creatures of instinct.

And they turned their parents into animals. These parents were, she noted, exhausted, they were in a state of animal exhaustion. They could not have cared less about themselves or their appearance, they were colorless, as though the children had sucked out all of their human energy surplus. They had become sexless, the women especially, they seemed milked dry, drained, desiccated.

Adam wanted to travel. He wanted to get on in the world. He wanted to make love. He wanted to look good. He wanted to be attractive and he was, he radiated energy. There were moments when Madelene pictured him not as a lion but as one of the little substations from her childhood in Vedbæk— tall, straight, bursting with volts and amps and with a sign on the back bearing a death's-head and the words "High Voltage."

She had been the very same, she knew that, it was what Adam had expected and naturally she had accommodated him.

To be the focus of an electrical charge such as his and to light up and glow, that had been her life.

Children had constituted a threat to all of this. Children had nothing to offer her and Adam, they would have appeared on the scene complete with a greed that would have discharged them and deprived them of everything they had. This they had both accepted. Together they had cut the switch to the question of children.

Now, when Erasmus placed his hand on her belly, a dazzling white light was shed on this darkness. And in this light Madelene could see that the ape's question was also an answer, a possible answer to where the mutual magnetism of two people may lead when it is strong enough.

The third and final question was the one put by every person who suddenly finds happiness, the one that asks: How long will it last?

For a long time this question seemed to answer itself by fading away and then vanishing altogether. There was nothing in Madelene's and Erasmus' life to suggest that it would not last forever, that this idyll of theirs was not to be depended upon.

In the mornings when they woke the garden was covered with a dew that caught and refracted the light like a mother-of-pearl veneer. Every leaf on a tree curled like an open pearl oyster around its own drop, the tree trunks were moist and slippery and when they walked hand in hand down to the river through the grass they seemed to be walking through cool, shallow waters on which lily of the valley floated like water lilies and from which the flowering meadowsweet rose like standing liquid columns. Down by the river they met the other animals in the garden, and at this time of day in this underwater world all natural enmities were suspended. Sable antelopes drank alongside elephants, alongside a cheetah, alongside a capybara, alongside a reddish-gray and white sarus crane, alongside a group of red lemurs. Even the monkeys held their peace and at times such as these the garden showed that side of itself which so many had dreamt of but so few had seen: in Old Testament harmony.

While Erasmus and Madelene washed, daylight broke. Not gradually but all of a sudden, and in a cloud of mist it swept the waters aside. Then came the heat, the sounds, the smells, and then the garden's heartbeat escalated from its resting pulse to its maximum rate.

Around noon a short hiatus occurred, not out of lethargy but because so great was the intensity of the place that every living thing in it had need of a break. Madelene and Erasmus rested then too, in their tree, on their air mattresses, and often when they awoke they would just sit there, sit quite still, surveying the burgeoning life around them. The fiery rays of the red lemurs, flashing like miniature comets through the treetops. Birds of paradise like some divine joke, three feather boas knotted together and tossed into the air. The stillness of the cheetah, its infinite patience, its impossible, slingshot acceleration. The indefatigable industry of the she-gorillas. The dominant males' endless forbearance with the young ones. The wariness of the field mouse, a wariness so unconfined that it prompted Madelene to think that here at last was a creature which was undeniably more afraid than she had ever been. They witnessed the extremes of the adder, from deathly inertia to movements too swift for either Madelene's or the ape's eyes. One day a golden eagle flew over their heads—first high above, rectangular, like a flying door, then quite close—and this time Madelene did not wave, this time she simply thought: We are just like it.

They ate early in the evening. When darkness began to fall the ape lit a fire in the fork of a tree, a tiny fire, for all the world as if it had grabbed a fistful of flame from the sun now fading from view. Not setting—for in recent nights even the sun had seemed too elated to go down—but withdrawing behind the midnight-blue membrane of the skies on which throughout the long, light night it would recline, permeating it with a luster that would filter down to the dark earth in the form of a reddish-gray glimmer of light.

In this life there was no time—or at least only of a sporadic and soon forgotten sort—and hence no question of duration, and so Madelene and Erasmus lost all interest in the problem of how long. They lost interest in time.

The truth, when it presented itself, sneaked up on them all unnoticed like a beast of prey one noontime, in the shade, in the middle of a lesson.

They had abandoned any idea of a systematic approach to their language lessons. Madelene had stopped trying to call to mind the fragments of grammar she had once learned and they were now journeying through language on instinct. She would gauge where the ape had not yet been and take it there. On this particular day she had conducted it to the Danish conditional conjunctions.

"If I could," said the ape, "I would fly."

"If I could," said Madelene, "I would fly with you."

"If we could," said the ape, "we would stay here forever."

At this Madelene felt the earth give way and sensed that it was too late to turn back.

"If we wanted to," she said, "couldn't we?"

The ape shook its head.

"There are all the others, you see," it said.

They fell silent. They listened in disbelief to the echo of what they had said.

They were less than a yard apart. A space now populated by living creatures, by apes like Erasmus. In a vision, a shared mirage, they saw a congregation of apes, a body of apes, a nation. Madelene could tell that Erasmus was every bit as overwhelmed as she herself was. That the reason he had not spoken about the future was that, like her, he had forgotten it. But somewhere there were hundreds of apes like him, maybe even thousands. Their existence must be threatened. And he, with his insight, must owe them something. His situation differed from her own. Her departure from civilization had been a quite definitive one. She had put everything behind her. There was not one soul on earth with whom she had shared anything she feared to lose.

Once she had thought this far the space before her grew very crowded. Between her and Erasmus, mingling with the imaginary apes, there appeared a new group, a group of people. In the forefront, Adam and Madelene's parents and Susan and her children, and behind them other acquaintances, relatives, forgotten school friends, and behind them again the faceless silhouettes of people who had once meant something to her. All of them were looking at her, like children who have asked a grown-up a question and not yet been given an answer.

"Yes," said Madelene. "The others. We'd almost forgotten them."

What they hit upon, both together, at that moment was a natural law that always takes the form of a reminder, a law that has prevailed through every hermit and stylite regardless of religion or historical era and revealed itself to each and every pair of lovers. It is the reminder that there is no such thing, nor can there ever be any such thing, as a private Paradise.

Madelene shut her eyes and took a deep breath.

"What do you call yourselves?" she asked. "I mean, you don't say 'apes,' do you?"

The ape thought this over, trying vainly to reconcile two irreconcilable languages before coming up with an acceptable compromise.

"People," it said. "We call ourselves people."

"And us? What do you call us?"

"Animals," said the ape, "is what we call you."

Madelene opened her eyes.

"Do you miss them?" she asked. "Your people?"

The ape did not answer her straight out.

"Princesses," it said, "what was it they were again?"

For seven weeks Madelene had been living in one flowing here and now. It was with some reluctance that her memory began once more to function.

"Chosen," she said. "That there's something you have to do."

The ape nodded.

"There's something I have to do," it said. "That's why I came."

Around them the garden hummed, warm and drowsy. Everything was as before. But nothing would ever be the same again.

"The animals," said the ape, "here in the garden, they don't know what to make of us. That's why they're afraid of us. Why they run away. In order to stay invisible they run away. It's a good way of doing it. Something we all have to learn. But there's another way too. If you understand what is coming you don't need to run. You can hold your ground, hold it even at close range, and still be invisible. Because you know where to stand. That's how we live—we people."

"Are none of you ever seen?"

"It might be that we're sensed. It might be that your people sense us. As something missing. Or as something that ought not to have been there. But you don't see us. And even if you do, you still don't see us."

Madelene threw the last shred of caution to the wind.

"Was it a good life?" she asked. "Were you happy? Are the others happy?"

The ape nodded.

"And yet you are here," she said. "But maybe that was a mistake."

The ape drew itself up, with unquestionable arrogance it drew itself up and in a flash Madelene recalled the stiff-legged strutting of the male gorillas.

"Erasmus," it said, "*allowed* himself to be caught."

"And what about me?" said Madelene. "I suppose I was just meant to lend you a hand?"

It was a quiet remark, and those are the most difficult of all to answer, especially in a language other than one's mother tongue. But Erasmus had learned a great deal and to his lessons he had brought some of his physical agility.

"When we go down to the river to drink," he said, "sometimes, quite often, the sun appears. Even though that wasn't what we were after. Now and again, when you go looking for something small, you come up with something big."

Madelene shut her eyes, savoring her lover's rapidly progressing eloquence like a ripe peach.

"Even if one is content," the ape went on, "even if it was, even if it still is a good life for us, even if we are quite, quite content, there would still be, there are, always . . . the others, your people."

They looked at one another and knew that they had arrived at the answer to the garden's final question. They said not another word. They had reached the outer limits of language, and what now occurred, the last stage of their journey, its farthest point, was wordless. They sat on a promontory, a linguistic ultima Thule, and what they espied far off in the distance were the contours of an answer to their question: Why can't two people or a band of apes shut themselves off in Paradise?

They discerned that this question is part and parcel of a bigger, a much bigger one: Why hasn't everything gone on being the same as it was in the beginning, why is the paradisiacal condition not a *steady state*?

The answer one arrives at depends on the point from which one asks the question, and Madelene and Erasmus asked it from a position seventy-five feet above the ground in the Garden of Eden, sitting hand in hand on two air mattresses, and the answer they reached in the same breath was that when the world starts to move it does so thanks to love. They saw—they thought they saw—that either above or below them there sat a god, perhaps the Almighty, holding something or someone by the hand, perhaps an ape, and was happy and for that very reason could by no stretch of the imagination be sufficient unto himself.

part four

one

If, on that July evening, one had come gliding in over London and dropped down toward the city, close enough to make out the facial features of isolated individuals, one would at that distance have gained the impression that the city had forgotten Erasmus and Madelene. That it had picked up the threads of its life again as if nothing had ever happened.

In South Hill Park, at Mombasa Manor, Adam Burden stands before his bedroom mirror rehearsing something or other, something reminiscent of a conjuring trick, something which evidently calls for practice and a clear idea of the positioning of one's audience and of what they may and may not be permitted to see. Working away at this he seems quite his old self again, with all the assurance of a seasoned trouper.

Elsewhere, in Mayfair, Andrea Burden is in the act of trying on a hat, again in front of a mirror, looking as though she has not a care in the world, radiating serenity and vitality.

At the other end of town, at Millwall Dock, at the very

back of a pub situated at the very end of a narrow side street, Johnny peers down into the bottom of his beer glass. It is not so much his own dispirited reflection he is staring at but rather as though he were gazing out across that Sea of Futility which has for so many years been lapping at his feet and upon which he has now finally abandoned all hope of ever reaching land.

Some way from there, on the outskirts of the Isle of Dogs, the man who until not so long ago had gone by the name of Bally is gazing down into the Thames just at the point where it flows past the boat which not so long ago was called the *Ark* but which has now taken a new name, and the look on his face is, as it has been for many years, equable and inscrutable.

On the opposite bank of the Thames, at veterinary police HQ next to St. Thomas's Hospital, Inspector Smailes gets up from his chair and walks over to the window. What he is contemplating is not to be found beyond the glass; what he is staring at with something akin to jaded routine is his own face in the windowpane.

In another office, much bigger, in the Holland Park Veterinary Clinic, sits Alexander Bowen, jittery as ever, clutching a telephone receiver. He has dialed a number but this call goes—as is so often the case with telephone calls—unanswered. There is no one at the place he has called to answer, no one apart from Firkin, the veterinary odontologist, who is wandering up and down through suite upon suite of offices and laboratories paying no heed to the instrument's peal. He has stayed on at the Institute long after the end of his working day but even that, under normal circumstances, would give no cause for wonder.

At this distance, at such close range, it is as though Madelene and Erasmus had never existed.

But if one pulls back, just a little farther back, a new picture comes into focus.

Adam Burden has been made the new director of the New London Regent's Park Zoological Garden. He was elected to great acclaim, not one voice raised against him. His reputation as a scientist and his curriculum vitae are impeccable, he has the support of Andrea Burden and all the animal protection societies, he has the backing of the investors, he has the Department of National Heritage's seal of approval and comes recommended by the Royal Zoological Society. Furthermore, due to that dreadful incident with his wife he has the warmest sympathies of the public and the media. At the end of July—a week from now—he will be officially inducted into his new post.

It is his induction he is now rehearsing. This will be held in the assembly hall of the new zoo, in the presence of representatives of Her Majesty's Government, the patron of the Royal Zoological Society, Her Royal Highness Princess Anne, and other members of the royal family.

The subject of his speech will be Erasmus.

This will be one of the most momentous zoological speeches of the twentieth century. The totally unforeseen disclosure of the discovery of a new and hitherto unknown mammal, an apparently highly intelligent anthropoid ape. His speech will be supplemented by slides, drawings, the brain-scan results, a complete anatomical description of Erasmus, a physiochemical analysis of his feed, excreta and metabolism, an outline of his behavioral pattern and a genetic record compiled by the DNA laboratory at the Institute for Population Biology. It is Alexander Bowen who is supposed to furnish this last-named record but as yet it has not been forthcoming, hence his call and his impatience. The DNA laboratory is attached to the Institute of Animal Behavioral Research—where Firkin works. Which is how Firkin caught wind of the inquiry. Which is why he is roaming the laboratories after office hours.

Firkin is thinking about the ape and about Madelene. Since their disappearance he has not been able to get them out of his head. Nor has Inspector Smailes, and it is the unpleasantness of the memory of them, of the feeling of something left unresolved, that moves the inspector to gravitate toward his own reflection.

Once the scientific proof has been produced it is Adam's and Andrea's wish that one particular testimony dealing with the circumstances surrounding the ape's capture should be presented and it is the man formerly known as Bally who is to present it and it is for doing this that his boat and his liberty have been restored to him. There is, however, another testimony—having to do with Bally's true identity and how the ape actually arrived in London—which must absolutely not be given, and therefore one person who must on no account show his face, that person being Johnny, and as an incentive to staying well out of it he has received a number of threats and a sum of money which he is now in the process of drinking away. Johnny has been on the bottle for seven weeks, ever since Madelene and Erasmus disappeared, and whereas other people will take as much as twenty years to drink themselves to death Johnny has displayed such a unique talent for alcoholism that as far as he is concerned it looks as though the process is going to be speeded up considerably.

This speech is not only scientifically unique, not only the most critical of Adam's career. It is also of crucial importance to Andrea Burden. It is going to supply the zoo with its first official credentials. It will be made clear that it was this new zoo and its scientific resources which made the discovery and detailing of the new ape possible.

The speech will conclude with the announcement that the New London Regent's Park Zoo is to include a large—a vast— enclosure for apes like Erasmus, an ape island. And, last of all, Adam is going to name the new ape not—as has been the custom—after whoever discovered the animal, or after certain characteristics of the animal, or after the place where it had been found. Instead it is to be named after the place where it would be on display forevermore, home of the zoological pioneers who had unearthed it from its hiding place, site of the scientific bodies that had been the first to classify it. Erasmus was to be known as *Homina londiniensis*.

So, at such a remove, there can be no doubt that for these people everything over the past seven weeks has revolved around Erasmus and Madelene.

Or rather, around what they would like to remember them for. And around what they have dared to remember. Because there are some things, particularly concerning the moment when the ape sprang aloft with Madelene and disappeared, which they are trying to forget, things which—were they to rise to the surface—would ruin the impression of sensational credibility which Adam's speech is meant to create.

The woman and the ape have gone. Now it is a matter of getting the best possible mileage out of the trail they have left.

But Madelene and Erasmus have not gone. They are closer than anyone imagines, crouched on the edge of a wood atop a ridge overlooking Edgware, in northwest London. And from this point the city presents a third view of itself. From here its concrete silhouette arches into a dome not unlike the skull of a malevolent gnome creeping out from under the stone beneath which it has lain for two thousand years, to find a butterfly and rip off its wings.

They are hunkered down on a branch. The ape is naked and Madelene wears nothing but a bit of cloth around the top half of her body and another bit of cloth around her bottom half. Outwardly they look like two displaced apes—for Madelene too could pass for an ape. Erasmus rarely carries her now; she can manage on her own, even seventy-five feet above the ground. And the way she sits there on the branch, curling her toes around it, one might think she was growing fingers on her feet. Erasmus' face is clean-shaven—Madelene insists on this, she wants to be able to lay eyes and hands on him directly—but the top of his head is covered with a layer of fine white down. So too with Madelene's head. Her hair has been bleached white by the sun and cropped to make it easier to get at the head lice. And while she surveys the city she catches a louse and crushes it between her thumbnails.

There is a fresh coolness in the air and Madelene shudders. They look so frail sitting there on that branch, she and Erasmus, so helpless. They seem, on this night in July, like the feeblest, most unlikely hit squad ever to strike London Town.

two

There was someone else who had been thinking about Madelene and Erasmus, who had possibly thought about them more than anyone else, and that was Susan. Today was the first day in seven weeks that they had not been in her thoughts. She had forced herself out of the depression that had fallen on her upon their disappearance by coaxing her husband and children into vacating the apartment for an hour and a half. During which time her lover paid her a call.

Susan had a penchant for compact sexual encounters. They suited London life. There was something provocatively unnerving about knowing that even as such a tableau called for great care in its planning, implementation and cleaning-up—all while in a state of utter abandonment—the whole thing had to be over, leaving no trace of its passing, in ninety minutes.

Here she was getting undressed. Here she was stepping into the shower. Here she turned on the hot water.

"Are you coming?" she called.

In the living room Donny LaBrillo peeled off his jacket, unbuttoned his white shirt, slipped it off his shoulders and regarded his own reflection in a piece of Japanese lacquerwork.

Donny was one of a new generation of boxers—handsomer, slimmer and smarter than Henry Cooper in his heyday ever dared to dream of being. After seventeen wins in seventeen sensational professional light-heavyweight fights under the British Boxing Board of Control he had the look of an angel straight from heaven who had never donned a boxing glove.

He liked this setup. Very elegant. The woman had class. The fancy apartment and the parklike grounds in which it lay had class. He liked the thought of being in strange pastures. LaBrillo the Stud among another man's flowers.

He looked around him. He liked the exotic antiques. The lacquerwork. The blue porcelain elephants in the window bay. The life-size doll on the sofa. The elongated masks on the wall.

His eyes slid back to the sofa. It was not a doll that sat there at all. It was a man. With a squashed-in face and a blanket around his shoulders, like a punch-drunk boxer at a toga party.

"What the hell?" said Donny.

Erasmus eased himself onto his feet. This man was the first human being other than Madelene with whom he was to communicate. It was imperative that he be correct in every detail of grammar and etiquette.

"How do you do?" he said, slowly and distinctly. "Now let me show you out."

LaBrillo stared at the ape.

"I have an appointment here," he said.

"I am delighted to hear it," said Erasmus.

He ushered the boxer solicitously through the hall and opened the door.

"Thank you so much for calling."

LaBrillo made a little side step and dropped his right shoulder ever so slightly. Then he belted Erasmus in the midriff, just under the breastbone and level with the solar plexus, at a point where the layer of muscle is very thin.

It was not like hitting a concrete wall, because there was a certain superficial elasticity to the torso beneath the blanket. It was like ramming a fist into the wall of a padded cell.

LaBrillo straightened up and gaped at the ape. He had scored a few knockouts with that punch. Being hit like that would give any ordinary untrained man in the street a heart attack.

The ape's expression remained deadpan. Gently it nudged LaBrillo through the doorway.

"Very best wishes for the future," it said. "Come back soon."

Then it shut the door.

LaBrillo grabbed hold of the banister, seeking some sort of mainstay in his life. He stood there, outside the closed door, for some time. Then he turned around and slowly, barechested, he started down the stairs, walking away from his first defeat as a professional.

Erasmus and Madelene sat down opposite one another in the living room. The ape picked up the boxer's jacket and put it on. The sleeves were too short. It pulled a pair of sunglasses out of an inside pocket and placed them on its nose. Madelene reached for the ape's hand; it stretched out an arm that extended with ease from the sofa back across the coffee table. Madelene put its hand over her crotch and before her eyes the ape's face gradually changed color, from pale yellow to chocolate. It was blushing.

"Donny," called Susan from the bathroom. "Grunt like a pig."

The bathroom door opened. Susan stared at them.

"Donny left," said Madelene. "He wanted his mommy."

It was over fifteen years since Susan had begun experimenting with the quicksilver of hastily improvised sex and she had developed the reflexes of an explosives expert. Losing none of her outward composure, she wrapped herself in a large bath towel, hugged Madelene, shook Erasmus' hand and sat down on the sofa.

But inwardly she was terrified.

It was their poverty that scared her. The experience of being confronted, for the first time ever, by two people with not a thing to their name—not even clothes for their backs— and no social support.

"We've been . . . out of town," said Madelene. "We know nothing."

Every unforeseen disaster separates people into two groups. Those who panic and those who operate at maximum efficiency and save the fear and trembling for later. Susan launched into a precise, unexpurgated account of what she knew—of Adam, of Andrea Burden and of the New London Regent's Park Zoological Garden.

As she spoke, she became aware of a warmth which prompted her to glance toward the radiator and the grate, but both were out of action. The radiation emanated from somewhere on the other side of the coffee table and after a while she succeeded in placing it. It was the heat of people in love. It glowed in the space between Madelene and the ape as if they had brought along an invisible, transportable sauna from which they were constantly letting out heat. Susan snuggled up to this warmth and slowly, as the heat spread, while she was talking, she began to suspect that perhaps these two indigents were not totally lost after all.

For a while after she finished there was silence. Then she asked her first question.

"Couldn't we just try to get you two away from here?" she said. "Out of the country?"

Madelene shook her head.

"There are the others," she said, "apes, like Erasmus. If the outside world learns of their existence they'll be hunted down like never before. Trophy hunters. Reporters and photographers. The international zoological underworld. Hordes of scientists. Just the fact of knowing—Adam's way of knowing—destroys anything of which we have any knowledge. Or changes it."

She stood up.

"Johnny," she said. "The man who drove us. We have to find Johnny."

Susan looked keenly at her friend. The cloven-hoofed obstinacy upon which she had remarked not so long ago had now been joined by a new trait, the panoramic perspective of a bird of prey. She checked her watch.

"You'll need clothes," she said. "And money."

"Would it," asked the ape, "be too much to ask to have a hot shower? And if I might borrow a razor?"

Susan let them out through the back door.

Erasmus was attired in a pair of flip-flops, the baggy trousers from a karate suit, a T-shirt ripped at the sleeves—this, however, being covered by LaBrillo's jacket—sunglasses and a felt hat slit up over the brim and crown.

The overall effect, while not exactly harmonious, was in no way alarming. The ape paused for a moment on the landing, resting on its knuckles, then it straightened up, rectified its posture and tipped the sunglasses forward. Erasmus had entered the world of man.

Madelene and Susan stood facing one another. Madelene had borrowed some sandals, a long skirt, a blouse and a cardigan. She was her old self again and yet at the same time someone whom Susan had never seen before: a woman with a share in a sauna.

Susan followed Erasmus with her eyes. His careful tread, the mindfulness around hip level.

"We've never taken any of one another's belongings," she said. "But maybe sometime I could borrow him . . ."

It sounded like a joke and Madelene smiled at it too, and leaned forward to kiss her friend on the cheek.

But it was not just a joke and this Madelene knew and her kiss was not merely a show of affection. As she leaned forward—cautiously, consciously—she rubbed her temple against Susan's and ten head lice, ten bloodthirsty, ineradicable anoplura which Madelene and Erasmus had caught from the red lemurs and twenty-five of the lice's sticky, robust eggs passed from Madelene's cropped scrubland to Susan's rampant temperate rain forest.

"That," said Madelene, "we will have to talk about."

three

Kempton Park racecourse has accomplished the feat of lying on the same spot and maintaining the same appearance for twenty-five years while everything it has enclosed for all that time has been going downhill. The horses are going downhill, the jockeys are going downhill, as are the spectators. And on this particular afternoon no one was going downhill faster than Johnny.

The two thousand pounds and the threats he had received from Andrea Burden upon his inexplicable release from custody had produced much the same effect as if she had put a pair of gilded lead shoes on him and thrown him out into deep water. Now—seven weeks later—he was in the process of settling on the seabed.

At his side stood Samson. Johnny looked down at the dog with bleary but fond eyes. Its coat was thick and glossy, its nails clipped short, its eyes clear, its nose cool. It stood as only a Doberman can stand, as though perpetually posing for a photograph for next year's Kennel Club calendar. When—soon—Johnny was no more, the truck was to be sold and all the money raised from its sale would go to Samson, who would have a good life. Right at this minute the dog radiated all of the carefree contentment and the pluck that Johnny himself had never possessed.

Now, however, a sudden change occurred. The gleaming hair on Samson's back lifted and stood on end, making the dog look all at once like a wire-bristled brush. Then its ears were pressed back flat against its head and its teeth bared. Then it rolled over onto its back, gave a little whine and stuck all four legs in the air.

Johnny bent down. Samson was not sick. He was not having a fit, he had not thrown himself to the ground in pain. He had prostrated himself in an act of unconditional submission.

Johnny looked around. The only living creature anywhere near them was a man standing a few yards off, leaning on the railing, looking across at the horses.

"So what d'you think?" said Johnny.

Slowly the man turned around.

"I beg your pardon?" he said.

At the sound of his voice Samson turned to stone.

"Who's going to win?" Johnny asked.

"The horse in the red coat," said the man.

Johnny tried to focus on the face in front of him. Kempton Park is a popular spot for day-tripping loonies from London. The face across from him was broad and innocent-looking. The face of a loony. Sometimes idiots brought good luck. Johnny waved a bookie over and put his last hundred pounds on the horse with the red blanket.

It was some weeks since Johnny had sold his field glasses because he couldn't hold them steady anymore. Now he followed the field with the naked eye. His and the stranger's horse came in a full length ahead of the favorite.

Johnny collected his winnings. Then he focused on the man.

"How could you tell?" he asked.

The man removed his sunglasses.

"I could . . . smell the hormones," he said.

There was something disquietingly familiar about his face. Johnny turned around and started to walk away.

The man was right on his tail. Johnny speeded up. The man was still there. Johnny stopped dead, spun around and thrust half his wad of notes at him.

The man shook his head.

The hair on the back of Johnny's neck rose. He had not thought of the devil since he was little. Now seven weeks of alcoholic poisoning had toned down the present and revived his boyhood. The devil had come to get him.

He shoved the whole bankroll into the man's jacket pocket. The man stepped right up to him and Johnny inhaled the scorched reek of the flames of hell. An arm went around him and he was swept off his feet. Johnny closed his eyes.

"Take me," he said. "But spare the dog."

That night, two months earlier, when he had put up Erasmus and Madelene in his mobile home had been the most wonderful night of Johnny's life. Out of the mire that had passed for his life for so many years he had suddenly pulled a sparkling existential highlight.

He had known that what had been granted him that night was too intense to last. Meekly he had taken the moment off the hook and thrown it back without any hope of a repeat performance. Now the same situation was being reenacted, more forcibly than before. In the van, sitting at the table beneath which Samson lay quaking—close beside him—were Madelene and the ape.

"We were thinking of asking whether we could stay here for a while," said Madelene.

Faint with joy, Johnny stretched out a hand toward the sink in which dreg-sticky glasses had been dumped to make room for his guests. Madelene placed her hand over his.

"We were also wondering whether you would do the driving for us," she said. "So you're going to have to stop drinking."

She looked across at Erasmus.

"We have to talk to Bowen," she said. "If he recognizes us he'll call the police. How can we get him away from the hospital?"

"Perhaps," said Erasmus, "I could."

Madelene lifted Johnny's telephone onto the table, keyed in a number and handed the receiver to Erasmus. Only when a woman's voice said, "Holland Park Clinic," and Erasmus took the receiver away from his ear and looked around the back of the phone to see where the voice was coming from did Madelene remember that this was the first telephone conversation of the ape's life.

She curled her fingers around the receiver and pressed it gently but firmly to his ear.

"I would be extremely grateful to you if I might please speak to Dr. Alexander Bowen," said Erasmus.

"Who may I say is calling?"

"If you would be so kind as to say that it concerns a large ape that has disappeared."

It took the vet five seconds to extricate himself from whatever he was doing.

"Do you remember," said Erasmus, "the man in whose garden you picked up the big ape? It's back. The ape. The same one."

Several seconds passed before the vet was capable of answering.

"What is its general condition?"

Erasmus glanced down at himself.

"Good," he said. "What do you think we should do?"

"Stay where you are," said the doctor. "I'm on my way."

The line went dead, and instinctively the ape pulled the receiver away to see where the doctor had gone. Madelene took it out of his hand and handed him the hat and the sunglasses. She stroked Johnny's cheek.

"Let's go," she said.

Madelene and Erasmus climbed from the gloom of the van into the bright Dulwich sunlight. They then walked fifty yards down the road to the house in the garden of which, two months earlier, Andrea Burden had first set eyes on Erasmus, and rang the bell. A maid opened the door.

"My uncle has been taken ill," said Madelene. "Could we possibly come in and sit down?"

There were black and white marble tiles in the hall and white lacquered furniture. The maid brought two chairs.

"I'm very thirsty," said the ape.

It searched its increasing, but as yet incomplete, vocabulary.

"A bucket," it said. "Could you please let me have a bucket of water?"

Three months earlier the man who came walking toward them would have scared Madelene out of her wits. Now—from her new viewpoint on society and the people in it—she nonchalantly classified him as a layer cake: a base of irritation at being disturbed, a layer of fear of burglars in disguise, a layer of insecurity at the prospect of physical closeness, all topped off by a frosting of urbane politeness.

"We're terribly sorry for bothering you," she said. "An ambulance has been called. It will be here any minute."

The man relaxed and walked over to the ape.

"How are you feeling?" he asked.

"Very well, thanks," said Erasmus. "How are you feeling?"

At this most inappropriate of moments Madelene learned something new about the man she loved. That he was incapable—physically and mentally incapable—of lying.

The man blinked.

"I'm glad to hear you're feeling better," he said.

"I'm glad that you're glad," said Erasmus.

The man started to rock back and forth on the balls of his feet. The maid brought a bucket. Erasmus raised it to his lips and drank down ten quarts of water.

The man stopped rocking. Now he stood stock-still, looking at the ape.

The doorbell rang. No one moved. The door opened and Alexander Bowen walked in. Wearing his white coat and carrying a small leather bag.

Dazzled by the sunlight in the street, all he could make out in the hall were the owner of the house and the maid.

"Where is it?" he asked.

The man motioned toward Erasmus. The doctor moved a little closer, then stopped short.

"We're so pleased to see you again," said Madelene from the shadows.

She and Erasmus positioned themselves one on either side of the doctor and escorted him to the door. The owner of the house took a couple of hesitant steps after them, caught up in an overwhelming moment of déjà vu.

In the doorway the ape doffed its felt hat and bowed to the maid. The man stared at the white down covering its cranium.

"Many thanks for the shelter and refreshment," it said. "Both to you and your husband."

four

The ambulance was parked twenty-five yards away. They got
into the back. Up front, on the other side of the Plexiglas
partition, sat two porters. It was Madelene who slid back the
partition but it was Priscilla who gave the order.

"Drive around the corner and pull in to the curb."

The doctor's eyes had not left Erasmus.

"It's true, then," he said. "It does talk."

The ambulance drove around the corner and stopped. The
doctor was still staring at Erasmus.

"You're going to be rolling in it," he told Madelene. "I
hope it's got a good agent. And a good accountant."

Hysteria drew a snigger from him.

"Its first tax return is going to be a farce. There's no law
governing the income of apes."

Madelene poked a banknote through the partition.

"You've got the rest of the day off," she said. "Take a taxi
home. And buy your wives some flowers on the way."

The two men got out. Madelene drew the ambulance's gray curtains. She opened the leather briefcase the doctor had brought with him. Nestling in blue velvet lay an air gun, a hypodermic syringe and two glass ampules, one of them filled with a pink liquid.

"Sleep-away," said Madelene. "Sodium pentobarbital. Adam says it homes straight in on the central nervous system. Two seconds and you're dead."

In the ambulance all was silent.

"I could cry out for help," the doctor said.

Madelene did not answer.

"I suppose it's those results you're interested in. They're from the DNA laboratory. At the Institute for Population Biology. The best in the business. They're the ones who back-crossed Przewalski's horse. DNA sequencing. That's what it's called. They set pseudogenes side by side. Then they can see the number of phenotypically neutral differences. These differences go to make up a molecular clock from which they can tell the length of time between two species. How long ago they broke away from one another. It's by means of this method that they've been able to show exactly how close we come to chimpanzees. Six million years. Give or take a million."

He paused, a market trader's tactical pause.

"What do I get for telling you all this?"

It was the ape who answered.

"The best we can do for you," it said quietly, "is to allow you to go on living."

Thoughtfully Madelene noted this fresh expression of her lover's characteristic candor. The ape had not made a threat, since a threat is all part of a game and the ape possessed none of the strategist's craft. It had stated a lethal fact.

The vet had gone white around the gills. He looked at Madelene, at the ape, and reassessed his position. Then he gave up.

"The first time I saw it—I'm sorry, I mean you—I thought

to myself, it's some new species of chimpanzee, that's what we all thought, Burden and his sister too. A sensational new type of chimpanzee. From a temperate zone. That's what we took as our starting point. That's what we told the molecular taxonomists. Of course, we didn't show them any pictures. All they were given were the cell samples. They sequenced thirty thousand genes. It must have cost Miss Burden a fortune. But we had it wrong. It—I'm sorry, you—were not close to the chimpanzee. It came close, horrifyingly close to—was impossible to tell apart from—ourselves. It—I beg your pardon, you—are, at least in genetic terms, not so much an ape as a human being."

Madelene gazed around. She saw the gray light on the built-in cots, the oxygen cylinders, the instrument drawers, the bags and the tubes for blood transfusions. She looked at what the doctor had said and she looked at the doctor himself, at the triumph with which he was regarding them. She opened her mouth to say something nasty, but the ape stopped her.

"We are very grateful to you," it said steadily. "And we take the liberty of asking you to do us one more small favor— to drive us to Mr. Bally."

"I don't have my driver's license on me," said the doctor. "I haven't been behind the wheel in ten years. And I've never heard of anyone by that name."

Gently Madelene and Priscilla lifted the pink ampule free of the blue velvet.

"Oh, but you have to," she said. "Otherwise I'll need to ask you to swallow this."

five

The man who had some months previously been calling himself Bally was, at this particular moment, doing quite nicely, thank you. After having been fished out of the Thames by the London Port Authority, after having been identified and then put in solitary for three weeks, he had received a visit from Andrea Burden, had been released and had *The Ark*—with a market value of half a million pounds—plus another quarter of a million pounds' worth of veterinary equipment, returned to him. In three days' time, once he had given his testimony—under the immunity granted to him—he would set sail from London, on course for an objective which, for the first time in a good many years, was not primarily money-oriented and which filled him with a hopefulness he had not known he possessed: Bally had made up his mind to catch another ape like the one that had given him the slip. Not in order to sell it, but to sit once more across from it in the cramped confines

of the cockpit, to once more encounter something like Erasmus.

In recent months he had returned again and again in his
thoughts to his last few minutes with the ape and it was on
this memory that he was reflecting, leaning on the boom that
had swept him overboard, when an ambulance from the Holland Park Veterinary Clinic drove out onto the wharf and drew
to a halt.

A woman in a blue lab coat got out and walked over to the
boat.

Making no other move to speak of, Bally slipped his hand
down through the hatch and released the two catches around
a shotgun, the barrel of which had been sawn off just above
the head of the stock. Not that there was anything menacing
about the woman as such, but Bally had not been expecting
her, and it was just this insouciantly cautious approach to the
unexpected that had made him a prince in the hazardous international principality of those who made their living by
breaking the Washington Convention.

"Mr. Bally," said the woman. "Dr. Bowen is over there in
the van."

Bally nodded politely. Then he stepped onto the quayside
and followed her, the shotgun hanging down at his side like
a gleaming rolled umbrella.

A man, also wearing a blue lab coat, opened the back door
of the ambulance. Looking past him at the driver's seat, Bally
recognized Alexander Bowen. He ducked his head to climb
inside.

"Excuse me," said Erasmus, pointing at his weapon.
"Would it be too much to ask you to leave that outside?"

Bally looked at Erasmus. He sensed the danger but could
not figure out from whence it came.

With an obliging smile he bent down and propped the gun
up against the pressurized cylinders in the ambulance. Then
he kicked Erasmus.

There are not many people who can boast of having kicked the legs out from under a berserk fifteen-hundred-pound rhino calf on the rampage but Bally could. He caught the outer edge of the ape's right kneecap; the leg gave way and Erasmus dropped to his knees, never uttering a sound.

Then Bally aimed a kick at the ape's head.

His first kick had been first-rate, but it had been delivered with the left leg and this was Bally's weak side. The second was made with the right; it was all one could have asked for and it wrenched the vehicle's bumper free of its bodywork. But it did not make contact with Erasmus because Erasmus had suddenly—and, to Bally, quite unaccountably—dodged a foot and a half to one side.

Keeping his eyes pinned on the ape, Bally lifted his gun from where he had left it. But he had no chance to use it. He had no chance even to cock it. Just as he was about to draw himself up Erasmus hit him.

It was a wild blow with the flat of the hand, and had it been dealt by a human being, it would have amounted to a casual clip around the ear. But it was not dealt by a human being. It struck Bally with all the force of a pneumatic hammer, produced a crack like a pistol shot, lifted him off his feet and hurled him up against the ambulance door.

At this point he momentarily lost consciousness and, left unsupported, he would have collapsed. But the ape supported him. Its left hand shot out, grabbed him by the jaw and held him upright.

But it also cut off his air supply and it was the feeling of being suffocated that brought Bally around. He opened his eyes, and looked along the length of the arm at the ape's face bearing down on him. When Erasmus was about as close as he could get, a bare inch away from Bally's jugular, he drew his lips back and opened his mouth. Bally felt the ape's breath, the heat of its throat, saw its glittering, conical two-inch-long canines.

"Erasmus!" said Madelene.

Erasmus released his grip. Bally crumpled into a heap on the ground.

Alexander Bowen had flattened himself against the dashboard.

"I'm holding you responsible," he said. "You're going to reimburse me. For any and all damage to the vehicle and/or equipment."

The ape deposited Bally on a cot. Madelene lifted the receiver of the ambulance telephone.

six

Half an hour later there was a knock on the ambulance's rear door. Erasmus opened up and Johnny climbed in, dragging a trembling Samson with him. He glanced at Bally, then sat down.

A quarter of an hour went by without a word being said. Then came another knock. Erasmus let in Dr. Firkin, the veterinary odontologist. Five minutes later there was yet another knock.

"There is a limit," said Dr. Bowen, "to the number of passengers this vehicle is authorized to carry. If it comes to a fine . . ."

Erasmus opened the door. Outside stood Susan.

"I had to bring the children along," she said.

Confinement within a small space heightens and accentuates all human relationships. The ambulance now contained ten individuals—six adults, two children, a dog and an ape.

They had come because they had been forced or because Madelene had asked them to, and without knowing why. Now they looked at her, feeling giddy, like passengers on a ship that is too small, steering an uncertain course onto the high seas.

"The day after tomorrow," said Madelene, "Adam becomes director of London's new zoo. At the ceremony he's going to make a speech, revealing everything he knows about Erasmus. I've been married to Adam. I know that if you try to learn too much too fast, in his way, you wipe out whatever it was you wanted to learn about. I have been wondering whether those of us who are gathered here might not be able to persuade him not to say anything after all."

She had spoken softly but they listened; they heard every word. The children had forgotten the dog, the dog had forgotten the ape, Bally had forgotten his bruises, Johnny had forgotten his withdrawal symptoms.

"I thought we could give him a call. Now. And then we could each say something to him, just a few words. So he knows that we have joined forces, that our knowledge has been pooled, and that if he proceeds he is going to founder, his life will go under."

She lifted the receiver.

Adam Burden's secretary had had two months in which to forget, to recover, but as soon as she recognized that low, husky and penetrating voice on the telephone, she realized that while she might well be on the mend she was anything but cured.

"He's out of town," she said. "No one knows where he is. He has gone away with his sister. They're getting ready for the ceremony two days from now. I don't see what I can do . . ."

Madelene stood where she was, unmoving, with the receiver pressed to her ear. She did not try to argue, she knew the woman was speaking the truth.

"What about the day after tomorrow, before the ceremony?"

"He's going straight there. They'll be checking everyone at the door. And only two hundred personal invitations have been sent out. But I could fix up something after that . . ."

The secretary's voice had grown tearful.

"After that," said Madelene, "it will be too late."

She put down the receiver.

They were all watching her. She could sense their instability. And all at once it occurred to her that she must have been mad to pin her hopes on such a crew. What were they, after all, but children, dogs, quacks, smugglers and addicts. Losers, all of them, and she, the one who had collected this human flotsam and jetsam, was the biggest loser of them all. She sat down.

The ape placed a hand on her thigh. A dry, warm and totally steady hand. She relaxed, they all relaxed. The ape's steadiness coiled itself around them; like the onset of a fair wind, their wait proved suddenly fertile.

It was Susan who eventually broke the silence.

"My God!" she said. "Of course! Frank and I are invited. I have two invitations. And we can rustle up a couple more."

Madelene stared at her friend.

"You go in my place," said Susan. "And Johnny will go. And the man who's all battered and bruised. And when Adam sees you . . . I know him, I know all about men, Adam's cautious, if you gave him an apple he wouldn't bite into it until he'd had it tested in the laboratory . . . when he sees you . . ."

Everyone looked at Madelene. All his life Adam Burden had been a mystery to everyone around him. Madelene had been married to this mystery. Now they wanted her to solve it.

She gazed into space.

"I don't think," she said, "Adam has ever truly had any interest in animals. They were more . . . a sort of underpinning for him. When he sees me and Johnny and Bally there in the audience, he'll realize that now it's purely a matter of staying afloat."

They all sat there quietly, listening, rapt, like the crew of a vessel heading out of the doldrums. The ambulance was starting to pitch and roll. The wind had risen.

Madelene walked her friend and the two children to their car.

"So what was Adam actually heading for?" asked Susan. "By way of the animals, I mean."

"Sometimes I think it was me."

"And now?"

Madelene stared straight ahead with that expression of dearly paid-for lucidity accorded only to those who have staked their existence on another human being, lost everything and discovered that there is life to be found even on the other side of the great crash.

"That's a question he would always have been too busy to ask himself."

Susan helped the children into the car.

"What if their father asks where they've been?" Madelene asked.

Susan straightened up and scratched her head. Over the past twenty-four hours her scalp had begun to itch.

"D'you know what?" she said. "That's a question their father would always be too busy to ask."

Erasmus escorted Bally back to the boat, assisted him into the cockpit and climbed in after him.

"When," asked the ape, "is Mr. Burden making his speech?"

"Day after tomorrow. Friday."

"How many times do we have to sleep before it's Friday?"

"Two," said Bally.

"Do you happen to know where he will make this speech?"

Bally avoided looking the ape in the eye. He knew it did not waste time on irony. He stuck a hand through the hatch, took a telephone directory from the shelf under the guy, wrote the telephone number and address of the London Zoo on a slip of paper and pushed it across to the ape.

It did not touch it.

"In that book, can you also see where people live?"

Bally nodded.

"Could I trouble you to look for someone for me?"

Slowly, deliberately, it pronounced the first name for Bally.

Not until there were twelve addresses and telephone numbers on the sheet of paper did the ape pick it up without looking at it, fold it and tuck it carefully away in a pocket. Then it stood up. In its hand it was still holding the sawed-off shotgun. It raised it to eye level.

"Where I come from," it said, "we usually give one another presents. When we . . . understand one another."

It wrapped both hands around the gun. The muscles around its wrists flexed. With a series of muffled cracks, of bolts snapping, varnished wood splintering and clips being torn apart it bent the two cylindrical barrel stumps around to meet the neck of the butt. This done, it set the mangled weapon down on the seat.

"I would most earnestly request that you not tell anyone about our being here," it said. "And that you take care that nothing befalls Mrs. Burden on Friday. After we have slept two times."

The ape found the ambulance empty apart from Alexander Bowen.

"I'll be missed soon," said the vet. "They'll be looking for me."

The ape sat down.

"No one will miss you," it said. "You have no friends."

The doctor's unfailingly *en garde* expression gave way to

a stunned stare. The ape's clairvoyant candor affected him more deeply than any threat.

"It's true," he said. "Not a single one. Isn't that terrible?"

"But perhaps you can make one?"

"It's too late for that."

Out of its pocket the ape drew the sheet of paper given to it by Bally. He pointed to the bottom line.

"This place here," it said. "Pick me up there, in this van, before sunrise, after we have slept two times. And you'll have taken the first step toward having a friend for once in your life."

"That would be breaking the law. There's a hunt on for you two."

The ape's eyes gleamed, with a cocky, streetwise glint that would have elicited a nod of recognition from Madelene.

"But then," it said, "with you people nothing's for free."

At this point an amazing thing happened. Across Alexander Bowen's face there traveled a spasm which might possibly have formed the beginnings of a—albeit inhibited and strained but nonetheless, in a sense, sincere—smile.

"I can see," he said, "you really are beginning to get the hang of things around here."

seven

The full moon had always gone to Madelene's head. Formerly it had made her long to wander, to drink a quart of pure alcohol, to have three lovers in one night. Now it made her transparently happy.

She lay on the double bed in Johnny's mobile home and every fifteen minutes the moonlight shook her gently so she could reassure herself that Erasmus was lying beside her.

The tenth time she woke up he was gone.

On the other side of the panel, in the cab she could hear the deep breathing of Johnny and Samson. Even the dog had not heard him leave.

Over the minutes that followed, she suffered a relapse, a *de facto* physical slide back into an insecurity she had forgotten. In rapid succession she was presented with those sides of herself that she had in past months started to believe she had put behind her: the searing jealousy, the stupefying anger, the bitter vindictiveness, the porous self-pity, the bleeding vanity. Every one of the multitude of masks assumed by her self-loathing presented itself—as if for a party, a jet-black midnight feast, they presented themselves.

Once they were all assembled Madelene made them a speech, a speech that was very short but conclusive.

"He weighs over three hundred pounds," she said. "The way I figure it, if he loves me he can live with the lot of you too."

She had made her speech soundlessly and with eyes closed. Now she opened them. The van was empty. The guests had vanished. Through the glass roof fell a blue cone of moonlight.

The light was cut off by Erasmus' shadow.

There was no sound to be heard, all Madelene was aware of was a faint rippling of the mattress and quilt. And there he was.

She did not open her eyes. She did not say a word. All she did was to put out a hand and run her fingers through the thick coat. Deep inside, for the first time in her life, she came to terms with the fact that even the one you love you cannot ever fully understand.

eight

The two hundred people who had gathered on that Friday afternoon in late July to take part in the inauguration of the New London Regent's Park Zoological Garden and to hail its new director were far fewer than the assembly hall was capable of holding, but they had been selected with great care. Not one of them had been invited as an individual in his own right. They had been invited because they happened to represent hundreds or thousands of others, or because they had control over copious quantities of capital, or a copious measure of political and administrative power, or real estate, or knowledge, or because they tended to crystallize public opinion. And each and every one of them symbolized some significant aspect of society's stance vis-à-vis animals.

In attendance were representatives of the Corporation of London, Her Majesty's Government, the twelve largest animal protection organizations, the British society of zoological gardens, the European society of zoological gardens, the safari parks' association, the natural science faculties of Britain's universities, investors and sponsors, the veterinary police, the Royal Institute of British Architects, the British association of zoological museums, the association of practicing veterinary surgeons and the World Wildlife Fund. The royal family was represented by Her Royal Highness Princess Anne, patron of the Royal Zoological Society.

Twenty-two specially invited journalists and three specially selected television stations were to convey the afternoon's events to the nation, and not only the nation but every corner of the globe, since it was not only the British who rejoiced that afternoon but the world at large.

They were rejoicing because this inauguration was a touching demonstration of unity. A demonstration of how a group of well-to-do citizens and property owners, a national administration and the population of a city—in the midst of what was otherwise, in many respects, a heartless civilization—had seen reason and endowed the world and themselves and the wild beasts with a place of refuge. Internationally speaking, it was an occasion as uplifting as any sports event, though with none of the nationalistic aggressiveness of sport. And so on this day the world rejoiced; from Tristan da Cunha to Spitsbergen it was a day that had been awaited as eagerly as the start of carnival in Rio, and with a touch of the emotion aroused by the fiftieth anniversary of V-E Day or the fall of the Berlin Wall.

All this London knew, knew that on this day it had the rostrum to itself—hence the deliberate downplaying of the festivities. Like a coquettish little model well aware that no one will steal her limelight, the city paraded itself before the eyes of the world wearing a quiet smile and a ravishing yet understated outfit, for the benefit of the endangered species.

The mood of irresistible optimism in the air had penetrated even into those places where people live by expecting the worst; penetrated to the core of the Metropolitan Police Special Task Force, which had the job of guarding the assembly hall. With the result that—by showing the invitations and other proofs of identity procured for them by Susan—Madelene, Johnny and Bally experienced no difficulty in passing through the first two checkpoints in the security cordons set up by the police around Regent's Park, Primrose Hill and Albert Terrace.

For the first time in their lives Johnny and Bally were in evening dress. They looked and felt like two Antarctic penguins banished to the tropics, and the weather this afternoon was indeed tropical. The sun blazed in a cloudless sky, and alongside the two men Madelene, in the dress she had borrowed from Susan, resembled an Amazonian parakeet, bright-hued and glossy-plumed.

The entrance to the hall itself was manned by two security guards and a woman who greeted every guest personally, ostensibly to bid them welcome, but in actual fact to verify the identity of each one.

This woman was Adam's secretary.

She recognized Priscilla and stood stock-still.

"He says he doesn't know you," she said. "I've just asked him. He's never heard of you."

"That's what they all say when they've been having a bit of a fling," said Madelene. "What does yours say?"

The secretary backed away, one step at a time.

"I live alone," she said. "I have done so for several years."

Then she halted and summoned up all her courage.

"You can't threaten to go to his wife now," she said.

The two security guards were closing in. Madelene leaned forward.

"Look at me," she said.

The secretary looked at her. Madelene took off her sunglasses. The secretary felt a wave of heat wash over her, different from the meteorological heat of the day—a warm front carrying with it a smell of burning—as from a sauna.

"There is no Priscilla," said Madelene. "There never has been. There's only me. Madelene Burden. I *have* to get in. It's a matter of love. Can't you tell by looking at me?"

The two guards had arrived. Bally and Johnny stood rooted to the marble floor.

The secretary pulled back her shoulders.

"We're so pleased to see you," she said. "Please go on in."

The guards moved off, the secretary stepped aside, two glass doors opened. The way was clear.

Meanwhile, by the curb on Albany Street overlooking Gloucester Gate sat an ambulance from the Holland Park Veterinary Clinic. At the wheel sat Alexander Bowen, wearing a blue coat over his dress suit. In the back of the van, on the cot, knelt Erasmus, still attired in T-shirt, jacket, karate trousers, and sunglasses.

"There's a roadblock," said the doctor. "We'll need to produce some form of identification. And you don't have any."

His voice was thick, his hands shook. He had not been this scared since he took his finals.

"Could you please switch on the light on the roof," said the ape. "The one that flashes and says *mee maw*."

The doctor switched on the flashing light and the siren.

"If you would be so good as to drive very fast."

Light flashing, siren blaring, the ambulance pulled out into the road, heading straight for the entrance to the New London Regent's Park Zoological Garden.

A policeman stepped out into the middle of the road and signaled to them to stop.

"I'll lose everything," said the doctor.

Erasmus removed his sunglasses. His voice was almost passive in its calmness.

"You're carrying a sick ape," he said.

Bowen rolled down the window.

"This is an emergency," he said. "An ape. It's dying."

The policeman stuck his head through the window and peered into the back. Bowen closed his eyes. When nothing happened he opened them again and looked in the mirror.

Erasmus was laid out on a cot, covered by a white sheet and with an oxygen mask over his shaven face.

The policeman stepped back.

"We'll give you a motorcycle escort," he said. "I hope you make it."

Accompanied by the police motorcycle, the ambulance negotiated the second roadblock, inside the Outer Circle.

"You're learning," said Bowen. "That honesty gets you nowhere."

He waved the motorcycle away and carried on slowly past the assembly hall. The doors were closed. Outside stood Adam's secretary, the two security men and a number of uniformed police officers.

"Inside there are two hundred of the most influential people in Britain," said Bowen. "You'll never get in."

He drove around the corner and stopped. When he opened the rear door, Erasmus stepped down onto the pavement clad in a blue coat, green surgical apron and surgical cap. In his hand he held a foam extinguisher; into his pockets he had shoved an assortment of gleaming instruments.

"I've dressed up as a doctor," he said.

Alexander Bowen relieved the ape of the fire extinguisher, took off the apron and removed the instruments.

"The key to impersonating a scientist," he said, "lies in striking a balance between making use of all the means at one's disposal and not appearing conscious of that fact."

He removed the surgical cap from the ape's head.

"Now," he said, "you look like a senior physician. More than most senior physicians do."

Erasmus took Bowen's hand in his own.

"I would like to say thanks for now," said the ape. "In case there isn't another time. You have taken the first steps toward making a friend."

It was walking away when Bowen stopped it.

"The DNA analysis," he said. "There was something else."

The doctor clenched the surgical cap between his fingers.

"I didn't want to tell Burden's wife—sorry, ex-wife. I know what she would think. Here's science passing another turd. And taking it for a sacred pearl. But I will tell you. You see, it's very difficult to tell the difference between the brains of the larger apes and our own. The chimpanzee brain looks exactly like ours. But, all things being equal, what one can say is that the more convoluted it is, the bigger the neocortex, the more intelligent the animal. Your brain, I noticed the minute Mrs. Burden—sorry, your friend—showed me the scans, is the most convoluted ever seen. With the largest frontal lobe. The greatest volume. Now, I know we've had no chance to talk about your life. Probably never will have. All the same, I want to tell you that you . . . that is to say your ancestors, your race, after breaking away from us a million years ago on the shores of Lake Turkana, traveled northward. And after that you outstripped us. We had it all wrong. Burden, his sister and I. We thought we would learn something about one of those hominids which came before man. But you are not what went before. If anything, you are what comes afterward."

nine

That afternoon, Adam Burden was not representing himself either, appearing instead as a symbol of the historic compacts arrived at between the general public, the royal family, the zoological world and the investors, all of whom had made this new zoo possible. He personified the myth that exceptional people enjoy exceptional success. And—his wife having been kidnapped and presumably murdered by a crazed ape—he bore the stigmata of the self-sacrificing man of science, bore them meekly, as Livingstone his malaria at the Lualaba, as Darwin his failing health following his circumnavigation of the globe.

Circumstances can make a person greater in size than they actually are, and Adam had grown—Madelene noted this the minute he strode out and across the rostrum. He was no longer just a strikingly handsome man. Responsibility had rendered him charismatic.

On reaching the lectern, looking out across the footlights

at the upturned faces and the black cameras and television monitors behind which sat millions of spectators, he swelled even further. At that moment he caught sight of Madelene.

He turned pale, as though suddenly drained of blood, and would have keeled over had not a hand gripped his arm and held him upright. At his side stood Andrea Burden. She put out her free hand and cut the switch on the public-address panel. She and Adam were still in full view. But now they were out of hearing range.

"It's Madelene," said Adam. "And Bally. And the driver."

"They're ants," said Andrea Burden. "Industrious. But still nothing but ants."

"The press?"

Under such extreme conditions Andrea Burden's commanding nature blossomed like a lotus flower. She took her time, took plenty of time. As a coach will fuss like a mother with a newborn baby over a heavyweight champ already knocked near senseless, thereby cajoling him into going out and winning that final round, she stroked Adam's muscular back and whispered softly, slowly, clearly into his ear.

"This is England," she whispered. "They'll never get to speak to the press. And if they do, Toby will see to it that the papers don't print it. Toby could stop word of the end of the world from being printed. If it was seen as a threat to national security."

Adam shut his eyes for a moment. Then he relinquished his misgivings and his will and sank, so it seemed, at long last into arms he could trust.

He switched on the PA system.

"Your Royal Highness," he said, "ladies and gentlemen, honored guests. Nature is bountiful."

The spectators in the auditorium had seen him stagger and had held their breath. At his first words they breathed out. On hearing the sound of his own voice, Adam drew himself up to his full height, sparkling with zoological star quality. His rehearsals in front of the mirror stood him in good stead—the prepared text, his whole choreography of gestures, opened up before him like a highway. He raised his eyes and stepped on the gas.

"It gives me great pleasure to declare the New London Regent's Park Zoological Garden—the world's largest, most modern urban zoological garden—open."

The walls and the roof of the assembly hall were of glass, encased by a network of stainless-steel venetian blinds. The blinds had been closed; now they were gradually opened. Behind Adam, beyond the end wall of the hall, the zoo—its enclosures, its jungles, its savanna, its lakes and its cliffs—stood revealed.

"A pact," said Adam. "An understanding, between technological civilization and the natural world. Proof that peaceful coexistence between animals and humans is possible. A technological miracle. And yet even this pales when set alongside what I now have the pleasure of presenting to you."

A slide was projected onto a twenty-five-by-twelve-foot screen to Adam's left. A picture of Erasmus, photographed in the Mombasa Manor conservatory, with the plants forming a backdrop and in a light reminiscent of dawn over the rain forest.

"It is my moving duty today to bring you news of the most important zoological discovery of this century, perhaps the most important ever. A hitherto unknown mammal. More closely related to us than the chimpanzee. A highly intelligent anthropoid ape."

Adam had designed his speech as an emotive guided tour. After building up the suspense with his opening remarks and reaching an interim climax with the slide of Erasmus, he intended to explain, in a few restrained phrases, that the reason for his showing them a picture and not the animal itself was that this was the ape which had abducted his wife. He would then have moved on to a résumé of the scientific documentation.

He did not get beyond his opening remarks. As he opened

his mouth and spread his arms wide he became aware of a
surge of tension in the hall, a surge that went over his head,
directed as it was at something at his back. He turned around.

Behind the assembly hall lay a building that could have
been taken for a large greenhouse but was in fact the section
visible from the hall of the magnificent enclosure meant to
house *Homina londiniensis*. On the roof of this building stood
a figure in a blue coat. Just as Adam turned, the figure stepped
one pace backward, began to run and leapt into the air.

It was a stupendous leap. With the deep preparatory bound
of a trampolinist, the soar of a human cannonball and a suicidal trajectory aiming straight for the glass wall of the assembly hall.

The landing was as light as a fly's on a cube of sugar. The
man—for now it could be seen that it was a man—hung for
a second from the steel slats. Then he scrambled upward like
a sprinter on a flat track, up onto the roof, where a row of
windows stood open. To augment the organic lightness of the
building the structural framework of the ceiling had been left
exposed—a hexagonal system of slender steel piping, not unlike the rudiments of a honeycomb. Along these the blue man
swung until he came to one of the cables holding up the light
fixtures. Down this cable he slid, to the lamp, and from there
he dropped. To land right next to the lectern.

There were fifteen police officers inside the hall, all of
them armed, and any one of them could easily have shot the
new arrival. But none of them did. In these surroundings it
was impossible to perceive him as a threat. Adam, the man at
the lectern, exuded self-confidence, the invited guests exuded
self-confidence, as did the journalists and the policemen. The
entire building, the entire zoo, smacked of a torrid, yet perfectly safe flirtation with nature and its savagery, a flirtation
one can get away with because everything is under control.

Adam pulled back a pace or two. The blue man mounted
the lectern. He straightened his back, stood for a moment
quite still, surveying the gathering. Then he grasped his coat,

dragged it off and stepped out of his white trousers. There he stood, Erasmus the ape—naked, hairy, short-legged, colossal—for all the world to see.

Up to this point the audience had been stunned and confused. Now they understood. This scene that they were witnessing had been staged. It was all part of Adam's speech. An illustration of the amazing animal-training techniques they had heard of and observed at both London and Glasgow Zoo. An actual "live" presentation of the momentous ape. Not only tracked down and captured by British scientists but also already tamed, broken in and trained.

There was a burst of applause, wild applause. The policemen clapped, and the journalists, there was no end to it. It subsided only when the ape picked up a microphone.

"We have come," it said, "to say goodbye."

The members of the audience did not merely stiffen. They lapsed into lifelessness. Their sense of well-being and their view of the world were founded on the conviction that the horrors of this world can be identified, pinned down and kept within bounds. But the beast in front of them spoke a perfect dusky English, and out of the blue, with this language, it hit them where they lived—in the same way as unemployment, as the threat of war, as AIDS, as pollution.

"Where we come from," Erasmus went on, "we say that if a . . . person is on his knees you offer him your hand. If he rejects it you offer him both hands. And even if he rejects them both you still have to help him up. But if, even so, he turns his back on you, then you have to let go of him. I hope I won't hurt anyone's feelings when I say that you are on your knees, you are all on your knees. So we decided to try. But it didn't work out. We were wrong . . ."

By now the people in the audience were shivering; in spite of the afternoon heat they were shivering. In their evening suits and capes, beneath their jewels and medals, cameras and handguns, they shivered.

"We have tried, tried in many different countries at once, and mine was the final attempt."

Erasmus swiveled around, slowly he swiveled right around on himself, like a male model at a fashion show. Quite distinctly the members of the audience could make out the operation scars, the bite marks, the still-raw burns and the numerous shaven patches to which Adam's electrodes had been affixed.

"I tried to fit in," said the ape. "We've all tried. But things haven't been working out too well. We're all agreed that the time is not yet ripe. We cannot do any more. Not this time around. It's too . . . difficult. So now we're going home."

There was some movement on the floor of the hall. Up onto the rostrum strode a dean from the University of London. Well known and forever barred from becoming rector by reason of his criticism of the scientific world's contempt for the notion of global responsibility. He positioned himself alongside the lectern and for a second or so he stood there like that, perfectly still, a tall, gray-bearded man. Then he tucked the fingers of one hand in at his tailcoat lapel, gripped his shirtfront, yanked it up and ripped it off. Beneath it his chest was hairy. Not a human hairiness, though, but off-white in color, wavy and long as a full-bottomed wig. He pulled off his tailcoat, undid his trousers and climbed out of them. Stark naked he stood there now, next to the lectern, wearing nothing but a pair of enormous patent-leather shoes. An ape, a creature just like Erasmus, only larger, older, with silver-tipped hair.

A woman walked up to take her place beside him—a big woman, a distinguished celebrity, vice president of the Royal Zoological Society, a public figure, spokeswoman for the animal-rights lobby, an intellectual, an advocate of the total abolition of animal testing, the one person who had done more than anyone else to persuade fifty-two nations to take part in the Great Ape Project, which had accorded the anthropoid apes of the world the same legal, economic, moral and social status as mentally subnormal humans. As with the dean, she too stood, for a moment, quite still.

Out of the auditorium came a scream, heartrending, imploring. It came from her husband. Like one possessed, he struggled to push his way through the audience in order to prevent what was about to happen. But it got him nowhere; people stood as if frozen to the spot, like icicles they stood there, blocking his path.

The woman drew her dress over her head and tossed it aside. Her face was clean-shaven but for the rest she was long-haired, naked, clad only in a pair of underpants so vast they might have been sewn out of a lugsail.

Two civil servants from the Ministry of Agriculture made their way to the front of the hall. Although strangers to the two hundred guests, within the Ministry and in government circles they were notorious, singled out and long since ostracized and politically defused for their unremitting, unrelenting, unobtrusive underscoring of the fact that there is no way the question of the survival of wild animals can be dissociated from that of the insatiable, grasping materialism of the world's wealthiest nations. These two were followed by a policeman, two zookeepers and a television producer, people who until this moment had been quite unknown to the two hundred guests in the hall but whom their day-to-day contacts had long both feared and felt themselves attracted to for their unfathomable, radical integrity—acting as it did as a permanent, nonaggressive reminder that there was something—something or other—very wrong with the world today. People fell back before them and the little procession marched up onto the stage, where they divested themselves of their dress suits, their uniforms, their handguns and press cards, laying them aside. They were apes.

Later, at the hearings, not one member of the audience would be able to recall how many apes there had been on the rostrum by the end. But they all believed that they had filled the stage, that there must have been somewhere between one and two hundred of them.

In fact there were twelve. They stood very still and yet they raised a storm that swept through the brains of the guests, a storm of bewildering images of lions, prehistoric monsters, snakes, dragons, rabid dogs, crocodiles and demented mandrills. Their entire childhood chamber of horrors.

Erasmus picked up the microphone.

"When we are gone," he said, "you will forget us. Until we come again. Till then there is only one thing I would ask you to remember. And that is how hard it is to tell, in each one of us, where the part that you call human ends and the part you call animal begins."

He jumped down from the lectern and for an instant all twelve apes stood there, side by side. Then slowly they backed away, making for the rostrum steps, and after that they were gone.

For a minute the hall was held spellbound, stunned into immobility by terror and the vague recollection of the ape's words. Then people began to come to, their first signs of life irrational, devoid of thought and hence totally genuine. They were stricken by grief. They recognized that they had been forsaken, something precious had forsaken them, some great force had withdrawn its protection. They took to milling aimlessly around, like a bunch of toddlers looking for their mommies and daddies; they bumped into one another and only gradually, over a matter of minutes, did their distress give way to rage, to a child's urge to avenge itself on the adults who have abandoned it. They started yelling, they screamed, like animals they screamed, weapons were drawn, they would give chase, they broke down the doors to the dressing rooms backstage, they raced shrieking along the corridors and through the toilets, they tore up and down the stairways, but the apes were nowhere to be found.

Then, amid all this rancorous desperation, the old back-bone-of-steel reflex came into play. One man spoke from the rostrum, an evacuation was organized.

They filed out of the hall, apathetic, like cattle. They bore the marks of what had passed, they were shocked, sick with worry for the future, unsure whether the world to which they were returning would still be there.

ten

Even before the last guest had left the assembly hall, every corner of the British Isles, from Jersey to the Hebrides, had been thrown into a fever of activity that lasted for about two hours. Then the nation froze and ground to a halt.

The initial, frantic stirrings occurred when—on hearing the first, unclear live transmissions and the first alarming rumors—everyone, all and sundry, in the country and in the cities, dropped everything and rushed home. They panicked, they stampeded, they trampled one another underfoot, stole other people's cars, commandeered buses and forced the drivers to run taxi services. They all wanted to get home, as quickly as possible, whatever the cost, to see whether their husbands, their wives, their children were still there or whether they were actually apes and even now slipping away.

Once inside they locked the doors, drew the curtains, slammed the shutters, pulled down the blinds and switched on the television.

There was nothing on the screen but a laconic announcement that all programs had been temporarily interrupted.

Even the BBC, whose proud boast it was that come hell or high water it would always manage to broadcast and which would have made it a point of honor, in the event of a third world war, for the last person left alive on earth to be a newscaster sending a balanced and well-formulated report on Armageddon into the void—even the BBC had closed down. When the *Newsnight* team turned up for work, in response to an urgent summons, they had looked at one another and seen that any of them—or all the others—could be apes; that so great was the risk that any move might prove to be a false one, in which case it was better to do nothing and so, muttering inaudibly, they had turned their backs on one another and gone home.

At eight p.m. the announcement regarding the break in transmission also vanished, and the screen was blacked out, when the power stations that feed London shut down due to staff shortages. One by one they shut down: Dungeness A and B, the French interconnector, Barking in Essex, the coal-fired stations at Kingsnorth and Tilbury. And, deprived of its oxygen supply, the city fell into a coma.

With the setting of the sun London was plunged into darkness. The last of the traffic petered out, all the shops were closed, the streets deserted and black—pitch black they were, as they had not been since the wartime blackout. Every visible human activity ceased, even crime came to a standstill, paralyzed by a fear greater than greed. For even in the world of cutthroats, ticket scalpers, muggers, pushers, con men and organized prostitution you need to know that your partner, your bodyguard, your pimp, your bookie and, yes, even your executioner or victim is a human being and not an animal.

Seven million Londoners in four million homes suffered a psychotic identity crisis. They had no access to any information regarding the fate of the remainder of Britain, of Europe, of the rest of the world. They grew suspicious of their

own government, their own society. They could not be certain
of the identity of their bosses, or their friends. They eyed one
another fearfully, tried to remember how their children and
their spouses looked naked, wondered when exactly they had
first met their wives, frantically they wondered whether she
might be an ape or the daughter of an ape. They gazed into
the light of the kerosene lamps or candles they had lit and
contemplated the most solid and glorious thing they knew—
the Crown. They hardly dared entertain such an appalling
possibility but, on the other hand, they could not help themselves. Running over a long span of years, coronations and
outrageous questions concerning the order of succession, they
realized they had no guarantee that they did not have an ape
for a queen.

eleven

A light swept the night; a solitary car drove through London, at a snail's pace, past the barricaded shopwindows, through the defunct traffic lights, around cars abandoned in the middle of the road.

In the front seat, between Johnny and Bally, sat Madelene. White-faced, tense, she guided them through a city she barely recognized, through districts she had never seen while sober and which she had never before been responsible for finding a way through.

But find a way she did, with the blind certainty of a homing pigeon. By the time she gave the signal to stop, in the heart of Mayfair, Bally and Johnny had long since lost their bearings. They had been sniveling for some time, caught betwixt fear of the unwonted darkness and desolation on the outside and fear of the desperation in the woman sitting between them.

Madelene took them by the hand like children and ushered them across the road, through a gate, up a stairway and

through suite after suite of darkened rooms that seemed to
lead inward then close up behind them like a lobster creel.

At last they came to a door. Madelene turned the handle
and it led to another door, behind which the sun had not set
but burned white-hot in a stainless-steel basin positioned
alongside an electric shredder and a pile of kerosene cans.

Dazzled, they remained standing just inside the door.

"Come in and have a cup of tea," said Andrea Burden.

She was standing by the fire, her arms full of papers in
yellow folders. She dropped all she held in her embrace into
the steel basin, the files landing like bricks and flaring up
like gasoline. The heat of the blaze could be felt all the way
to the door.

"As a child," said Andrea Burden, "I was very fond of
jigsaw puzzles. 'Sunrise over the Savanna of the Serengeti.'
Seven thousand pieces. The other children never so much as
made a start but once you got your teeth into it there was no
stopping. Finally, when there were only a couple of dozen
pieces left, always of the sky—well, there were three thousand
pieces of blue sky, all virtually identical—it became like an
obsession. Mother told me that during the war, during the
Blitz, people were killed because they just had to see that last
piece of the sky. They ignored the air-raid sirens. Ever since
the first time I laid eyes on you I've had it in mind that you
might be such a person."

"Where's Erasmus?" said Madelene.

"The ape? On his way back, I suppose."

"Back where?"

"Didn't it tell you? To the forests. Around the Baltic. The
Swedish and Finnish forests. This one—Erasmus—was captured on that Danish island farthest to the east, the rocky
island, what's it called again?"

"They must have had someplace here where they could
meet," said Madelene. "They may still be there. They may not
have gotten out of London yet. I had an idea you would know
where this place might be."

"Does it matter? Do you know what we have here?"

"She's in love with it."

Beyond this room lay yet another. In the open doorway stood Adam, holding a stack of files.

For the first time in a long while, perhaps for the first time ever, Madelene saw the man to whom she had been married with perfect clarity. She saw that she had loved him for the unguarded vulnerability that shone out of him at that moment to be extinguished the next moment and supplanted by that painstakingly cultivated indifference which had ruled out any possibility of her love enduring.

"The country is falling apart," said Andrea Burden. "I've spoken to Toby. The government is to stand down tomorrow. There's a rumor going around that half the ministers are apes. A commission of inquiry is to be set up. Let's say, just for argument's sake, that there were a thousand apes. In high places. Their intelligence is, of course, indisputable. The chaos they've left behind them will have to be cleared up. Steps will have to be taken to ensure that they don't come back. That they aren't still here. I have been offered the post of secretary to the commission. Adam is to be scientific consultant. The commission will be accorded legislative status. Provide an ad hoc government. Ahead of us lies a time of cataclysmic upheaval. One thousand is a conservative estimate. Adam and I estimate it could be more like ten thousand. One hundred thousand is not out of the question. In Britain alone. But what about the rest of Europe! The New World! We have no idea of their breeding capacity, but what if, on a global scale, what if there were . . . ?"

"Twelve. What if there were only twelve?"

The heads of everyone in the room turned. One of the windows high up in the wall stood open. On the sill sat Erasmus. Cardinal numbers were still new to him. Wanting to make sure that he had been understood, he held up first ten fingers, then two.

It was not the ape at which Andrea Burden stared. It was the figure its fingers were underlining.

"But that's impossible!" she exclaimed.

"Ten," the ape's fingers reiterated, "ten and two."

With an inhuman effort of will Andrea Burden reviewed her strategy.

"Nobody knows that," she said. "The confusion will still be tremendous. What about the other countries? Denmark? Sweden? Germany?"

The ape did not reply. Its face was expressionless.

Everything fell quiet. No one uttered a sound and yet above the rustling of the flames every one of those present could hear something, a sound not physical but mental: the sound of covert, far-reaching schemes coming crashing down.

Andrea Burden began to laugh, a manic laugh. Despite the shock to her system, despite the deeply problematic nature of the situation, she laughed, and her laughter was catching, catching as a respiratory infection. Bally started to chuckle, Johnny was giggling, Adam smiled—an uneasy smile but nonetheless a smile—and finally the ape's face cracked. Even the pyre of paper and kerosene seemed to be laughing along with them, an absurd mirth spread throughout that high-ceilinged room.

Only Madelene did not laugh.

"You let me down," she told the ape.

There is nothing as annoying as a spoilsport, sabotaging everyone else's fun, and Andrea Burden did try to stop her.

"Get out of the way," said Madelene.

The other woman moved aside. Madelene advanced on the ape.

"You used us," she said, "me and the others, like decoys you used us."

"I'm afraid there was no other way," said the ape.

"Through those roadblocks, in front of the cameras, surrounded by hundreds of people. All because we thought we could help you."

"I had to have help to get in," said the ape. "People watch television. We wanted to say what we had to say on television."

Andrea and Adam Burden had moved back against the wall; Bally and Johnny had their backs pressed up against the door. The floor had been cleared for the first confrontation between Madelene and Erasmus the ape.

"You told me nothing. You left me to do all the worrying, all the agonizing alone," Madelene said.

"Among my people we say the plans that are carried through are the plans you keep to yourself."

The ape looked down from on high with an air of statuesque self-importance. But Madelene was close enough to discern the escalating panic behind the animal's half-shut eyelids.

"You've forgotten who you're talking to," she said. "Take a good look at me. Do you know who I am? I'm the woman you love."

The ape looked at her.

"I never regret anything," it said. "Where I come from we cannot have regrets. But if I had been capable of it I would have said I was sorry."

Erasmus could not edge away, since, had he done so, he would have tumbled backward out of the window. But he was now squeezed up against the window sash.

"I don't want an apology," said Madelene. "You don't have to say anything. What you have to do is to shut up. Keep your mouth shut for two minutes. So I know you've gotten the message. And if you don't, I'm the one who'll be heading off home to the forests. And you'll never see me again."

There was silence; for one minute, for two, for three, there was dead silence. Then Andrea Burden shifted, fidgeting, like someone trying to get comfortable on a baking-hot sauna bench.

"The last pieces," she said, "the last pieces of the sky."

It was a small room. Once it had been a maid's room; now it served as a built-in strong room, ten by ten feet with ample headroom. The walls could not be seen on account of the yellow files arranged on green enameled shelves stretching from floor to ceiling.

"These are interesting times we live in," said Andrea Burden. "Human beings are forming closer attachments to animals than ever before. Dogs and cats sleep in people's beds, get kissed on the mouth, stroked between the legs. The media are overrun with animals. Children's rooms are crammed with them. It's extremely interesting."

There were only three of them in the strong room: Madelene, Erasmus and Andrea Burden. Bally and Johnny and Adam had remained in the doorway.

"Everywhere you turn there are animals. When people die, when others inherit, coming between adults and children, for protection, in the garden, in the house, at sports events, in children's bedrooms, in nursing homes, close by the people there are always animals, closer than ever before. And deep within human beings, in their minds, on the fringes of their consciences, their outlook on life, their angst and passion, animals abound. So they come to me. Researchers, politicians, the rich—they come to me because they are all animal lovers. They come to me because I manage foundation funds, veterinary hospitals, homes for dogs. With an open mind I've managed them, taking no political sides, challenging no one's conscience. To them I am public servant, lawyer, psychoanalyst, priest and the lady who holds the purse strings. And above all else I am an animal lover, from their own class. It's to me they confide the story of the secret mistress's cat, the divorced husband's gundog, the children's pets, the pets with which they bribed the children, the snake he had her perform with for him, the watchdog he could no longer control, the animal that was witness to rape, breakdown, forgery, abuse.

In a way, when they are sitting across from me I become that animal, I take on its characteristics, its devotion, its dependence, while at the same time I am understanding and I listen, like a human being. And so they start to talk, they talk and talk, they cannot stop, it comes pouring out of them, for twenty years it has been pouring out of them. And afterward, once they have gone, I take notes."

She slid her fingers over the files on the shelves.

"Five thousand cases. Five thousand sketches of the true anatomy of Britain's upper classes. The decisive factor, without which the New London Regent's Park Zoological Garden would never have become a reality. Without any pressure being brought to bear. I have not pressured a single person. I have, however, given them a hint, provided them with a glimpse of what they themselves, or their mother, or their cousin once happened to tell me. I've left them with a vague notion that a room such as this might exist. I've dropped the odd remark. With the investors. In Whitehall. How else do you think we managed to have the area exempted from the standard planning regulations, by bringing it under a development corporation? Getting that sort of planning permission would normally set you back millions of pounds. But this way they've met me halfway. And then I and others have been able to fit the last pieces into place."

"That's blackmail," said Madelene. "You're a terrorist."

Andrea Burden's eyes narrowed.

"British slaughterhouses murder two hundred thousand animals a day. The last wild animal populations of any size are in the process of being exterminated. My conscience is snow white."

She stretched out her hands to Madelene and Erasmus.

"Come over to us," she said. "Right now. If the cataclysm doesn't strike today, then it'll hit us tomorrow. Prior to this we've been able to put the squeeze on a minority, an elite. But the elite count for nothing. Those in government do not wield power. I know, because I understand about power, it's my stock-in-trade. They merely administer it. It's not the rich who are destroying the world; they are too few and too insignificant for that. It is the common people who are devouring the earth. It's petty greed, the greed of the little woman, the greed of the little children, Joe Blow's piddling little car times sixty million in the United Kingdom, times two hundred and fifty million in the United States, times seven hundred and fifty million in Europe. That's what we have to shout from the rooftops, that's what we have to put a bomb under. The new zoo is the detonator, you two could help us prime the explosive. Come, and let's start by fitting in the pieces of blue sky."

Madelene shook her head. Andrea Burden looked at the ape.

"Where I come from," said Erasmus, "we're too . . . jumpy for anything that goes bang."

"You and your race will be wiped out," said Andrea Burden.

"I'll take that as it comes," said the ape.

It took Madelene's hand and they backed away—through the room, past the glowing embers in the steel container.

"You can't leave me," said Andrea Burden. "Not after the trust I've put in you both. We need support."

By her side stood Adam. Now with a rifle in his hands.

The ape stopped in its tracks and regarded the weapon.

"We have a saying," it said. "We say that on coming upon an enemy the first thing you have to do is try to make peace. If that fails you should employ charm. And if that fails you should resort to magic."

"And if that fails?" asked Andrea Burden.

"If that fails," said the ape, "you annihilate."

The room went quiet, very quiet, for one minute, for two, for three. Then Adam Burden put down his gun. Madelene and the ape retreated toward the door. Adam followed them, unarmed, awkward. He stopped in front of the ape.

"I would like . . . to wish you good luck," he said.

Then he turned to Madelene.

"I have come to the conclusion . . . now . . . here . . . that it is best this way. It was never going to work out between you and me. I . . . couldn't have borne it. I need someone . . . sweeter."

Madelene laid her hand on his shoulder, a tiny gesture but one imbued with great tenderness.

"And you will find her too," she said.

twelve

The last morning was a scorcher. The sun shone down on London as if through a burning glass and the city and its inhabitants awoke to this disagreeable light as though waking to the morning after an attempt to drink themselves to death. Uncertain as to whether the real world still existed, they proceeded to crawl out of their houses, to find themselves—as one always does after an attack of delirium—faced with the painful choice of repeating those mistakes that would in the long run be the death of them or making an effort to stay sober.

Alongside Klein's Wharf, Bally was taking in the *Ark*'s fenders. All that now bound him to London were two mooring lines, which would shortly be cast off and hauled aboard. A few minutes from now he would be leaving behind him the city and the traumatic events of the past two months. He would never be back and he would never give another thought to what had taken place there. In fact he had already given up thinking. Only when he heard the sound of a car engine somewhere among the warehouses on the deserted dock, and automatically stuck his hand through the hatch to release his shotgun and saw that it was bent like a horseshoe magnet did his mind cheat him and force him to think of the ape.

Johnny's truck pulled up. Johnny, Madelene and Erasmus got out. Madelene and the ape shook Johnny's hand, walked over to the quayside and the *Ark* and climbed on board.

Bally viewed his useless weapon. He felt a throbbing in the—still swollen—side of his face. He realized that, sadly, strong-arm tactics were not an option here and instead he toyed with the idea of calling the River Police over his short-wave radio, of citing the law of piracy. For the first time since his boyhood he contemplated appealing to someone's better feelings.

Before he could make a move, while he was still standing there confused and quiescent, the ape reached out, took the crooked weapon from him, straightened it out—almost absentmindedly, it seemed—and threw it overboard.

"We do hope we're not putting you to any trouble," it said. "We've brought our own food."

Bally glanced up. From the sleeping quarters at the back of the van emerged one ape, two apes, three, then three from the cab and another two from the same sleeping quarters—seven apes, ten apes, eleven, all of them enormous, as big as Erasmus or bigger still, all wearing life jackets, oilskins and sou'westers and carrying boxes and duffel bags.

"Now let me help you cast off those moorings," said Erasmus.

Even as Erasmus was coiling the mooring lines; as Bally, stiff as an automaton, put the vessel's engine into gear and swung away from the quay; as the eleven other apes spread out to bring the *Ark* back onto an even keel—at that very moment Madelene waved to London and to Johnny. And just as she raised both arms into the air she detected a movement which first-time mothers-to-be are not usually able to identify, at least not that early on in the pregnancy, but which she instantly—quite definitely, beyond a shadow of a doubt—knew to be their baby, her and Erasmus' baby, rolling around, like a little fish still, in its ocean of amniotic fluid.

Erasmus came down from the foredeck and Madelene took his hand and gazed up at the sky.

"Those last pieces," she said, "it's not only blue sky. There's an angel there too."

"What is an angel?" asked the ape.

Madelene shook her head.

"That's something I've never totally understood," she said. "But for all we know, it's one-third god, one-third animal and one-third human."